PAINTING BLUE WATER

PAINTING BLUE WATER

A Novel By

Leigh Fossan

Cover Design by Pink Ink Designs

Cover Photo by Leigh Fossan

Editing by Theresa Wegand

Blue Water Publishing

978-1-7322672-0-6

For James & Sophia, the loves of my life

CHAPTER 1

"I met someone."

Katherine stared at the two black suitcases standing together in unison. They seemed to stare right back at her, daring her to doubt their purpose.

"Kate . . . Kate, are you hearing me?"

All she could think in this moment was that she never really liked the name Kate. And why? Why did she always allow *him* to call her by a name she didn't even like? Her name was Katherine.

"Kate, please say something." He coughed and looked down to check his watch.

She wasn't experiencing any of the feelings she had imagined she might *if it ever happened to her.* Katherine had a few friends with respective tales of unfaithful husbands. She had listened to the resentful "I should have knowns" over bottles of rosé and the sobbing "What am I going to do nows?" over tubs of ice cream. She had imagined she would feel tremendous devastation, rage, and hopeless fear. She imagined she might throw things, glass things, things that make dramatic crashing and shattering sounds, emphasizing the volume of the anger within.

But with the reality now standing before her, begging her to respond so that *he* didn't feel worse than he already felt, Katherine only felt . . . blank.

"Look, Kate. I don't have a lot of time."

The confident suitcase duo continued to hold her unblinking gaze.

"Okay" was all she could manage. Numbness had taken over. She couldn't feel her hands, or her legs, or her mouth—much like when one returns home after a day at the dentist.

"That's all? You have nothing more to say to me?" He rolled his eyes. "Look, Kate. I'm sorry. But I have to listen to my heart, and you and I . . . This isn't a marriage. I'm not happy. I'm guessing you're not happy. It's hard to tell with you."

He was right, of course, only Katherine had never really allowed the true state of their marriage to enter the main stage of her mind. She had subconsciously pushed the humiliating and unsettling reality behind the curtain long ago, succumbing to pain and embarrassment, accepting everything the way it was, and settling, while other priorities in life stole the show.

But things were once very different. It hadn't always been this way.

Katherine had met Michael at a holiday work party almost eight years before. She was the host of the party, along with her business partner and best friend, Andi Bretton. It was a celebration for their exceedingly successful first year in the competitive real estate business, a salute to their thriving company, K&A Manhattan Realty. Katherine and Andi floated around the event with bottles of Veuve Clicquot, greeting guests, clients, and friends. "Merry Christmas!" "Thank you for coming!"

"Happy Holidays!" "Are you still loving the apartment?!"

Katherine wore a perfectly red dress, the kind of red you can only describe using food and car metaphors like "maraschino cherries" and "red Ferrari." It was a daring shift from her usual preference, classically and modestly inspired black & white ensembles. The red dress fit her like a glove, though.

"C'mon, Katherine, show some holiday spirit. It won't kill you to add some color to your evening. Let's have some fun! Remember fun?" Andi had said with a devious grin while they shopped together for the event.

As Katherine fetched a newly opened bottle of champagne from the bar area, her eyes caught a peripheral glimpse of an ever-so-clichéd tall, dark, and handsome party guest smiling at her from across the crowded room. She couldn't believe she did it, but she looked over both her shoulders to make sure she was, in fact, the person meant to receive his smile. Then he laughed and began to walk toward her. She laughed too. Of course, when a dreamy guy smiled at her confidently, she fumbled the opportunity to be totally cool and collected. Just once, she thought, I'd like to wow with a mysterious grin and, even one day, maybe a sexy wink! Fat chance.

Tall-dark-and-handsome was getting closer, and Katherine realized she had absolutely no idea who he was. She knew, or at least recognized, almost every other person at the party—as she should. She was the host after all!

"I thought I should come over here and clarify that I was smiling at you," he said smoothly with an amused grin perfectly poised between a killer set of dimples.

"Hi, I'm Katherine, Katherine Ross." She shook his hand, hoping it was dark enough in the room to conceal the fact that her skin had blushed dangerously close to the shade of her Ferrari-cherry dress.

"Happy to meet you, Katherine. I'm Michael Kristoff. Is this your party?" He looked at the bottle of champagne in her hand.

"Yes, it is. Well, along with my partner, Andi. We're sort of celebrating. New business and all that . . ." She made a concerted effort not to ramble, a nervous habit she had battled her entire life. A gift with words could be more of a curse in some situations.

"What do you do?" She silently applauded herself for the smooth segue.

"I'm an attorney here in the city. Actually, one of my clients is one of your clients, I believe." He gestured toward Susan Lennox, one of K&A's biggest deals to date. Katherine and Andi had recently helped her acquire a beautifully updated historical penthouse in the Upper East Side. Mrs. Lennox, in her late-60s, was from the South but had moved to Manhattan for her fifth marriage. Not too long thereafter, Dear Mr. Fifth Husband passed away from a heart attack, and Mrs. Lennox inherited his fortune.

"Ah, yes, Mrs. Lennox. Aren't you a bit young for her?" Katherine teased, hoping that he was not actually on a date with the southern senior serial wife.

"Sadly, yes." Michael faked disappointment. "Mrs. Lennox loves me only for my legal counseling. She asked me to accompany her this evening so that she could introduce me to her friends. I'm just getting started at the firm, and Mrs. Lennox has taken it upon herself to be my very own walking, talking, martini-drinking, bedazzled business card."

They spent the rest of the evening, talking and flirting by the bar. At one point, Andi actually had to come over and scold Katherine for neglecting the other party guests. But Katherine couldn't help herself. He was irresistible. Michael had grown up in New York. He had graduated at the top of his class from Columbia Law and had just become the newest partner at his father's prestigious corporate law firm in the city. Michael forthrightly admitted being the son of very traditional parents with endlessly high expectations, but it didn't seem to bother him. In fact, he seemed to find a rush in attempting to meet or exceed those expectations.

Despite his impressive resume and classic movie-star looks, Michael was also very funny. Katherine laughed so much that her face hurt. And not the pitying I-can-tell-you're-trying-to-be-funny-so-I'll-humor-you-to-make-this-less-uncomfortable kind of laughter, but real genuine laughter—the kind that makes your stomach muscles ache (in a good way) and brings tears to your eyes. Michael Kristoff was a catch, and, that night at the party, he caught Katherine.

~*~

"Kate! Dammit!" Michael snapped impatiently. "Forget it. I'm going now." He picked up the suitcases and shook his head as he glared at Katherine, who failed to move or say another word.

"Have a good life," he muttered as he walked away, the door slamming loudly behind him.

Suddenly, Katherine felt an icy chill creep slowly from the back of her neck, down her spine. And then, it was gone.

CHAPTER 2

"*Dr. Terrence P. Goldwater, PhD, Psychology.*" Katherine studied the simple business card. Though minimal, it wreaked of assured prestige and confidence.

"He is FAB-U-LOUS," Andi enunciated dramatically as her eyes basically popped out of her perfectly botoxed forehead. She sipped her skinny latte, sat back, and smiled as though she just handed Katherine a forbidden fruit.

"*And* he's GOOOORGEOUS!"

"I didn't know you went to a therapist," Katherine responded, still staring at the card.

"Who *doesn't* go to a therapist?!" Andi laughed. "He's a lifesaver. Really, darling, you should give it a shot. It could help you move on from this . . ."

Andi let her words trail off as Katherine shot her the don't-push-me look. Though they were nearly opposite in personality and interests, Andi had always been a loyal friend. And after nearly a decade of working together, they could read each other quite well. Katherine never told Andi the dark details about her marriage. She was too ashamed. She felt degraded and foolish. Instead, she told her dear friend that she and Michael had simply grown apart, and that the affair was inevitable.

"Well, just hang onto the card, in case you change your mind."

Andi let the issue go and shifted the conversation to tales of her latest love interest: a twenty-three-year-old CrossFit instructor from Ireland, with a sexy accent that made her "weak in the knees." Katherine was grateful for her friend and for the distraction. They finished their lattes and kissed cheeks, *Mwah! Mwah!* as they always did when saying good-bye.

"Call me later so I know you haven't done something drastic," Andi yelled from the corner and gave a little wink.

Katherine hadn't talked to Michael since he walked out of their apartment two weeks ago. His secretary had emailed the divorce papers this morning; it would be a fairly simple process due to their iron-clad prenup—something Michael's family had insisted on during their engagement. "No offense, Katie, it's not you. We adore you, and you two will *obviously* be together forever. But no Kristoff is to marry without a prenup. You understand, don't you?"

She was glad for it now. The divorce was hassle-free and required no face-time with Michael, no petty negotiating about who gets the blue vase and who gets the Warhol print. Yes, the Kristoffs were one of the wealthiest families in the city, but she had done so well with K&A that her financial situation was one thing she did not have to worry about. She couldn't imagine ever seeing Michael again. The thought of his face alone made her stomach turn and her throat burn.

Their loft apartment technically belonged to her. She had purchased it after her first successful year in the real-estate business. It had everything she loved: floor-to-ceiling windows, tons of natural light, an open floor plan, and modern lines. It felt like a proper artist's studio—a space Chagall or Van Gogh would have loved to work. And while she personally didn't get to use it for that purpose, she fell in love with the artistic spirit it embodied. Michael had agreed to move into the loft. It was close to his work, and he had been living with some friends across town. It wasn't his personal taste—he was more a black-lacquer-and-marble kind of guy—but he loved that it made Katherine happy. *Ah yes, those selfless newlywed days, when their love for one another was the only thing that mattered . . . Those days felt so far away. Perhaps they never really existed at all.*

Katherine checked her watch. She had an hour until her next meeting. She was on the west side of Central Park, and her meeting was on the east side. It was a perfect autumn day, with air cool enough to wear a scarf but warm enough to wear a skirt. For the first time in a long time, she decided to walk through the park rather than hail a cab. She crossed the busy street and strolled down a sidewalk through one of the many historic, charming brick overpasses. And just like that, she was in a different world. It was strange and a bit enchanting, this magnificent forest and green meadowland, rich with trees and flowers, ponds and lakes, wide open to the blue sky, nestled smack-dab in the middle of one of the biggest concrete jungles in the world. As Katherine walked through the park, she smiled at kids riding their bikes and watched an elderly man expertly drive a remote-controlled sailboat in the pond. She breathed the fall air deep into her lungs and let her thoughts engulf her for the first time since Michael had left.

She had been a robot the past couple of weeks, refusing to address the life-altering shift that had occurred, refusing to accept that all she had built, everything she had become, and everything she had prioritized over the past eight years, was done so in vain. No, instead she dealt with the blow by burying herself in work, following up with old clients and schmoozing prospective ones, networking with other brokers and homeowners all over the city. When she got home at night, she only collapsed into a deep, comatose sleep, an all-consuming sleep that would surely go on endlessly if she hadn't programmed her insanely loud alarm to violently jolt her awake each morning.

But here in the park, on this beautiful day, Katherine surrendered to her dreadful reality. The tears started, slowly at first, reluctantly creeping from the corners of her eyes and then slowly crawling down her cheeks. She found an old tree near the path, tucked behind a pile of giant boulders, and there she collapsed with her head against its trunk—just in time for the full-on ugly, uncontrollable sobs that suddenly consumed her with great force. It wasn't heartbreak; it wasn't remorse for the loss of *him*. It was an overwhelming feeling of valuable time wasted and a terrifying notion that she truly did not know herself anymore.

How had she gotten caught up in this life? How did she become this person? A person driven only by success, prestige, and appearance—even within her own marriage? She had become Kate Kristoff, real estate mogul, submissive wife to successful, alcoholic husband. What happened to Katherine Ross, Fine Arts major? The Katherine Ross who loved to cook and read? The Katherine Ross who loved to travel, explore, and create?

Her tears fell relentlessly for several minutes, and she feared she might drown in them here behind these rocks, where no one would ever find her. Only after what felt like an eternity, her eyes began to dry, and Katherine was able to catch her breath. It was time to call for reinforcements.

Hey, can you show the 79th St penthouse to Mr. Belvedere in 15 mins? I NEED the afternoon.

Andi, always loyal and *always* on her phone, responded to the text immediately.

No problemo. I gotcha covered hun. Call me later. We'll wine! ☺

Katherine found some tissues in her purse, wiped the snot and tears from what was left of her face, and took some deep breaths, hoping the oxygen would erase the red blotchiness that covered her cheeks and chest (an irritating side effect she had dealt with her entire life). She had always envied girls who could shed some tears and then wipe them away with no evidence of the sadness that had occurred. When Katherine cried, it was obvious from a mile away.

Weak and wobbly at first, she eased herself up from the faithful tree trunk. She felt as though she had shed about twenty pounds. Still breathing deeply, she continued her walk through the park. Now that her afternoon was free, she had no destination in mind.

Not far away, a harpist sat with her beloved instrument, her fingers dancing across the strings, her head swaying with her eyes closed. She was smiling and appeared to be completely content. Her music was the only company she required. She was unperturbed by a crowd, and she was equally unperturbed by the absence of a crowd. Katherine watched her with admiration. She didn't know what the harpist's life was like beyond the borders of the park, but she imagined it was simple and full of love.

Was it too late for Katherine to find true happiness? Was she too broken to start over?

As she wandered on, she thought about Michael. It would be natural for her to want to pick up the phone and beg him to reconsider. Maybe he was just lost. Maybe he still loved her. Maybe he regretted all the pain he caused her. She pulled her phone out of her purse and stared at the screen.

Nothing.

Not a single bone in her body desired to contact him. She did miss him, or at least the *idea* of him when they were younger and when their days were joyful and full of laughter. But things had changed. He had changed.

Had she changed?

Did she somehow become a repellent, self-involved creature that failed to give her husband what he really needed? The question stopped her in her tracks.

Was the divorce completely her fault? Had she sent him subliminal I-no-longer-care-about-you messages without even realizing herself that she felt that way?

The image of Michael above her in bed, drunk and angry, swept over her. She closed her eyes tightly and willed the memory away. When she opened them, she looked to her left and realized she was standing just behind the Met.

The Metropolitan Museum of Art had captivated Katherine since she was a girl. A beautiful and formidable structure, conveniently accessible from the ever-bustling 5th Avenue, it sat perfectly on an invisible line separating the ambitious and hectic city from the serene natural beauty of Central Park. The Met held an air of undeniable grandeur, but Katherine had always found it very inviting. It beckoned to those who walked down 5th with its alluring stairway entry, grand columns, and tempting food carts lined up along the sidewalk, hoping to entice museumgoers with their lunchtime aromas.

She hadn't been to the Met for a long time. The last visit had been maybe four or five years ago. *Could it really be that long*? She felt as though she had carelessly neglected a dear friend and now she must make up for lost time. She made her way across the backside of the building and around the corner to 5th. As she walked toward the entrance, Katherine smiled at the caricature artists and street vendors selling iconic prints of Manhattan's main attractions. Her pace quickened. Suddenly, she couldn't wait another minute to lose herself in the halls of the majestic place that had brought her so much happiness throughout her life. Maybe among some of history's most important paintings, the international tourist groups sneaking forbidden photographs of famous works, and the seemingly impenetrable marble sculptures, she would find some comfort or, perhaps, even a tiny hint of clarity.

Passing giggling gaggles of teenagers and an older couple resting their feet and enjoying hot dogs from one of the carts, she climbed the massive stairs and walked through the front door. While security searched her bag, she smiled and looked around the grand lobby. The enormously high ceilings created a muted echo of the crowds talking in their "museum voices" just above a whisper. To some, a lobby of this scale and subtle-but-powerful energy might be intimidating, but for Katherine, it was *home*. As she approached one of the admission desks, she remembered she had an annual membership that had been set to auto-renew every year for the past ten years. She was embarrassed that it had been so long, but she was delighted and proud to produce her card.

"Thank you for your annual contribution, Miss Ross," the attendant remarked as he handed it back to her.

Miss Ross . . . Katherine had applied for her membership before she was married to Michael and had never taken the time to change her name with the Met. She hadn't been addressed by her maiden name in years, but she liked the sound of it, and she warmly welcomed its return.

Katherine Ross.

CHAPTER 3

Katherine committed herself to spending the rest of the day in the museum. In the past, she would prioritize her valuable time and focus entirely on the European Paintings section, bypassing the other significant realms of international art history: Egyptian Art, Armor, Photographs, Sculpture, etc. But today, she would take a few hours and explore the other parts of the museum, while still looking forward to her favorite collection as a final-stop reward.

As she walked through Arms and Armor, she marveled at the intricately decorated weaponry, imagining the soldiers and royals who had once wielded the beautiful swords and sported the bejeweled armor. She had always loved the idea of a knight in shining armor. *Didn't every girl?*

She had been certain that Michael was her knight. That he was her forever. *How could she have been so wrong?* Rather than protecting Katherine, he had hurt her. He had caused her more harm than anyone.

Would this fair maiden ever find her knight?

She shook her head as she moved onto the next wing. *First, she needed to find herself.*

The European Sculpture Court transported Katherine to a time when only survival and passion mattered, a time when life consisted of love, war, and family—nothing else. The flawless, clean surfaces of the sculptures reflected the copious amounts of natural light flooding in through the floor-to-ceiling windows on the far side of the room. The ceiling rose to an impossible height, as if the architect wanted the gods themselves to have access to this court and its collection of their stories carved into pristine marble. She walked by each piece, marveling at the artists' abilities to create soft, porcelain-like curves of human skin from what was once a hard block of rock.

Back in art school, Katherine had been gifted the pleasure of visiting Michelangelo's *La Pieta* while completing a couple of semesters in Italy. She had stood in front of the masterpiece for what seemed like hours, tracing each line of precious anatomy and each delicate fold of fabric with her eyes, trying to catch her breath, which had been swept away by the shock of the extreme beauty seeming to live and breathe within the work itself. It was one of those pivotal moments all those years ago that had convinced her that art really *was* important and that it held a deep and sometimes mysterious power. Art had the ability to make people feel and respond, sometimes even against their own will. She held onto that belief firmly during her time in Italy, where she spent most of her hours in the art studio, devotedly painting and sketching.

Her own artistic talent had been evident when she was very young, when her teacher in the 6th grade recognized her unique ability and encouraged her to take an oil painting class at the local community college. At twelve years old, Katherine had created a painting that rivaled those of the adult students in the workshop—the same adult students who had initially found her presence in the class to be nothing more than adorable. They weren't expecting the excellence she produced effortlessly with only a few general instructions on how to use the medium. Katherine hadn't expected it either. From that point on, she was hooked. She took every art class available through high school and received the highest possible scores on her senior-year portfolio.

When it had come time to choose a major in college, she never once hesitated. Katherine had completed her Bachelor of Arts degree in Fine Art, with the hope of spending her life as a professional artist.

She found a seat in the middle of the sculpture court, along the edge of a small pool created by water spouting out of the mouth of some exquisite mythical creature with fangs and fantastical wings. And there, she mentally scanned her life over the past decade in search of some answers, like skimming through a movie at 2x fast-forward, hoping to catch the scene that causes the plot to take such a dramatic turn.

What happened after school? I was so sure of my path and my purpose.

Katherine recalled her time working as an intern for a couple of art galleries in Chelsea. She had hoped that, by learning the business of art, she'd be able to break through as a practicing artist. But as time went on, she was exposed to the many complexities and corruptions in the art world. Talent was of little-to-no relevance. All that mattered was that someone "important" in the art world discovered you and declared your work to be great; then all the galleries and collectors would come running. It didn't take long for this brutal realization to weigh heavily on her plans, as well as on her bank account.

As she became increasingly jaded by the impossibility of making it as an artist, she began exploring other career options. She swallowed her pride, got her real estate license, and built K&A with Andi, who had been a good friend in school, and who had been relentlessly nagging Katherine to join her in the venture.

While the starving artist could be a romantic concept, Katherine knew she wasn't cut out for a life of struggle—eating ramen noodles and desperately seeking out benefactors. She ultimately made the decision to set aside her dream to make a life, and that was that.

Feeling suddenly lost among the giant marble men in the giant marble room, Katherine tossed a quarter into the fountain over her shoulder and decided it was time to go visit her old friends in the European Painting wing.

She could never quite pinpoint what it was that pulled her to the European paintings. She wasn't a strict traditionalist in her art appreciation; in fact, she herself had been more of a modern abstract painter during art school. But in the European Paintings collection at the Met, Katherine had always felt a very strong connection with the work, almost as if the paintings were deliberately whispering too quietly for her to hear what they were saying but begged her to listen. She would lose herself in the symphonies of color in the landscapes and felt a kinship with the kind-eyed girls sitting patiently in their bonnets and gowns. She imagined the French Impressionists wandering around Paris in the 1920s: drinking, smoking, and philosophizing together, outwardly encouraging one another in their ambitions while inwardly resenting the others and competing to be the best.

Katherine stood in front of a simple Van Gogh landscape. She marveled at the wistful beauty, paint applied with such freedom and vibrancy, and she wondered if the notoriously troubled artist ever felt that kind of true joy within his own heart.

Had Katherine ever felt true joy?

Yes, in Florence. One wonderful rainy day when she was alone in the art studio, she'd listened to her favorite music, spread out her supplies, and sipped on a cheap bottle of Chianti while she worked. At that moment, she had not cared about a single thing beyond what her hands were doing with the charcoal and paint. And in that moment, her heart had sung with pure joy.

Surely the great Van Gogh experienced at least a few of these blissful moments while he blended his lively greens, golden yellows, and seductive blues. For an artist, the creation of beauty opened the doors to the path of escape.

Escape . . .

Katherine meandered through the collection aimlessly. Her thoughts were unfocused, chaotically swimming around childhood memories and critical self-evaluations, pending work deals, and Michael. It was a wonder she didn't walk into anyone. She continued to float around in her daze until she was brought to a halt by a Monet painting she had never seen before.

Claude Monet had always been a favorite of hers, but not in the cliché oh-his-*Water-Lilies*-are-so-pretty kind of way. She was fascinated by the artist's subtle yet commanding use of light and its interaction with equally subtle yet captivating color palettes. Monsieur Monet seemed to have the ability to communicate divine messages through his delicate whispers of light, his hushed colors, equally natural and transcendent. To Katherine, Monet was the ultimate champion of capturing only the best qualities of our visual world, the way she supposed a soul mate would bring out the best qualities in his partner.

How had she never seen this particular painting before? Maybe she had seen it but failed to notice it?

She believed the painting had probably been there all along, but she likely had been distracted by Michael's efforts to hurry her along so that they could go do something "more exciting."

This was a different sort of work by the famed French artist, a departure from his more familiar romantic garden or Parisian scenes. Upon close inspection, *The Valley of the Nervia* was undoubtedly a Monet because of the signature brushstrokes and typically brilliant approach to subtlety of hue. But the subject appeared to be in a place far from the artist's homes in Paris and Giverny. In the foreground, a vast valley was kissed by the sun, the warmth of the ground finding reprieve in the presence of a calm stream quietly wending its way across the canvas. Beyond the valley floor, the palette became cooler among scattered greens and lavender hills. And in the far distance, majestic snow-capped peaks reigned over the land. They intimidated in scale and wintery whiteness, but they beckoned to the viewer, welcoming a journey to their summit, where perhaps the mysteries of the world and of the heart would ultimately be revealed.

Katherine studied the painting. Her eyes traveled from each corner to the center vanishing point. She was in the valley, dipping her feet in the stream, seeking shade in the trees at the base of the hills. There were no buildings, no cars, and no people—a far cry from her usual surroundings. She deeply inhaled the fresh open air as she ventured toward the snowy mountains, daring herself to go further.

"Ahem," coughed the gallery security guard.

Apparently, Katherine had lost herself so much in the mysterious mountain valley that she had forgotten proper museum etiquette. Her nose pointed dangerously close to the painting, as her upper body bent at a nearly ninety-degree angle to lean over the protective barrier placed along the base of the walls to prevent museumgoers from touching or otherwise damaging the priceless paintings.

"Sorry!" she whispered and clenched her teeth in an I'm-innocent-just-a-bit-stupid smile, as her cheeks warmed and turned a nice shade of Monet water lily pink.

Returning her attention to the painting from an appropriate distance, she imagined the sounds surrounding Monet as he worked on it.

A comforting quiet.

Not the uneasy quiet when something is wrong, or when a storm (literal or metaphorical) is about to strike, but the kind of quiet when all is well, and excessive sound is simply unnecessary. In her mind, the quiet of this valley was only occasionally interrupted by the song of a small bird or by the wind jostling the leaves of the trees, and those who listened very carefully might be lucky enough to hear the graceful roll of the stream dancing over smooth rocks, carrying the icy cold water from the mountain majesties above.

Katherine closed her eyes. Her life had become a distracted life full of noise. Not all of the noise was bad, but it simply never ceased. She feared one day she might wake up an old woman, still drowning in noise and searching for happiness.

She opened her eyes and smiled at her new favorite painting. Suddenly, she knew exactly what she needed to do.

CHAPTER 4

"Colorado?" Andi nearly sprayed an entire mouthful of rosé out her nose. "You've got to be kidding me." She stared at Katherine, her wide dumbfounded eyes waiting for her friend to concede, "Yes, ha-ha, it was just a joke," and then they would continue to talk about their latest deals, upcoming parties, and Andi's recent romantic flings.

But Katherine made no such concession. "It's time for a change. I'm ready for a change."

"Yeah, but *Co-lo-ra-do*? You might as well be going to *China*." Andi always had a flare for drama and exaggeration, qualities that nicely lent themselves to her success in selling exorbitantly priced real estate. She looked around uncomfortably, shifted in her chair, and chugged the remainder of her $18 glass of wine as though it were a shot of cheap tequila, waiting for Katherine to admit the absurdity of her plan.

"Oh come on, Andi, it's not that far. I used to go all the time when I was a kid. Four-hour plane ride and you're there." Katherine recalled the summer vacations to the Rocky Mountains with her family. Her parents had met in a ski town in Colorado when they were in their twenties, and they lived there together for a couple of years before moving back to New York to start their careers. For a few wonderful summers, her parents had made a tradition of returning to the mountainous state with Katherine and her older brother.

As a kid, she'd fallen in love with the mountains. She found them gloriously exotic—colossal piles of earth and trees reaching higher than the empire state building. She had imagined that the dinosaurs must be buried beneath them. That, of course, was the only way to explain their massive size.

Her family had always rented a cabin in one of the small mountain towns, and they would spend their trips hiking, fishing, and toasting marshmallows around a campfire. Katherine couldn't believe how different the smells and sounds were in the mountains. She would breathe in traces of fresh cut wood and lake water upon the cool breeze, while listening to the birds sing to one another from the branches of towering pine trees. As a child, she likened the experience to Snow White and her quaint little cabin with the dwarfs, among friendly musical animals and far away from the pressures of the castle and its dangerous evil queen.

Her favorite trip had been to an old one-street town called Bluewater Lake. Appropriately named, the town ran alongside a lake so vividly blue it appeared to glow, even in the middle of the night. Katherine had been convinced it had magical powers, and she would sit on the dock for hours, trying to capture the mesmerizing hue with her pastels. Even as a kid she was fascinated by the power of color, and something about the crisp blues and greens in this particular place spoke deeply to her young artist's heart. Like Snow White, Katherine found peace and happiness in the woods, and she had often wished she could stay there forever.

But as time went on, her parents fell more deeply into obligations with work and life in the city. Their leisurely family trips to Colorado became less and less frequent, until they simply did not have time to go at all. Katherine couldn't quite remember the last time they visited. She estimated that she had been around nine years old, and come to think of it, she remembered her father spending most of that final trip on his cell phone, frantically wandering around with his arm held up in the air, trying to find a spot where he had enough service to conference back to New York.

Colorado became an assortment of fuzzy recollections. After many years had passed, Katherine couldn't discern her real life memories from her imagination. Did her father really burn the steaks that one hot summer and throw them into the lake, announcing in a goofy English butler's voice that they would be "Dining on s'mores!" instead? And had her brother really stirred her from her stiff cabin bed one early morning to take her fishing on the dock while their parents slept? Perhaps it was all just one big beautiful daydream.

"But for how long? Like, a week?" Andi's question snapped Katherine out of her nostalgia.

"No." Katherine cleared her throat nervously. "I was thinking for . . . Well, I was thinking more like . . . permanently." She looked down at her barely-touched glass of prosecco. While she was excited about her decision, it broke her heart to look her best friend in the eye and admit that this was the beginning of a good-bye.

Andi's jaw dropped and her brows furrowed, as if she had just witnessed an obscene crime. Her eyes darted around anxiously, and she moved her mouth in an attempt to say something, but for perhaps the first time in her life, Andi appeared to be speechless.

"I want to start my life over. I want to do it right this time," Katherine began, her voice shaky, but her undertones resolute. *I have to erase Michael from my memory,* she thought to herself.

"But *how*? *When*? What about K&A? What will you *do* there? Oh my God, are you going to turn into one of those mountain people who don't shave their legs or armpits and who, like, *hunt* for their food?!" Andi apparently found her words again.

Katherine tried not to laugh. Her friend was obviously very upset. "I'm not sure. I was thinking, maybe, I will paint again." She paused, hoping for a response resounding with positive encouragement, but Andi appeared to still be in shock. "Besides, you are more than capable of taking over K&A. I have no doubt you'll be great. You deserve it all to yourself anyway; your heart has always been more invested than mine. We both know that."

She sat back and sipped on the bubbly prosecco, giving Andi a few moments to process the news. Katherine adored her friend, and she knew she would miss her terribly. Andi was bold and daring. She had a killer business sense, while still maintaining a free spirit. And while she hoped Andi might someday find true love and settle down, she envied her lighthearted and carefree approach to men. Andi and

Katherine were perfect complements to one another—harmoniously different, like robust balsamic vinegar paired with a subtle and earthy olive oil. Their beautiful balance had allowed them to become brilliant business partners, and their friendship, like a fine red wine, only got better with age.

For a moment, Katherine wished Andi were enough reason to stay here in the city, in this routine, in her comfort zone. But she knew she had to go.

"Andi, please say something. You're killing me here."

Andi cleared her throat and waived her empty glass at the waiter.

"I want you to be happy, Katherine. I just don't want you to regret making such a big move. And I just don't know what I'll do without you!" Andi smiled her I'm-fine-and-everything-is-fabulous-even-though-it's-really-not smile as the waiter brought her a refill. She unfolded her cloth napkin and elegantly wiped a tear from the corner of her eye. "But I understand you need to do this, and I'm sure I'll see it as a good thing . . . *eventually*." Andi sighed and lifted her glass. "Here's to my little Katie and her new beginning as a lumberjack!"

Katherine laughed. "And here's to you, Miss Andi Bretton, the fearless leader and goddess of K&A Realty!"

They clinked their glasses proudly as they welcomed, if slightly tentatively, their new chapters in life.

"Cheers!"

~*~

Katherine woke up the next morning with a heavy prosecco hangover. So many beautiful dancing bubbles shimmering in the New York City rooftop sunset, glass after glass, the exquisite liquid with its inherent prestige should not have such an intensely raw and dreadful effect on its purportedly fancy victims. She rolled over and tried to breathe meditatively in an effort to coax the thunderous throbbing out of her head.

They had had quite the celebratory night full of colorful cocktails and mixed emotions. They laughed and talked; they cried; they reminisced. They even danced with some handsome investment bankers visiting from out of town.

It all started coming back to Katherine in foggy tidbits, each detail from the night reentering her mind with a short but powerful shot of pain to her temple.

Playfully dodging his attempts while they danced, she hadn't let the handsome banker kiss her. Even in her alcohol-induced lack of inhibition, she knew she wasn't ready to feel the touch of another man's lips. As enticing as he was with his fetching smile and dark brown eyes, Katherine couldn't bear the feeling of his hands on her waist. It was too soon. Her body stiffened, and her stomach still tumbled with thoughts of that terrible night with Michael. She felt used; she felt disgusting. After a few songs, she kindly excused herself from the dance floor, desperate to go home alone and collapse into bed.

Andi, on the other hand, had helped Katherine into a cab, before walking away arm in arm with the other, also devastatingly attractive, banker. Katherine remembered sloppily turning around in the cab seat to look out the back window just in time to catch Andi's giddy wave and signature I'm-about-to-be-very-naughty wink.

Ouch.

Andi's text made Katherine laugh, which in turn made her head feel like someone was taking a wrench to it, in an attempt to pry it off her body.

Meet for lunch in an hour? I need something to soak up my idiocy.

She smiled and squinted in pain as she texted back.

Soaking sounds good. I hate you by the way. ☺ I can only hope they do NOT have prosecco in Colorado!

Katherine willed herself out of bed. She had grown accustomed to living in her apartment alone after Michael left. While the nights sometimes felt lonely, and she jumped at even the smallest unfamiliar sound, she mostly loved having the place all to herself again. She made her way to the bathroom at a sloth-like pace and finally got her hands on the bottle of aspirin. Taking three with water, she braced herself as she looked in the mirror.

She had always been what she considered to be average: not too big, but not thin, not at all tall, but not too short. She didn't despise her face, but she didn't find it remarkably beautiful or exotic either. She had her mother's eastern European features, but was cursed with her father's rouge-prone coloring. The slightest moment of embarrassment, nervousness, or unexpected warmth would transform her skin to a red and blotchy mess in less than a second—an attribute that for her entire life caused strangers to mistake her temporary blushing for sunburn and offer unsolicited sunscreen advice.

Unlike her skin, Katherine's eyes had always been her proudest feature. On most days they were a calm inviting blue, but they would shift to a vibrant forest green seemingly at their own discretion. This morning, however, her eyes were only red and bloodshot, struggling against the heavy weight of the mascara-stained bags beneath them.

She jumped in the shower and then brewed an offensively strong cup of coffee. The aspirin began to work its magic, and finally she could move without wincing. After getting dressed, she decided to walk to meet Andi. It would be a long walk, twelve hungover blocks, but she wanted to soak in some of the city she had called home for so long.

Katherine had a love-hate relationship with Manhattan. Overall, she had always felt a bit overwhelmed. She was sensitive to sound and had been a claustrophobe ever since she could remember, so she never felt the cool sense of ease she so often witnessed on the faces of other New York commuters in the clattering crowded subways and along the congested sidewalks. But tucked between the noise and the crowds, she had found so many special pockets of beauty in the city, and she knew she would miss her favorite spots, like Romeo's Flower Shop on the corner of her building, where she could rarely pass without Romeo himself handing her a single daisy or carnation, always accompanied by a "Good morning, Bella!" and a wink. She would desperately miss *Trattoria Vivaldi*, her favorite little Italian place and the *only* restaurant that produced dishes resembling the authentic Tuscan food she had eaten while studying in Florence. She would miss Central Park in the fall with its warm cinnamon and pumpkin-colored leaves and cool crisp air kissing the cheeks of city dwellers after a long hot summer.

She would always cherish her memories of the occasional brunch at the Plaza Hotel with all of its glamorous patrons and glistening chandeliers, and the iconic painting of a chubby disheveled Eloise—the famed fictional girl who lived in the Plaza and caused all sorts of mischief in an otherwise immaculate and perfectly elegant establishment. Katherine had read the Eloise books as a girl, and she always looked for the little troublemaker every time her family visited the Plaza, hoping to someday catch a glimpse of the naughty yet charming creature she secretly hoped to befriend.

And then, of course, there was the Met.

Could she actually leave the Met, her one constant beacon of light and comfort, behind?

The Met was like a lifelong friend, always waiting for her with open arms, offering her a safe place to think or to escape. As she walked, her chest tightened at the thought of leaving the museum, her sanctuary. But she knew it would always be there, faithfully waiting for her to come back someday, even if only for a visit.

Katherine turned the corner to find Andi slouched on the railing in front of their lunch spot, O'Finnigans Irish Pub, a sure bet for greasy hangover sustenance. She almost laughed out loud at the miserable version of her usually fabulous friend— only because the sight was so shockingly pathetic and unfamiliar it caught her off guard.

"So, should I prepare the wedding invitations?" she teased.

"Ha-haaaaa." Andi groaned. She was in far worse shape than Katherine and attempted to hide the effects of last night behind enormous black sunglasses.

They found a small table in a dark corner of the pub, trying to escape any painful glares from the bright sunlight.

"He was fun. And I think he *did* propose to me at some point during the night. They usually do." Andi smirked proudly and flopped her forehead down onto the table.

They nursed their nausea and headaches with orders of grease-soaked fish and chips and Diet Cokes, as Andi filled Katherine in about her night with her southern banker. She always told Katherine about her sleepovers, whether she wanted to hear it or not, and Katherine always blushed as her friend so comfortably shared intimate tidbits and raunchy details. She often suspected Andi found joy in her obvious discomfort, and that she found Katherine's much more reserved and private nature extremely frustrating.

"C'mon, tell me more! What happened with that tall, dark, and dreamy dessert you met last night?"

Andi had begged her desperately when she first met Michael all those years ago at the K&A party. Of course, Katherine, with rapidly reddening cheeks had brushed it off as "no big deal" in an effort to avoid diving into an overexcited conversation destined to curse any potential future with the man.

Once they finished their plates, feeling both revived and guilty for the excessive calorie consumption, Andi's skin color and spirit had improved, and she was ready to get down to business.

"So, what's your plan?"

"Well, I think I'll go to this town I visited once as a child, Bluewater Lake. I loved it so much, and, well . . . Anyway, that's where I'm going." Katherine didn't know how to justify her choice, and it was obvious in her nervous fragmented response. She really had no specific reason or directive for her selected destination, other than the impression it had left upon her all those years ago.

"Ohhhkay, sounds lovely?" Andi joked. "And what will you be doing when you get to Bluewater Lake?"

"I'm not sure. I mean, after selling my half of the business to you and with selling my apartment here, I guess I'll be set for a while financially."

"Wait! You're going to *sell* your apartment?! What if you decide Colorado isn't the answer and you want to come back?!" Andi's voice was getting louder and drawing the attention of the other pub dwellers, many of whom also appeared to be nursing hangovers.

"Well, I guess I'm afraid that, if I hang onto my place here, I won't really be able to properly let go and move on. You know. I need a clean cut. I could always come back and buy a different place. After all, I *do* know a great realtor here in the city." Katherine winked, hoping to lighten the tense mood brewing at their table.

Andi was quiet for a few moments as the reality of permanence set in. Katherine tried to comfort her dear friend, "Besides, you *will* be coming to visit me in Colorado. You have no choice in the matter."

Andi smiled reluctantly. "Only if you find me some devastatingly handsome and rugged backwoodsmen to shack up with by a fire."

CHAPTER 5

The week flew by in one big blur. Katherine and Andi settled the K&A business details with their attorney, and Katherine tied up loose ends with important clients and visited with friends. She spent her evenings packing up the apartment, sometimes with Andi and a bottle of wine keeping her company. She and Michael had gone fairly minimal in their lifestyle. Aside from impressive art on the walls and chic designer furniture, they did not have a lot of stuff.

She had grown attached to some of the art pieces, original paintings collected from artists and galleries in different places around the world, each work with its own unique story. She wasn't a snob when it came to art and never bought a painting simply because a trendy dealer told her it would be a good investment. Rather, Katherine chose pieces for herself, pieces that caught her attention and held it.

She was not one to ignore a talented street artist, vulnerable and humble, hoping that busy passersby would notice his work and appreciate its beauty. In fact, her favorite piece within her personal collection was a small canvas by a street artist in Prague. She had visited the enchanting city during her year abroad in college, and early one morning while her friends were sleeping off their night of indulging in too much absinth and disco, Katherine had decided to find coffee and go for a walk. She wandered through the city, following the streaks of sunlight warmly caressing the cobblestone streets between the magnificent buildings.

Morning Prague was very different from nighttime Prague. The previous night had been so alive with energy and music and dancing, students touring and laughing, locals peddling their wares. It had almost felt like the city was moving, bouncing, unable to contain the excitement within. But in the morning, everything was still, and Katherine believed she might be the only living, breathing person there—almost as though the colorful characters from the previous night had vanished into the wind and had simply forgotten to take her along.

She enjoyed the thought of Prague belonging to her alone, and she smiled as she explored. But after a few blocks, she discovered that Prague was not hers to claim. She shared it with a crazy-haired artist painting along the river. He was young, maybe even her age, and he was working on a delicate capture of the water glowing in the golden morning light. A cigarette hung loosely from the corner of his mouth, and his curly chestnut hair darted in all directions, shifting wildly each time he moved. He nodded at Katherine as she sat on a bench about twenty feet behind his easel. She did not want to disturb him, but she couldn't tear herself away.

The artist worked so naturally, showing no signs of struggle or frustration as he added splendid yellow and soft pink reflections to the painted river. Katherine marveled at his effortless brilliance for the next hour as he completed the painting. The canvas was so tiny, measuring only about ten inches, but it was the most magnificent achievement she had ever witnessed. She shyly approached the artist and offered him $200 for the work, which he gladly accepted with humble surprise. Yes, it had been her only spending money for the remainder of that month, but she didn't care. She'd eat only day-old bread and feast her eyes on her scrumptious new painting.

Katherine studied the small Prague painting now, as she removed it from the wall and held it in her hands. She smiled as she thought of that young Czech artist, and wondered if he was still painting. She decided this would be the one piece of art she would take with her to Colorado, as she couldn't bear the thought of parting with it. The rest of her art collection would be safely stored at Andi's place for a while, and her furniture would be sold with the apartment. She wrapped the painting in tissue and placed it in the center of the folded clothes in her large suitcase.

Her flight was departing at 7 a.m. the next morning, and from there, she would make her way to Bluewater Lake.

"I can't believe you're moving across the country with only two suitcases. I wouldn't even be able to fit my jewelry in two suitcases." Andi came into the bedroom after paying the cleaning staff. The apartment was going on the market the next day, and Katherine was going to stay at Andi's for her last night in the city. While Andi, of course, wanted to make a big lavish night of the occasion, Katherine insisted they lie low with takeout.

"Ready to go?" Andi asked tentatively.

Katherine sighed and looked around. The beautiful apartment had been good to her, and she would miss it. But it was also home to the life she had shared with Michael, the love and then the darkness, and that was something she was ready to leave behind.

"Yep. Let's go." Katherine choked back tears as she grabbed her bags and left her keys on the counter.

~*~

Two suitcases. Katherine checked her bags at the ticket counter. For a moment, she thought of the two suitcases that had stood in solidarity with Michael the evening he left. Only a few weeks had passed, but to Katherine, it felt as though years had gone by since she numbly watched Michael walk out the door.

"Just the two bags today, ma'am?"

The woman at the counter cleared her throat.

"I'm sorry?" Katherine shook the image of Michael and his suitcases from her mind. "Oh, yes, just the two. Thank you."

After security, she had some time before her flight. She stopped at a snack and souvenir shop to load up on gum, Tums, and trashy magazines—vices to distract her from her inevitable in-flight claustrophobia. As she waited in line to pay, she mindlessly browsed a display of New York City postcards. One particular card caught her eye, and she added it in with her purchases.

At the gate, Katherine took a seat and fished a pen from her purse. She held the postcard, admiring the image on the front: Central Park in its finest autumn glory, trees splendidly draped in reds and golds, almost glowing against a perfect cobalt blue sky. And fixed stoically in the center of the picturesque fall splendor was the Metropolitan Museum of Art. *Her* Met.

On the back of the card, Katherine wrote Michael's name and addressed it to his office in the city. Then she wrote only two words.

Thank you,

-K

She pulled a stamp from her purse and found a mailbox in the terminal. Katherine exhaled as she dropped the card into the bin, just as the final boarding call for her flight was announced.

CHAPTER 6

Katherine wandered through Denver International Airport with a green face and wobbly legs. The nearly four-hour flight had been turbulent, and her excessive gum chewing and Tums-popping provided only slight comfort to her nervous stomach. The very large and very cheerful gentleman who had been sitting next to her was a chatty grandfather of ten. Katherine did her best to ignore his giant legs and Santa-like belly spilling over onto her seat, and tried instead to focus on his comical, endearing stories about his grandchildren. After all, it wasn't his fault the airplane seats were obviously designed to hold only small children, elves, and the occasional Oompa Loompa.

Little did her jolly neighbor know that, behind her polite smile, she battled a desperate internal panic attack. She spent the entire flight subtly trying to control her breathing and convince herself that her seat was not trying to squeeze her into suffocation and that the walls of the plane were likely not shrinking inward.

At the baggage claim, Katherine took a seat on a bench facing the carousel. She closed her eyes and took a few deep breaths. Slowly, her nausea subsided, and her legs regained strength and stability. She had always been a nervous flyer, but when she and Michael had traveled, she would simply take a Valium and sleep, trusting that he would wake her up if necessary. Flying alone for the first time in years, she had made the executive decision to remain coherent and alert for her trip to Denver—a decision she regretted, especially because she was now convinced that kind Mr. Santa Man would have taken good care of her in case of an emergency.

Finally able to stand confidently, Katherine realized for the first time since the plane had landed that she was in Colorado. *She made it!* It felt so surreal to think that she would not be returning to New York, or at least not anytime soon. This was not a vacation; this was life. This was the start of *her new life*.

She collected her bags from the carousel and walked over to the rental-car desk. She didn't have a plan. All she knew was that she would rent a car and use her phone GPS to map the drive to Bluewater Lake. She only hoped that she could find a nice place to stay when she arrived and, from there, would figure out the rest. The uncertainty of her next steps made her nervous, as she had always been somewhat of an obsessive planner. But Katherine found it all a bit exhilarating. She didn't need concrete plans right now. What she needed was adventure. She texted Andi to let her know she survived the flight.

I made it. Miss you already.

Shaking her head, she smiled at Andi's predictable response.

Good. Glad you got that out of your system. Ready to come home yet? ☺

Katherine took a deep breath and tried to process her own words as she typed them.

I am home. ☺

Because it was still daylight, she opted for a MINI Cooper convertible at the rental park. It was late fall in Colorado, and she decided to make the most of her drive to Bluewater. She squeezed her two suitcases into the back seat and pulled out a light jacket to wear for the trip.

As she plugged the address for Bluewater Lake into her phone, she looked toward the mountains lining the western edge of Denver. They seemed to consume all space beyond that side of the city, rolling into one another in an endless pattern of dark green pine trees, golden Aspen trees, and purple rocky summits. Much to her surprise, she noticed the tallest peaks were already covered in snow. It wouldn't be long until winter made itself at home in the mountains, and she made a mental note to shop for more weather-appropriate clothes when she got settled.

Katherine spent the first half hour on the road, relearning how to drive. Her parents had insisted she take Drivers Ed and get her license when she was a senior in high school so that she would have the ability to drive if she ever ventured out of the city. And she certainly did go on a few road trips the following summer and during college. But that was a long time ago, and in the city, she always took cabs

43

or company cars when she couldn't walk to her destination.

After a couple of close calls during some tricky merging situations, accompanied by angry horns of fellow drivers notifying her of her navigational mistakes, she began to get the hang of it and merged onto Interstate 70 heading west. The Colorado air was cool and dry and so pure it sent her city-soaked lungs into a brief shock. She breathed it in slowly, believing for a moment that the air itself might have healing powers. Perhaps it would erase the darkness that lingered within, replacing all sadness and insecurity with clean, bright hope. *Or at least it would be a good start.*

Having finally found a confident groove with her red MINI Cooper, Katherine put both hands on the wheel, took another delicious deep breath, and headed toward the snow-capped mountains.

The two-lane interstate leading out of Denver climbed higher in elevation, curving around steep slopes and through vibrant valleys. Katherine believed this had to be the most exquisite drive in the world. The air grew even cooler as she wove her way deeper into the mountains, and the sun tiptoed closer and closer to the horizon, while the autumn leaves on the aspen trees shifted in magical golden translucence.

She played her favorite album of all time, Norah Jones' *Come Away With Me*, and laughed a bit as she could hear Andi's eyes rolling from across the country. "Norah Jones! Don't you mean SNORE-ah Jones?" But Katherine had always loved it. The artistic melodies had a way of calming her. And for today especially, Norah was an obvious choice of musical accompaniment to the visual symphony dancing around, welcoming her to the stunning new world.

After a couple of hours on the interstate, the GPS instructed her to exit and turn onto a small highway heading north. She stopped to fill up on gas and put on another layer. Her hands were freezing, but she didn't have any gloves, and she was too excited to mind. According to the directions on her phone, she had only another hour or so before she would reach Bluewater Lake. She hopped back in the car and nearly peeled out of the parking lot. The anticipation was almost too much too handle, and she wanted to drive 100 miles an hour. What would she find in Bluewater? Would she find happiness? Would she find a purpose? Would she even be lucky enough to find love? Katherine quelled her childlike excitement and convinced herself to be reasonable. First, she should be happy enough to find a warm room and some dinner—she was starving.

The northbound highway twisted through lush green fields speckled with fallen yellow leaves. It wound around thick aspen groves, running parallel to a strikingly pristine river, occasionally passing small towns consisting of only a gas station, a few little homes, and a church or school. Katherine found such towns to be quaint and charming, but couldn't help wondering what life was like in a place where the gas station is the Friday night hangout spot. If her memory served her correctly, Bluewater Lake, albeit a small mountain town, had a bit more to offer. She hoped she was right, as she watched the sun burrow between the distant peaks, while the sky embraced a cooler, more subdued version of its formerly vibrant blue.

Just as the last strokes of warm light bid farewell to the taller branches of the trees, and the darkness of night announced its imminent arrival, Katherine, now completely an anxious wreck, spotted the sign for Bluewater Lake. She nearly missed the turn because the wooden sign was partially covered by the branch of a huge pine tree, and there was no light to clarify the few letters that *were* visible.

Whipping the MINI Cooper abruptly onto the road, her heart began to beat faster, and her freezing hands trembled with nervous anticipation.

Bluewater was just as she recalled: a long one-street town with family-owned restaurants, gift shops, galleries, and candy stores. An old playground marked the center of the town on the left, with a tree-covered mountainside climbing upward behind it. And to the right, between The Saloon and Ralph's Grocery, was the unmistakable glow of the cerulean blue water—even more vivid than she had ever remembered.

Against a tugging impulse to turn right and visit the lake, Katherine decided she must first find a place to stay. She hadn't eaten since that morning before her flight, and her low blood sugar teamed up with the high altitude at Bluewater (it rested at just over 9500 feet), inducing an extreme case of lightheadedness. *She must eat and sleep. She would visit the lake first thing in the morning.*

As she neared the end of Main Street, she saw a sign for The Bluewater Inn and pulled into one of its few designated parking spaces, desperately hoping they had a vacant room.

Even in her hungry exhausted stupor, Katherine could appreciate the timeless beauty of the small inn. The building appeared to be quite old, maybe even historical, but extremely well kept. The wood was painted white with blue trim, and each window was outfitted with a planter full of colorful Colorado wild flowers. A warm glow radiated from the lobby windows, and Katherine could hear someone softly playing the piano inside. As she walked through the door, she was pleasantly assaulted with an array of tantalizing smells: wood burning in the fireplace, cinnamon, and freshly brewed coffee.

"Hello! Can I help you?" A small elderly man with perfectly white hair and quirky round glasses sitting atop a giant, almost cartoon-worthy, nose smiled at Katherine from behind the baby grand piano. The exquisite instrument sat in the middle of a warm and welcoming living room. To the right, she noted a small desk and a table full of brochures, and to her left, a stone fireplace framed by an impressive collection of books. Straight ahead, behind a sofa and two giant armchairs, was a large window overlooking the lake.

"Hello. Do you happen to have a vacancy for this evening?" Katherine felt as though she may burst into tears if the answer was no.

"Why you are in luck, young lady! I just had a cancellation!" He smiled warmly, seeming to sense her delicate state.

The man introduced himself as Eli Trust, the inn's proprietor. His family had built the inn over ninety years ago, and it was the first official business to open in Bluewater Lake. With great pride sparkling in his eyes, the kind host took Katherine's bags and led her up a beautiful staircase with a wood bannister matching the elegant wood of the piano.

The walls were decorated with framed black-and-white photographs, and Katherine made a mental note to study them when she was better rested. She marveled at Mr. Trust's ability to carry her suitcases with such ease. He must have been at least eighty years old, but there was plenty of spring in his step, and she envied his childlike energy.

At the top of the stairs, they walked down a narrow hallway, passing some closed wooden doors, each accompanied by a lantern-style light and a wood plaque with a room number. Mr. Trust escorted Katherine to the final door at the end of the hall, Room #8.

"Here is your room, darling. When you are ready, come down to the dining room. The kitchen closed an hour ago, but I'll have the chef cook up some dinner for you. I bet you're hungry." Mr. Trust tipped an invisible hat on his head, and with a slight bow, he smiled and shut the door.

The room was perfect. Along one wall, a queen-size bed rested between two log nightstands. The bed was covered in several blankets and what looked to be a hand-stitched quilt crafted with love by someone in the Trust family, Katherine suspected. A matching desk and dresser stood along the opposite wall, as well as the door to the bathroom. In the center of the room, a large soft rug protected bare feet from the cool hardwood floor, and in the far corner, a cozy chair, worn but inviting, sat next to a large window. She pulled back the curtain and smiled as she greeted the glow of the lake peeking through the dark silhouettes of pine trees.

CHAPTER 7

Katherine awoke to a beam of sunlight piercing through the edge of the curtain. She stretched her legs and her arms and marveled at the incredible comfort of the bed. The quilt had kept her warm in the brisk fall night, and she couldn't believe how well she had slept.

Her first evening in Bluewater Lake had been utterly wonderful. As promised, Mr. Trust had dinner prepared for Katherine despite her late arrival. After unpacking her bags and changing into yoga pants and a sweater, she'd shyly walked down the stairs into the empty dining room. Mr. Trust introduced her to Murray, the inn's chef, who had whipped up a Gruyere grilled-cheese sandwich and a side salad.

"I'm sorry it's not very extravagant," Murray said as he set the plate in front of her. "But please come again tomorrow, and I'll show you what my dinners are all about."

Murray was probably in his mid-60s. He had salt and pepper hair, with a well-trimmed beard surrounding a huge ear-to-ear smile. He spoke with one of the thickest Boston accents she had ever heard, and his chef's belly was perfectly round. Katherine liked him immediately. She could tell he took great pride in his work.

"Are you kidding? This looks amazing!" The smell alone almost made her drool.

Katherine took a bite out of the sandwich and sighed. The cheese was heavenly, savory and dripping, and the bread was perfectly warm, melting in her mouth. She tried to eat slowly, for the thought of the meal ending was enough to bring tears to her eyes. Yes, she was beyond starving, and her judgment might have been slightly impaired, but she suspected this was the best grilled-cheese sandwich ever made in the history of all time.

She had been an unofficial foodie most of her adult life. Her mother was always an amazing cook, and Katherine herself enjoyed cooking when she had the time. The year she spent in Europe had elevated her already-established love of food to an entirely new level, creating within her a deep appreciation for true culinary craft. To Katherine, cooking was as much an art as painting or music, and here at this little inn, Murray the chef had already proven to be a master of his art.

Willing herself out of bed, she went to the window and pulled back the curtain. The lake, reflecting the bright sunlight on its surface, was nearly fluorescent. It was completely undisturbed by any wake or wind and stood enduringly in its powerful glare.

Katherine checked the time as she dressed. It was already nearly ten o'clock! She couldn't remember ever sleeping so late, and for a moment, she was angry with herself for failing to set an alarm—so much of the day was already wasted. But then, she remembered that this was only the first of many days at the lake. Time was not confined to a short amount of vacation hours or limited by work deadlines. She was here for the foreseeable future, and this was just the beginning. She unpacked the rest of her suitcase, carefully placing the small painting from Prague on the center of the dresser.

Down in the lobby, she filled a to-go cup with hot coffee and smiled and waved at Mr. Trust, who was sitting at the desk, taking a reservation over the phone. He tipped his imaginary hat in return and smiled with a wink.

A few other patrons lingered in the lobby. An older couple sat on the sofa and flipped through one of the *Scenic Colorado* coffee table books. Another couple, much younger, sat on a bench by the fireplace, giggling and sharing a scone. Katherine could hear a few more voices and the delicate clanks of dishes coming from the dining room, accompanied by the mouth-watering smells of hot sizzling bacon and something with cinnamon and sugar. *Maybe fresh-baked cinnamon rolls?*

Despite her late night dinner, her tummy growled, begging her to partake in Murray's undoubtedly delicious breakfast. But she suppressed the tantalizing urge and focused on her mission at hand. It was time to see the lake.

Outside, the town was already bustling with activity. A group of older ladies huddled together on a bench to read the paper and catch up on town gossip, while storeowners set up displays and swept their doorsteps. Several tourists wandered along the sidewalks, peeking in shop windows and stocking up on sweet souvenirs from the candy store.

How very different this scene was from her usual morning walk to work back in Manhattan. There she would step onto the busy sidewalk outside her building and be immediately besieged with a cacophony of taxi horns, sirens, clicks of high heels on the sidewalk, and indomitable New Yorkers negotiating on their cell phones as they hustled to their ambitious workplaces.

Katherine strolled along Main Street for a block, until she intersected a dirt path that led down to the lake on her left. Sipping her coffee, her pace quickened as she followed the trail, twisting through impossibly tall trees, passing a few quaint cabins. It was only a minute or two before she reached the lake, her path ending at a grassy clearing nestled along a small rocky beach.

She giggled, *actually giggled*, as she removed her shoes and dipped her toes in the water. Here at eye level, the lake adopted an entirely different personality. Still smooth as glass on the windless day, the water continued to reflect the brightness of the sun. But as Katherine stared at the lake from where the water met her toes in a cold but gentle embrace, the colors seemed to multiply and dance in playful transitions.

In the shallow waters nearest to her, aqua blues, similar to those found in the water along Caribbean beaches, played with cool minty greens shimmering in the sunlight and dodging any notion of permanence. As she looked farther into the deeper waters at the center of the lake, the aquas and greens blended into luscious velvety teals. And finally, at the farthest point across the lake from where she stood, Katherine observed deep indigo and midnight blue water dotted with sporadic specs of sun—looking very much like a star-studded night sky.

Log homes and A-frame cabins bordered the lake to her right and to her left, but straight ahead, the indigo water along the far edge merged only with the pure deep green of the untainted pine forest sheltered from behind by the steep slope of a massive mountain peak. She remembered the mountain from when she visited as a child. Back then, she had imagined that, if she stood at the top, she'd be able to see around the entire world and that the mountain was the wise protector of Bluewater Lake and all its inhabitants.

I have to paint this. I have to paint these colors!

The inspiration bombarded her with an unexpected urgency. Of course, the lake would be there today and tomorrow and the next day, but she had to paint it *now*, at this very moment. Her elation morphed quickly into frustration when Katherine realized that she had no painting supplies. And she doubted she'd find any in the tiny town. She had planned to order supplies once she was settled, but that would take days. She dried her feet on the grass and put her shoes back on, before sprinting up the path, coffee spilling all over her hand.

When she reached the street again, she turned left and headed for Ralph's Grocery. Maybe they'd have *something* for her to use, at least for now. She combed the small aisles, desperately looking for things she was almost certain she wouldn't find. And then, on the bottom shelf by the Band-Aids, pens, and Scotch tape, there was a children's set of watercolors! It would have to do. She grabbed a blank notebook off the shelf above and hurried over to the register.

"Good morning." The girl at the counter smiled nervously at Katherine as she scanned the watercolors and placed them in a bag with the paper. She seemed a bit concerned as she studied Katherine, who, at that moment, realized she was panting quite loudly.

"Good morning!" Katherine smiled widely as she paid. "Thank You!" She grabbed her bag and nearly sprinted out the door.

Back at the beach, she settled on a large rock and placed the pad of paper on her lap. She balanced the little watercolor set next to her and pulled out the tiny paintbrush. Taking a deep breath, she squinted at the water. Katherine didn't know if she remembered how to paint; all she wanted to do was attempt to capture the colors dancing in front of her. She delicately mixed the blues and greens from the basic palette, creating vivid variations of the primary and secondary colors. In some mixtures, she added a hint of red to create cooler purple shadows, and in some, she added a touch of yellow to amplify the lightness of the green highlights visible in the shallow parts of the water.

Katherine painted sheet after sheet. A few compositions featured the entire lake with a rough outline of the mountain standing proudly behind it. Others were only drenched in color from top to bottom—as though she had dived in and painted them from within the lake itself. The quality of the work was not good. The paper was so flimsy it wrinkled and nearly tore under the weight of the water and cheap pigment. And Katherine could not achieve the level of vibrancy she wanted. But the act itself was exhilarating.

She was painting!

Working on her last sheet of paper, scraping out the last bits of paint that remained in the diminutive plastic palette, she had completely filled the notebook, and her hand was beginning to cramp. Nevertheless, she savored the final moments of her spontaneous artistic adventure. As she mixed a blue-green teal and brushed it carefully across the page, she heard someone walk up behind her.

CHAPTER 8

Katherine jumped when she turned to see the man standing there. In doing so, she sent the empty paint palette tumbling to the ground while her pile of painted papers flew up and then drifted down all around her like feathers falling from a bird in flight.

"Sorry, I didn't mean to startle you." He spoke so quietly she had to strain to hear him clearly. Now she knew how her grandpa had felt at all those family dinners over the years, smiling and nodding, politely pretending to hear everything despite his dysfunctional hearing aid.

Katherine smiled nervously as she slipped her shoes back on and bent down to clean up her mess.

"Oh, not at all, I was just finishing up." She sputtered, trying not to appear as flustered as she felt. She could feel the blood rushing to her cheeks and chest. She had been so caught up in painting, completely tuning out everything else. All she could see was the lake, the water, the mountain, and the sky. All she could hear was the soft touch of the brush on the smooth paper and the lapping of the water where it met the shore by her toes. Her mind abandoned all other thought or care and became entirely obsessed with the blending of colors. She had no idea what time it was or how much time had passed.

It had been the same for her in art school. Once she got into a groove, it was like those scenes in movies where all ambient sound suddenly disappears and everything in the background moves in blurry slow motion while the camera zooms in on the main character experiencing some dramatic epiphany or plot-twisting realization. Only for her, the epiphanies and realizations unfolded during her painting process. With each artistic creation came discoveries of fresh color combinations and daring new approaches to layering the paint. Perhaps not exciting enough for most movie scripts, but it was nothing less than thrilling for Katherine.

"There isn't usually anyone down here. Are you visiting for the weekend?" The man continued to talk at whisper volume. And while he was being polite enough, she sensed a subtle undertone of irritation— *another tourist interrupting my fishing routine.* He carried a tackle box and a fishing pole and wore a heavy flannel shirt. A knit beanie, slightly too small for his head, revealed a thick mop of messy dirty-blond hair underneath.

"Um, no, not visiting. I'm . . . I'm moving to town, here, to Bluewater. I'm in the process of moving here." There were so many times in her life when she wished she could physically remove her foot from her mouth. *Why couldn't she just answer a simple question with a simple, confident response?*

The man raised his brow in disbelief. If it weren't for the understated, yet very present, condescension in his tone and mood, Katherine realized she would find him quite attractive. He was average height, but taller than she, and he appeared to be in very good shape. *Probably from all of the fishing?* Despite his almost annoyingly soft voice, he had a strong, prominent jawline hiding behind a perfect five o'clock shadow. His eyes and brow appeared to be fixed in a steady squint, as if they were locked in a permanent state of deep thought or skepticism. His skin was tanned from the intense mountain sun, and his dirty blond hair was speckled with strands of silver. He looked to be in his forties, at least a decade older than Katherine.

"Well, okay then. Welcome to town," he said flatly as he made his way to the edge of the water and opened the tackle box.

"Thanks." Katherine had cleaned up her mess. She felt childish with her sloppy little paintings, standing next to this slightly older, apparently very serious man who moved slowly and gracefully, confident in his routine, in his comfort zone. He didn't say anything else, but just gave her a quick glance and a single nod as he cast a line into the water. The color of his eyes was a piercing blue, the exact unbelievable blue of the lake by which he stood.

Katherine gave a clumsy little wave and ducked her head as if to say, "*I'm sorry I intruded on your sacred fishing spot,*" and hurriedly made her way up the path back toward town. She didn't need a mirror to know that her cheeks were about fifty shades of red.

~*~

When she returned to the inn, no one was in the lobby, but she heard some muffled activity coming

61

from the kitchen. She was starved again and tempted to go in for a snack, but she didn't want to ruin her appetite for Murray's dinner. So she grabbed an apple from the well-supplied fresh-fruit basket at the front desk and climbed the stairs with her disheveled pile of paintings, returning to her room to freshen up.

She couldn't believe the time. It was nearly four o'clock. She had been down at the lake for almost six hours.

Katherine remembered how fast time had passed in art school. She would work on a painting in the studio and become so lost in a swirl of inspiration and adrenaline that she would forget to eat breakfast, lunch, and dinner. More than once, the elderly Italian custodian would come in and kindly ask her to leave, as it was nearly midnight and the studio was technically closed.

It was times like those, and like today, where she recognized the insanity that consumed some of the great artists throughout history. If one allowed oneself to become so completely enraptured on a daily basis, consistently missing meals, social interactions, and other aspects of life, one was bound to lose one's mind. And so, in her still slightly fragile state, Katherine made a conscious mental note to ease into her own artistic practice at a steady pace. She decided for now to take a hot shower and then to call Andi with an update before dinner.

~*~

"Oh my gosh, this is *incredible*!" Katherine tried to savor small, attentive bites rather than give into her ravenously hungry animal instincts and shovel the heavenly food into her mouth. Murray had prepared the world's most perfect filet mignon with homemade basil vinaigrette and a roasted apple, cinnamon, and sweet potato salad on the side.

"See? I told you I could do better than grilled cheese," Murray said with a wink. He was beaming with pride as he looked around the dining room full of inn patrons and other Bluewater visitors. It was obvious that everyone was enchanted by Murray's dinner, and he happily visited each table, greeting the guests and collecting numerous bits of praise.

Mr. Trust walked up to Katherine as she took a sip of her wine. "May I join you?"

"Of course. Please do!" She was happy to have company. There were a few couples sharing romantic meals, talking closely and sharing bites of their entrees. Other tables were filled with small families, kids laughing as their parents recounted the day's fishing and hiking adventures.

In New York, Katherine had never dined alone in a restaurant. She hadn't been opposed to the idea per se, but she never really had the opportunity to try it. Even as her marriage with Michael began to dissolve, people constantly surrounded her. She was always with *someone*, whether it was Andi, clients, or other friends. Her alone time in the city had been scarce, and she cherished it: her solo walks through Central Park and, of course, her visits to the Met.

She didn't mind being alone in the dining room tonight, but was pleased to gain the company of Mr. Trust.

"So, how was your first day in Bluewater?" he asked with a gentle smile as Murray brought him a glass of wine and a plate with the same filet entrée.

"It was nearly perfect," Katherine managed to articulate through bites. "I still can't believe I'm here."

"*Nearly* perfect?" Mr. Trust inquired curiously, pushing his glasses back into place upon his remarkable nose.

"Well, I think I may have upset a local fisherman. Maybe I was sitting somewhere I shouldn't have been. I don't think I saw any signs or anything, but he didn't seem happy when he found me at his fishing spot." As Katherine spoke, she thought about the slightly perturbed, ruggedly handsome man with his fishing pole. He had been civil, but not warm, and she was happy to get away from him, even if he did have the most astonishing blue eyes she had ever seen.

"Grumpy fisherman. Hmmm. Scruffy fella? Flannel shirt?" Mr. Trust asked.

"That's him," she said with a dramatic eye roll and an I'm-so-annoyed intonation.

"Oh, don't you mind him. That's just Will. He's a bit rough around the edges, but he's harmless." Mr. Trust smiled and changed the subject. "So my dear, what brings you to town?"

Mr. Trust took a bite and closed his eyes in a moment of satisfaction. Then he glanced across the room at Murray and mimed a salute of appreciation. Murray put his hands together and bowed back.

"I'm moving here. Permanently." Katherine finished her last bite and debated asking Murray for another plate as she scraped the remaining sauce onto her fork.

"Really? That is wonderful, dear! And where, might I ask, are you moving from?" Mr. Trust's eyes opened wide with excitement. "We don't get many newcomers here in Bluewater!"

"I'm from Manhattan, but I vacationed here with my family when I was a kid. My life in New York . . . Well, it was time for a change." She thought of Michael and how callous he had been as he left their apartment for the last time. Shaking the memory from her head, she smiled. "And so . . . I picked Bluewater."

Katherine sipped her wine and looked out the window, trying to shield the uncertainty in her voice. She still didn't have a plan, and she still hadn't completely processed the move. For now, it was a bit of a fairytale playing around in her head. She was simply an actor, performing an idea, an idea she hadn't yet accepted as being a reality.

"Well, on behalf of the residents of Bluewater Lake, I warmly welcome you, Miss Ross." He smiled and raised his glass. "And please, stay at the inn as long as you like while you get settled. I'm happy to help in any way that I can." Mr. Trust patted her hand, and they poured another glass of wine.

After dinner, Murray served a sinfully delicious dark chocolate gelato cake for dessert and offered coffee to the remaining guests. Everyone gathered around the piano while Mr. Trust performed a myriad of popular songs by request.

Katherine sat on the sofa, sipping her coffee and enjoying the entertainment. She thought about the lake and about her day of painting. She felt inspired to do more, but would need real supplies, and decided to order some materials online first thing in the morning, before exploring the town.

For a moment, she also thought about rough-around-the-edges Will and his not-so-rough blue eyes. Tomorrow, she would also spend some time walking around the lake in search of good places to paint. Hopefully, she would not intrude on any other coveted fishing spots.

CHAPTER 9

Early the next morning, Katherine got dressed in the most casual mountainy outfit she could find: skinny jeans from Neiman Marcus, a cream-colored turtleneck sweater (designer, but hopefully no one would notice), and her favorite navy Fendi sneakers. Then she took her laptop down to the lobby in search of coffee.

She hadn't checked her email since she left New York, and her inbox was overflowing with new messages. Most of the emails pertained to work, and she forwarded them to Andi with a less-than-regretful *I'm sorry I can't help you with these ;) Love you! xoxo* in the subject line. For just a fleeting second, she missed the crazy pace and daily excitement that came with big deals and new clients. She had become accustomed to her life as a successful businesswoman, and it was strange to wake up in a quiet place with no sense of urgency or defined purpose. She was certain she made the right choice, but that didn't mean it wouldn't require some time for adjustment.

She thought about Andi, probably in her second meeting of the day by now, and she smiled, knowing that her dear friend was undoubtedly charming the socks, and maybe even the pants, off of whomever she was with. Taking a deep breath, she decided to charm Murray into making her some breakfast.

"Good morning, beautiful!" Murray greeted Katherine with a hot cup of coffee as she entered the dining room, and told her to brace herself for the "best eggs Benedict west of the Mississippi."

As she waited, Katherine found a national art supply store online and began to browse through the endless varieties of paint, canvas, brushes, and palettes. It all seemed so much more complicated than when she had last painted, just after art school. Back then she would wander into any little art supply shop in the city, grab a stretched canvas, some oil paints and mixing medium, and whatever brushes she could afford. Now, with every possible choice in front of her and with no financial restrictions, she felt overwhelmed and lost.

Murray came out of the kitchen with a beautiful plate of eggs Benedict, just in time to save her from her online shopping woes. With one bite, Katherine forgot her ordering troubles. She melted into the eggs topped with an exceptionally fresh and vibrant slice of tomato.

"Murray, what is *in* this hollandaise sauce?" She couldn't pinpoint the flavor, but it was savory and incredible, and it was different from any hollandaise she had ever tasted.

"That, I'm afraid, is a secret I'll never tell." Murray smiled and lifted his chin in posed snobbery.

"Well, you're going to have to stop feeding me like this, or I'll soon be too big to ever leave your dining room," Katherine said as she savored another bite. "May I ask you something?"

"Sure, shoot kiddo." Murray took a seat across from her. Most of the other guests were still upstairs in their rooms and would be coming down soon for their own scrumptious breakfasts.

"Why are you cooking *here*, in this little town? Surely, you could wow the culinary world with your food. Why aren't you in LA? Or New York?"

Murray smiled. "Thank you for your compliment, darling." He paused and looked down at his cup of coffee. "I did that scene for a while. It just wasn't for me. I like this place, these people. I get to spend time with the people I'm feeding, and I have more freedom."

"Do you ever miss that world?" Katherine asked.

"Well, sure, once in a while. It was a rush at times: some good memories, but some not-so-good memories too. I'm just glad I ended up here." He slapped the table with his hand and stood up. "I better get busy back there." He smiled and waved at one of the couples entering the dining room as he walked back to the kitchen.

Katherine took a sip of coffee and savored another delicious bite of eggs Benedict then opened her laptop to browse the art supplies once again.

Just pick some things and order.

She settled on one of the more affordable brands of oil paints. There was no point in ordering the fancy stuff when she didn't even know if she remembered *how* to actually use the stuff. She also selected a handful of various canvas sizes and brushes. Finally, she found a transportable easel and checked out, reminding herself that everything didn't need to be perfect right away and that she just needed some basics to work with. If she decided to continue painting, she would explore more options.

After breakfast, Katherine made her way out to the lobby. Mr. Trust was talking with some new guests by his desk, and she decided to wait and say good morning. She wandered by the piano, lightly grazing the beautiful wood with her fingers. She had never learned to play piano or any instrument for that matter. But she had always deeply loved music and found it to be an important companion while painting. She had never worked in the studio without music playing in the background: classical, opera, café music from France and Italy. Music set the tone for her artwork; it inspired her to be bold, to be romantic. It guided her energy as she mixed colors and applied them in daring layers on the canvas. Music had been a muse.

Beyond the piano, she browsed the collection of photographs staggered along the wall. In one, Murray and Mr. Trust stood proudly smiling and shaking hands in front of the inn. It must have been taken twenty years ago, as Mr. Trust's hair was much darker in the image, and he stood a bit taller. Murray had a bit more dark hair as well, and a slightly smaller belly. They hadn't changed much otherwise.

Another more recent photograph featured Mr. Trust standing next to a beautiful young woman. As she studied the photograph more closely, Katherine's jaw dropped and her eyes widened when she realized the woman was the famous model and actress Ginger Mayrose.

Ginger Mayrose had been a bit of a Manhattan goddess a decade ago. She and Katherine were near the same age, and as Katherine and Andi were building K&A, they often read about Ginger and her many extravagant affairs. They never crossed direct paths with the starlet, but had many clients involved in her world—a world full of lavishness and scandal. The last Katherine heard of Ginger Mayrose was that she had been sent away to rehab after nearly dying from the effects of a particularly heavy party week. As she thought more about it, she found it strange that it had been years since she had heard anything about such a popular celebrity. *What ever happened to Ginger Mayrose?*

"Ah, my beautiful granddaughter." Mr. Trust was standing behind Katherine, smiling over her shoulder.

"Oh, good morning, Mr. Trust!" She jumped a bit in surprise. "Wait. Ginger Mayrose is your *granddaughter*?" she asked carefully, not wanting to upset him if anything tragic had happened.

"Yes, she is. My sweet Ginger. 'Mayrose' was just her stage name, her alias, or whatever you call it." He waved his hand, dismissing the concept. "To me, she is Ginger Trust. You should stop by and meet her today while you're out and about." He smiled innocently.

"What? You mean she's *here*? In Bluewater?" Katherine tried to keep up.

"Well, of course she is. She runs *Le Café Bleu* down the street. I think you'd like her. You girls are about the same age, and she lived in the Big Apple too for a while. You'd probably have a lot to talk

71

about." He winked and gave Katherine a pat on the arm.

Wow, so this is where she's been.

Katherine made a mental note to call Andi later to fill her in. She wouldn't believe that Ginger Mayrose was hiding out in a little mountain town, running a coffee shop.

She giggled at the irony as she put on her sunglasses.

"Have a great day, Mr. Trust. I'll see you at dinner."

The Bluewater Inn was located at the very end of Main Street. As Katherine walked out onto the sidewalk, she decided to explore the south side of the street, the side closest to the lake. Then she would cross over and return along the north side. Rather a far cry from 5th Avenue, Main Street was small and quiet, and not a single building stood taller than two stories high. The two-way street had only a handful of intersections with smaller cross streets and, at each intersection, a pedestrian crosswalk. There were no car horns, no traffic lights, no taxis, and no subways rumbling beneath the ground.

Neighboring the inn was Nonna's Candy Shop, with an old-fashioned ice cream window on the front wall, where kids could walk right up and order afternoon treats. After Nonna's there was the Bluewater Bookstore and a few restaurants. As she walked, Katherine encountered the path down to the lake. She wondered if Will was down at his fishing spot, and then quickly shook the thought of him from her mind.

She crossed the path and continued on her journey, past Ralph's Grocery and The Official Bluewater Lake Souvenir Shop. Then she walked by the Bluewater Bakery, a tiny and charming establishment releasing the tantalizing aroma of warm, fresh baked bread, teasing her as she willed herself to keep walking.

Beyond the bakery was Fallen Leaf Lodge built of massive logs and decorated with whimsical wooden bear sculptures. The lodge staff was bustling about, in and out the front entrance, carrying handfuls of linens, bouquets of mountain flowers, and trays of champagne glasses. It looked as though they were preparing for a wedding.

What a lovely place to get married, Katherine thought. Marriage . . . failure. Michael . . .

Katherine and Michael's marriage had been wonderful in the beginning, but after the honeymoon season fizzled out, the passion in their marriage shared closet space with irritating quirks and respective imperfections. They fought like any other normal married couple—stupid fights about meaningless things like whose turn it was to do the dishes or whose family they were going to spend the holidays with. But they also made up, which was always fun, and for a while at least, the making up always seemed to reaffirm their love for one another.

As their careers blossomed, they tirelessly attended prestigious business dinners and events:

some for his work and others for hers. Michael always held out his arm in the traditional crook for her hand to rest upon as they discussed lawsuits and square footages with various clients and partners.

"This is my wife, Kate Kristoff. Kate's company is closing on a West 82nd Street penthouse this week." He often bragged eloquently about her achievements to his high-profile clients.

While she hated the spotlight, and always blushed with a touch of embarrassment, she loved him for having pride in her work. Yet sometimes she couldn't help but wonder if he bragged about his successful wife so that he would seem more impressive to his clients? When the thought entered her mind, she pushed it out of her head and silently reproached herself for doubting his intentions.

A few years later, Michael and Katherine still had love, but it was a love that only showed itself sporadically when it wasn't suffocated by the pressures of their careers. It was no longer a passionate I'll-forgive-your-every-flaw-because-I-must-have-you-right-now-no-matter-what kind of love, but rather a we've-been-through-a-lot-we-make-an-awesome-married-couple-on-paper-and-we-respect-one-another kind of love.

Michael's work at the firm had consumed him more and more each month, and while he still had his classic movie-star good looks, they came with some stress-induced wrinkles and gray hair around his temples. Michael had gone from a James Dean to a Humphrey Bogart in less than twenty-four months: still handsome and charming when necessary, but aged and a bit weathered nonetheless.

Katherine wasn't getting any younger herself. K&A had become one of the most sought-after realty groups for Manhattan's wealthiest property shoppers. She and Andi regularly worked eighty-hour weeks and had built an entire staff of brokers and assistants. She didn't need to go to the gym because she never stopped moving and she hardly had a moment to eat an actual meal. One would think she'd sleep like a rock each night—that her body would succumb to the exhaustion while it could. But she struggled to find sleep, despite her exhaustion.

Late at night, with Michael snoring beside her (he never seemed to have trouble finding sleep–the man could sleep through a hurricane), Katherine battled a relentless case of heartburn, obviously stress-induced, accompanied by a funny feeling in the pit of her stomach, the feeling some get when a plane descends too quickly. She sat up night after night, taking handfuls of Tums and propping up several pillows. Scattered thoughts would dance in her head and team up with the heartburn, teasing her. She felt like she was on a long trip and forgot to pack something very important or like she was nearing the end of a crucial semester at school only to realize she had missed several classes and would fail her exams.

Sometimes, to calm her mind, she'd imagine walking through the halls of the Met. It was a wonderful meditation she'd naturally developed over the years, and it was something that was all her own. She'd visualize the peaceful pastel colors gracefully dancing across a Renoir painting, and she would breathe in the simple beauty. She'd stare in the eyes of a Bouguereau girl, and she would imagine living alongside her, working with her hands in the field. Then she'd swim among Monet's water lilies.

Katherine often wondered if she even remembered how to paint. She imagined herself back in art school, spending endless hours in the studio—playing with colors and different brushes. She was so free and creative. What happened to that girl? Was she still in there somewhere? Well, even if she was, there was no time for her or her paints right now. She could barely keep up with life as it was.

Renoir, Bouguereau, Tums, Monet, Picasso, Tums, Raphael, and finally . . . sleep.

Over time, something began to shift, like a slow-moving weather system creeping into the city, subtly swallowing the light of the sun. Just as one can smell the rain in the air before a storm hits, Katherine sensed a transformation in her husband. Michael still had his humor and wit when he entertained clients and partners at the firm, but it debuted less frequently when he and Katherine were alone. When he spoke to her, his patience dwindled, and his tone frequently featured an air of annoyance or frustration. And when they made love, it was more . . . mechanical . . . something out of physical necessity, rather than desire. Brushing it off, she figured it was just a phase, and she repeatedly told herself that it must be something every couple goes through when they're exhausted from life's many demands.

Eventually, Michael just simply existed in her presence, and he rarely granted her any sincere attention. She suspected he was suffering from some kind of work-related depression, but he would shut her off abruptly whenever she tried to talk about it.

"Don't be preposterous! I work hard, Kate. I'm a Senior Partner. I don't have time for this." Then he'd shove her away as though she were a frivolous child. "Why don't you go walk around the Met and spend some time with your beloved paintings?" he'd suggest bitterly. Michael hadn't accompanied her to the Met, or any other museum, for years. While he used to find her love of art endearing, intriguing even, he now found it ridiculous. Her "obsession" with art, as he often referred to it, was no more than an intrusive distraction in his very important life.

Katherine hadn't felt warmth or affection from Michael in months. Sometimes the thought crossed her mind, "Is he having an affair?" But she refused to fully accept the possibility. She just couldn't. They were a power couple—Michael and Kate Kristoff—and the thought of life without him was just too scary.

When they attended galas and dinners, Michael would magically "turn it on" and shine the way he always had, putting his hand on her lower back and winking at her while they talked with other important couples, as if they were still so in love and happily married. At this point, it all felt so staged, so unnatural. Katherine wondered how many other couples hid behind such fabricated façades, and she could feel the acid rising in her throat as Michael schmoozed away so suavely. And then, just like clockwork, as soon as they would get home, he'd depart for the kitchen, pour himself some scotch, and turn on ESPN, wanting to be left alone.

"What are you wearing?" Michael had said one day, shutting the front door behind him and throwing his keys on the floor.

Katherine looked down at the white tee shirt and sweatpants she had just changed into after a long day of touring properties in an unbearable dress suit and stiletto heels.

"What do you mean? Why? Do we have dinner plans?" She scanned her mind. She was certain they didn't have a work dinner tonight; she would have put it in her calendar. If nothing else, Katherine was very organized.

Michael looked at her with disgust. "Kate, for God's sake, you're a Kristoff. Kristoffs don't wear sweats. You look like a slob. Does my name mean nothing to you?" He spat a little as he uttered the word sweats as though it were the most appalling word he'd ever said. His eyes were unrecognizable slits of ice.

This was not her husband; this was not Michael.

Katherine stood frozen in place, staring at him, too terrified to say a word, hoping the offensive intruder would peel off his mask and reveal the loving man she used to know. As he walked past her and into the kitchen, she felt a chill in the air and caught a strong whiff of scotch. He reeked of it.

That night, she left Michael alone with the liquor cabinet and went straight to bed. Her tears stained her pillow as she tried to understand what had happened to them. Where was the smiling stranger she met at her holiday party all those years ago? Where was the charming man who swept her off her feet? The man who used to strip off his suit the second he walked in the door because he couldn't stand it for another second? The man who used to sit on the floor with her and eat Chinese food, laughing hysterically late into the night?

She often went to bed alone, but Katherine was too busy and too tired to let herself fret about it. Michael had become passive and inattentive, but he had never spoken to her with such anger, such disdain. That was, not until then.

At some god-awful hour later that night, Katherine woke to the foul stench of scotch and kept her back turned as she listened to Michael stumble around the room, grunting as he clumsily removed his shoes. She clenched her teeth and remained motionless, hoping that Michael would simply fall onto the bed and pass out. She heard him struggle with his belt before he ripped it free from the loops on his pants, the leather hissing against the fabric.

With another grunt, Michael rolled violently onto the bed, causing the mattress to bounce. Katherine could feel his hot breath creeping closer to the back of her neck, and the stench of the scotch was suffocating. Michael reached over Katherine's waist and grabbed her crotch with his hand as he sloppily kissed her neck with his open wet mouth. The tears began to form in the corners of her eyes, as Katherine grabbed his hand and shoved it away.

"What?" He growled, as he reached again between her legs.

"Michael, don't." Katherine wanted to be strong and firm, but her heart was breaking. Don't cry, you fool. He doesn't deserve it.

Michael stumbled to his knees on the bed and forced Katherine onto her back. He dug his palms deeply into her shoulders so she couldn't move, and straddled her, making sure she looked at him as he spoke angrily threw his teeth. "You are my wife. You have an obligation to me, dammit!" Katherine stared into the bloodshot eyes of the man she no longer knew. Memories of Michael flooded her mind, memories of his smile, of his quick wit, of the way he used to gently kiss her cheeks. This stranger—this liquor-soaked, uncaring beast—had devoured the Michael she married and was now forcing her tee shirt off her limp, devastated body.

Don't cry. Don't be weak!

But Katherine began to shake with waves of silent sobs as Michael overtook her. He grunted as he moved back and forth roughly, coldly, like a machine programmed to a repeat-motion setting.

The next morning, Michael was gone before she awoke, and they never once spoke of that night.

Katherine snapped out of her reflections and discovered another trail down to the lake. This one was shorter than the one by the inn, but it was steeper. She stood at the top and looked down at the path winding around big rocks and juniper bushes, leading down to an old gazebo. The structure rested on the surface of the water just off the shore and was currently unoccupied. Katherine decided to make an unscheduled stop and go check it out.

After creeping carefully down the steep path like an apprehensive toddler braving a big staircase, she finally arrived at the short bridge to the gazebo. There was a small gold plaque on a post in the ground, and it read:

For Jacqueline,

My calm water on a quiet morning.

My love, my life.

Forever Yours,

Eli

Eli. *Eli Trust, the inn proprietor?* Katherine realized she didn't actually know much about Mr. Trust. He was always the one asking her the questions, while he himself remained relatively private. He probably *had* been married. He was a catch in her opinion. If this Eli on the plaque was indeed Eli Trust, Jacqueline was obviously someone he loved very much. Maybe one day Mr. Trust would tell her all about Jacqueline. It would be nice to hear a real-life love story.

Katherine walked into the gazebo and leaned on the railing, its wood chipping off in a natural, poetic pattern. The lake shimmered in the morning light, and the water danced in soft ripples as a few small boats motored across. This was an entirely different view of the lake from where she had been yesterday. From the gazebo, she could see more of the great mountainside on the south side of the lake, currently draped in a sea of gold and red from the changing leaves. The warm colors reflected and whirled in the water below, like sparkling sunken treasure. The mountain peak continued to dominate the skyline on the far end of the lake, and it looked as though it may have gathered a bit more snow overnight, making it even more majestic than it was the day before.

Taking a seat on the battered bench, Katherine admired the gazebo from within. Its paint was all but gone, and the structural angles were imperfect, worn and pulled one way or another from the effects of time and weathering. But it was beautiful all the same. This . . . This was where she decided she would paint next—as soon as her supplies arrived.

After prying herself away from her peaceful solitude in the gazebo, she clumsily climbed back up the hill. At the top, a worn-down mini golf course sidled up to a hardware store, and a few children ran about smacking the tiny golf clubs against multicolored golf balls, ricocheting them off a miniature, rotating windmill. On the other side of the mini golf was Bluewater Outfitters, a clothing store with a display rack out front. Katherine perused the rack full of ladies flannel shirts, soft fleece pullovers, and some jeans made of strangely thick material, cut the old-fashioned way: no skinnies, no boot-cut, just the straight-leg design she had probably only worn as a very young child before she knew any better. She needed to stock up on some warmer clothes, but she didn't want to stop her tour, and she made a note to come back the next morning.

Who knows? Maybe flannel would suit her.

After noting the pharmacy at the end of the street, Katherine crossed to the north side near the entrance she had nearly missed just days ago when she arrived. In such a short time, she had reacquainted herself with the lake and had found some dear new friends in Murray and Mr. Trust. Perhaps her luck would continue in this place she was already beginning to love, and she only hoped her thoughts of Michael would fall away with the autumn leaves.

The north side of the street was lined with more souvenir shops and restaurants, another lodge hotel, and a year-round Christmas shop. She walked by the playground she had seen when first driving in. There was a small stage off to the side and rows of picnic tables. A banner hung from the roof of the stage advertising:

BINGO SATURDAYS!

She shook her head and laughed to herself. Would she really be able to handle this way of life? It could not be more different from the pace of New York. Sure, it was charming and lovable now, but it was still very fresh and new. What if, after some time, she became incredibly bored? What if she could never truly fit in with the small-town crowd? She certainly had never been the bingo-playing kind. Maybe Andi was right. Maybe Katherine rushed into this drastic move without really thinking it through. Yes, she was excited to paint. But what could that do for her beyond fulfilling her childish desire to create?

Michael's voice rang loudly in her head, "Art is so frivolous. It's . . . *decoration*. I can't believe how much people spend on decoration," he'd whispered irritably as they attended an auction at Christie's with his firm the year before. "It's idiotic."

Maybe it is frivolous. Maybe I'm wasting my time.

Katherine's spiral of doubtful thought was brought to a halt as she spotted a lovely coffee shop situated on the corner of the far end of the park. The windows were dressed in white lace curtains, and blue bistro tables scattered the sidewalk out front, each with a small vase and single red rose in the center. She looked up and saw the sign *Le Café Bleu* beautifully printed on the awning. Curious and charmed all at once, she decided it was time for a late morning latte with Ginger Mayrose.

CHAPTER 10

Le Café Bleu was bustling, and Katherine struggled to find an empty table. She finally made her way over to the bar and sat in the only vacant seat near the end.

"Hello again," Will mumbled. He was sitting on the stool directly to her left, wearing flannel, again, but without a hat today. His hair was disheveled, which nicely complimented his unshaven face. His relentlessly blue eyes looked right into hers as he dipped his chin and then turned back to his cup of plain black coffee.

"Oh, hello. Again." She had been so happy to find an empty seat that she failed to notice him sitting right there next to her. Her cheeks burned.

What is it about this guy that gets me all flustered? He's not even nice, really.

She tried to ignore Will's presence and appear nonchalant as she looked around the café. It was an adorable little place—something right out of an old French movie. Ginger Mayrose obviously had great taste and paid attention to detail. From the vintage and rustic furniture to the simple classy menus, from the French music playing quietly in the background to the original oil paintings on the walls, everything was comfortable and casual, but also, splendid.

"Good morning! What can I get for you today?"

Katherine looked up from her menu to see Ginger Mayrose standing right in front of her, smiling and holding a pot of coffee. Her face was free of makeup, and she wore her blond hair tousled up in a messy bun on top of her head. Her white tee shirt was stained with jam and coffee, and she wore torn blue jeans. Yet, even in her present nearly unrecognizable state, she was unbelievably beautiful.

"Hi! I'd love a latte . . . please." Katherine was star-struck. *I just ordered a latte from Ginger Mayrose. Ginger Mayrose is making me a latte.* In New York, Katherine had become indifferent to celebrity sightings, especially in her line of work with prestigious clients, often famous themselves in one respect or another. But something about coming face-to-face with Ginger Mayrose here in this little town, in the middle of nowhere, made her stardom seem bigger and stranger.

She was just glad she could suppress a completely embarrassing *"I know you! You're Ginger Mayrose! What happened to you? Why are you here?!"* outburst. After all, Will was still sitting next to her, and she felt embarrassed enough around him as it was.

"Of course. That'll be ready for you in a moment!" Ginger looked younger than she had appeared in the tabloids. She seemed refreshed and healthy, and she was so sincerely friendly.

Will pushed his stool back and stood up. "Thanks, Ginge. I'll see ya later."

"Later!" Ginger yelled over her shoulder. She was busy at the other end of the bar, clearing some plates.

Were Ginger Mayrose and Will an item? It certainly didn't seem like it. They weren't lovey-dovey or anything. Maybe they were just friends, fellow Bluewater locals. Katherine wondered why Will didn't acknowledge her when he left. Then she laughed at herself. *He doesn't even know my name. I'm just some strange girl that keeps showing up and getting in his way. He doesn't have to acknowledge me . . .*

"Here's your latte."

Katherine spun around. She realized she was still looking out the café door.

"Thank you. It looks wonderful!" She blushed and took a sip. It was delicious.

"Do you know Will?" Ginger smiled. She could tell Katherine had been watching him leave.

"Um, well, no. Not really. I kind of met him yesterday, I guess." Katherine blushed more. Here she was, talking about boys with Ginger Mayrose. It was all so surreal.

"He's a doll. One of my best friends. Good guy," Ginger said casually. "So, where are you from? And I *love* your Fendis by the way." Ginger motioned over the counter to Katherine's shoes.

"Oh, ha-ha, thank you. I need to go shopping. I didn't come with many practical options. I'm from New York, Manhattan." Katherine didn't want to carry on a charade, pretending that she didn't know who Ginger really was. It seemed rude or fake or something. So she continued, "I'm staying at the Bluewater Inn, and I met your grandfather. He recommended your café."

"Aw, Gramps. He's the best. You know I lived in Manhattan too for a while." Ginger smiled and winked.

"Yes, I know." Katherine smiled back. "I'm a fan." They both laughed. Katherine was glad to break the ice. Ginger seemed really nice, and perhaps they could be friends. "I love this place. You may be seeing more of me. I just moved to Bluewater, and I have a serious latte problem."

Ginger laughed. "Looking forward to it! I'm Ginger by the way, but you already knew that." She grinned.

"Yes, I did. But it's nice to meet you. I'm Katherine."

"Very nice to meet you." Ginger wiped her hand on her apron and reached over to shake Katherine's hand. "Hey, a few of us are going out tonight. There's always live music on Saturdays at Dale's Pub down the street. You should come!" Ginger said as she refilled coffees along the bar.

"Okay. That sounds fun!"

"Great. See you there around eight!" Ginger walked out the front door to take orders from customers sitting at the tables outside.

Katherine finished her latte and left a few dollars on the counter. She waved at Ginger as she walked out onto the sunny sidewalk.

~*~

"You're kidding me! That is so bizarre!" Andi squealed on the phone. "Well, then I am *definitely* coming to see you!"

"Ha! Thanks a lot. You'll only come to see me because Ginger Mayrose lives here?" Katherine smiled. She missed her friend. "Don't come yet. I need to get myself together, get grounded a bit. I'll invite you out when I can be a proper host."

"Are you house-hunting yet? Did you find me a mister yet? Wait. Scratch that. Have *you* found any steamy mountain suitors yet?" Andi giggled mischievously.

"No. And I'm not looking for any suitors, remember?" Katherine insisted. She couldn't imagine being with anyone anytime soon. Michael had hurt her so gradually, but in a way that made her feel like she could never trust another man. She sighed and added, "There's this one guy, Will. He's gorgeous in that totally rustic sort of way. You'd be all over him."

"Hey! I resent that . . . kinda." Andi joked. "So? Tell me more about him. Do you *liiiiike* this Will?"

"I really don't. I mean he's wonderful to look at. But he's cold and kind of unwelcoming. I don't know. I feel weird around him. I've only bumped into him twice, but he makes me nervous. Bad energy or something . . ."

"Or *yummy* energy!" Andi laughed.

"I miss you, friend." Katherine smiled.

"I miss you too. You're happy, right?" Andi asked.

"Getting there."

CHAPTER 11

Katherine dressed in a new wool sweater she bought from the outfitters store that afternoon. While she couldn't yet bear the thought of buying the shapeless jeans, she was at least able to find a few cute tops and some mountain-style boots.

She rarely wore her hair down. In New York, it just seemed to get in her way, and it tangled too easily in the humidity. Andi had always teased her for her relentless "Audrey Hepburn bun," a style Katherine had comfortably worn for as long as she could remember. Michael had always liked her hair up. He said it made her look elegant and professional. But tonight, she decided to wear her hair down. She curled it slightly and let it fall over her shoulders. Perhaps, with the relaxed hair and her new, more practical attire, she'd fit in better with Ginger and the other locals at the pub.

After another wonderful Murray dinner and wine with Mr. Trust, Katherine bundled up and made her way down the street. She was excited to meet new people, but mostly nervous. She still found it strange that she was going to hang out with Ginger Mayrose. As she walked, she wondered who might be at the pub. *Would Will be there?* She hoped not. She just wanted to relax and have a good time, and for some reason, he made her feel anything but relaxed.

~*~

Dale's Pub was an old saloon-style bar. Neon beer signs hung in the window, with dark wood and low lantern light inside. An old jukebox stood in the far corner, and bar stools crowded around a handful of high-tops. In the front window bay was a small stage area, or at least a portion of floor raised a few inches higher—a nice cozy spot for tonight's four-piece bluegrass band.

The band, a scruffy collection of happily bearded men, played a comical song about hunters and hippies. Their fingers danced quickly across the strings of their mandolins and banjos, and their feet tapped along to the lively tempo.

The bar was packed, and Katherine had to stand on her toes to get a good look around. Finally, she spotted Ginger at a table in the back by the jukebox. She inched through the crowd—a mix of locals and tourists drinking beer, eating peanuts, and dancing to the music.

"There you are! Guys, this is Katherine." Ginger jumped up to give her a hug and gestured toward the group crammed around the table. "This is Matt and Tony—they run the marina. This is Lolo—she owns the bookstore. And I believe you know Will . . ."

Katherine smiled at everyone around the table. When her eyes met Will's, he nodded and half-smiled. *A courtesy smile?*

"Hello. Nice to meet all of you." Katherine felt shy, but Ginger's friends were immediately warm to her. Tony stood up from his seat next to Ginger's and insisted that she sit down. He ventured off to find another stool and to fetch her a drink.

"So, Katherine, where you in from?" Matt asked. He was a big guy, probably late twenties. His head was shaved, and his tan arms were both muscular and chubby. Upon his left bicep, Katherine noted a slightly faded tattoo of a pirate ship.

"I just moved here from New York." Katherine had to raise her voice so she could be heard above the music. Tony returned and handed her a bottle of beer. She looked at it and then took a tiny sip. She had never really been a beer-drinking girl. It just didn't occur to her to order beer when she could order wine or vodka cocktails.

"Not much of a beer drinker?" Will sat to her left and seemed to notice her slight hesitation. Even in a loud bar, he spoke in the same quiet tone he had before. Katherine could barely hear him.

"Not really. Not yet, I guess. I just haven't been afforded many beer-drinking opportunities." She blushed and took another sip. "But this is delicious."

Afforded beer-drinking opportunities? I'm such a moron.

To her surprise, Will let out a little laugh.

"So, New York, huh? What brings you here? Are you an old friend of Ginger's?" Tony asked. Tony was the opposite of his buddy Matt. He was tall and lanky, with big gawky eyes and floppy hair.

"I actually just met Ginger this morning at the café," Katherine said.

"She's a new Bluewater implant!" Ginger stated proudly and squeezed Katherine's shoulder.

"That's fabulous! Welcome to town, doll." Lolo was probably in her late 40s, voluptuous, and eccentric, with bold makeup, colorful jewelry, and a glittery scarf. She wore several rings on each finger. Katherine thought she looked more like a fortune-teller than a bookstore owner.

"To implants!" Tony yelled and held up his beer. Everyone laughed.

"I'll drink to that," Matt chimed in, the pirate-ship tattoo expanding momentarily on his flexed arm as he held up his beer.

"To implants!" Ginger and Lolo yelled and held up their beers. Katherine blushed and laughed. Will smirked only slightly and sat back in his chair, shaking his head with his arms crossed, refusing to participate in the silliness.

The group became even more colorful as the night continued. Tony ended up dancing with Lolo in front of the stage, attempting to dip and twirl her as if they were listening to ballroom music rather than bluegrass. Ginger and Matt started smoking cigars and playing cards at the table.

"Cigar?" Ginger offered one to Katherine.

"No, thanks." Katherine laughed and watched in awe as Ginger Mayrose sat casually with one foot up on the stool next to her, elbows on the table, cards fanned out in her hand, and a huge smelly cigar hanging from the corner of her mouth. Manhattan would never believe it.

Will said very little throughout the night. He mostly sat back and watched his entertaining friends make fools of themselves, while nodding to the beat of the music. He seemed to be in his own world, deep in thought. He would look over once in a while and nod or smile at Katherine, but he did not initiate any conversation beyond offering to get her another beer when he went to the bar.

After two or three drinks, Katherine felt more relaxed. She was thankful to Ginger for inviting her out. Everyone was so fun and friendly. Despite his massive and rough exterior, Matt turned out to be a big teddy bear and told Katherine she had to visit the marina sometime soon so he and Tony could take her out for a boat ride.

Tony was the comedian of the bunch, the Gilligan to Matt's Skipper. His scrawniness added visual whimsy to his hilarious banter, and he laughed at himself along with the others. At the moment, he was attempting to perform some kind of Riverdance for Lolo, who sat on a bar stool, clapping along encouragingly.

While Katherine hoped to talk more with Will, she did not want to disturb him or ruin the progress they had made tonight. He didn't say much, but there was a new air of acceptance about him. He smiled over at her a few times, and he no longer seemed irritated by her presence. She decided not to push it. If Will wanted to talk to her, he would.

The band finally conceded to the early morning hours, and Katherine and Ginger and their friends were some of the last conscious patrons left in the pub. Tony was snoring on a bench, and Matt picked him up and threw him over his shoulder.

"Night, guys. Great to meet you, Katherine," Matt said as he carried his buddy down the sidewalk toward the marina.

Lolo wrapped her arms around Katherine in a tight embrace. "Lovely to meet you, dear. Come see me at the bookstore!" She smelled of flowers and spices.

Ginger gave her a hug too. "See you later for a latte?" She smiled.

"You bet," Katherine said, covering her mouth to shield a huge yawn.

"Night." Will smiled slightly over his shoulder as he tucked his hands into his pockets and journeyed down a side street.

"Night," Katherine responded, but he had already turned a corner and was out of sight.

At noon, she heard a knock at her door.

"Miss Ross? Are you feeling okay?" Mr. Trust sounded worried. He spoke softly and hesitantly, not wanting to disturb his guest.

Katherine had been in the lobby each morning for coffee since she arrived, so she wasn't surprised to hear the concern in his voice.

"Yes! One minute!" she replied, attempting to sound alert and chipper.

She rolled out of the warm bed and wrapped her robe around her nightgown. The floor was freezing! She quickly fetched her slippers out from under the bed, before opening the door.

Mr. Trust held a steaming cup of coffee out to Katherine. "I'm so sorry to bother you, dear. I just wanted to check on you."

"Thank you." She gladly accepted the mug and reveled in the comfort of the warmth embracing her hands. "I'm wonderful. It was just a late night. I was at the pub with Ginger and her friends."

"Oh, I am so glad you girls hit it off!" He smiled widely. "Well, I'll let you be. Come on down for lunch when you're ready. Murray is making soup!" He tipped his invisible cap and bowed before her then turned on his heel and walked happily down the hall, whistling. He reminded Katherine of Dick Van Dyke, so charming and ageless. Ginger undoubtedly inherited some of her spark from her grandfather.

"So, you were at the pub, huh?" Murray served Katherine a heaping bowl of minestrone, with warm French bread and butter on the side.

"Yes, with Ginger and her friends. It was fun!" She tried to articulate with a full mouth. Murray's soup warmed her from the inside out, and the bread soaked up the beers she'd had just hours before.

"Ah, yeah, that's a good gang." Murray smiled and shook his head then returned to the kitchen.

Katherine didn't know if she'd ever get used to living in a place where everyone knew everyone. The concept was comforting in some ways, but she was beginning to sense fragility in such community closeness.

In New York, if you engaged in any sort of conflict—perhaps with a surly store employee or cab driver—you could react impulsively, say whatever you wanted in the heat of the moment, no matter how insulting or ridiculous, and walk away knowing you would likely never see that person again. But here in Bluewater, Katherine was beginning to understand that she would have to be careful with her words and actions. She smiled as she thought of Andi and her spitfire ways. *She would never survive here.*

~*~

"Thanks for joining us last night! I hope you had a good time." Ginger smiled warmly and slid a giant latte across the counter. She looked well rested and energized, whereas Katherine was hoping to erase the all-to-evident bags under her eyes with heavy doses of caffeine throughout the day.

"I had a great time! Thank you for inviting me. Your friends are wonderful." Katherine relived the night in her mind as she sipped her delicious latte. As happy as she was to meet Lolo and Matt and Tony, she couldn't help but think mostly about Will and his subtle smiles throughout the evening.

"You and Will looked like you were hitting it off," Ginger replied with raised eyebrows.

"Really? We didn't talk much. But he's nice." Katherine tried to appear casual and indifferent, but she could feel the color rising in her cheeks, betraying her efforts. "What's his story anyway?" she asked.

Ginger sighed and almost looked sad for a moment. "Will's story is a *long* story. He's a fairly private person. But my gramps has been like a second father to him, and we've known each other for a long time. He's a really great guy; he's just been dealt more than one rough hand."

"He does seem a bit standoffish. But I guess we all have things we don't want to share with the world." She thought of her tainted life with Michael and her misdirected career path.

"Oh, don't I know it!" Ginger laughed and rolled her eyes, clearly alluding to her own dark past.

"Have you two ever . . . been . . .?" Katherine's voice faded when she realized she was probably being too forward.

Luckily, Ginger was a lot like Andi and didn't seem to get easily offended. "Me and *Will*? Noooo! Never! He's like a brother to me! Iccccckkkk!"

Katherine laughed. "Okay, okay, I get it."

"You should get to know him. He can be standoffish at first. But there's a lot of good there. You'll see." Ginger winked.

Katherine made arrangements to have her rental car picked up from the inn. She hadn't required it since arriving in Bluewater—everything she needed was within walking distance. She supposed she would need a car someday, at least to travel beyond the town and into the mountains or down to Denver once in a while. But she would buy something when it was necessary. She had enough to explore on foot for the time being.

Back at the inn, she greeted Mr. Trust at his desk. "Mr. Trust, may I speak with you for a moment?"

"Of course, dear. For you, I will give two moments." He smiled and they made their way to the couch in the lobby.

"What can I do for you?" he asked as they sat down.

"Well, I just wanted to talk to you about my room here. I don't want to be a burden, and I don't want to be the reason you have to turn away reservations. I was thinking maybe I'd start to look for a house today . . ." Katherine was surprised to hear the indecision in her own voice.

Mr. Trust put his hand on hers. "Miss Ross, you are anything but a burden. Your presence here at the inn has been a treat." He grinned. "And Murray adores you! We have all been eating like kings since you arrived. Please stay. Are you happy here? At the inn?"

"Of course! I feel more comfortable here than I have anywhere! I would stay here forever if it were up to me."

In New York, she had cherished her privacy and alone time. If someone had told her that she would one day live in an inn that was frequently occupied by others, with an innkeeper who checked on her if she did not attend breakfast, she would have laughed and said, "No thanks!" But she meant what she said to Mr. Trust. She truly was happy and contented at the inn, and she would love to call it *home*. At least for a while . . .

"Well, then it's settled. You are Bluewater Inn's permanent resident. Our very own VIP!"

They worked out the details for her stay. Mr. Trust insisted on giving her a lower monthly rate. It was just his nature to be a protector, a caretaker: with Ginger obviously and apparently with Will as well. Now it was Katherine he wanted to take under his loving wing. Katherine was adamant though, and insisted she would help out around the inn however she could.

When all was discussed and decided, Murray brought out a bottle of champagne, and the three of them toasted to her new home.

CHAPTER 12

The next morning Katherine walked sleepily into the lobby, ready for her warm cup of coffee.

"Good morning, Miss Ross! You have some packages behind my desk!" Mr. Trust exclaimed from across the room. He was chatting with an attractive young couple near the window, pointing out the marina and other Bluewater attractions along the lake.

For a rare moment, Katherine completely forgot about her quest for a cup of coffee. She was too excited about the packages—*her painting supplies!* She gathered the three large boxes in her arms, precariously balancing them upon one another as she made her way upstairs.

Back in her room, she sat on the floor and began to open the boxes with reckless abandon like a young child on Christmas morning.

The first box was full of oil paints, palettes, and brushes. She organized the paint tubes, making sure that she had the right combination to create any color she may desire. She gently touched the paintbrush tips against her hand and her cheek. They were so soft and delicate—she was almost sad to think about ruining them with paint.

The next box was full of canvases of various sizes, and the impulsive artist within begged her to grab the largest canvas and dive right in. But she ignored the temptation, figuring she had better start small, reacquaint herself with the practice, and work her way up.

Finally, Katherine found her travel easel in the third box. It was beautifully crafted and smelled of fresh cut wood. She breathed it in, remembering her old easel from art school. She had carried it around Florence with her, constantly hunting for irresistible painting opportunities. Her friends had teased her, calling her "the box lady" always walking around with her wooden box.

After years of use, that easel had become entirely covered in paint splatters and charcoal smudges. The handle had broken, and one of the clasps no longer worked. Katherine loved it, though, and couldn't bring herself to throw it away. To her, it would feel like throwing away an old friend. For now, the retired easel was safely stored with her other valuables at Andi's place.

She packed up the new easel, free of stains and fully functioning, and loaded it with the paints and brushes so habitually it was almost as if she never stopped painting. Then she dressed in several layers and put on the only pair of gloves she had. It was still morning, and Katherine could tell it was cold outside; there was frost on her window. But she had become well acquainted with the power of the sun here, and knew that, as it climbed higher into the sky, over the peak at the end of the lake, it would cast incredible warmth onto the town by lunchtime.

Securing the smallest canvas of the bunch, Katherine grabbed her supplies and made her way downstairs. It felt good to carry a loaded easel again. Maybe, just maybe, the box lady was back.

~*~

Steam rolled off the top of the lake, and the little old gazebo was freezing. Katherine shivered and jumped up and down in place, hoping to generate some internal heat. She breathed into her cupped hands. The gloves were not working as well as she hoped, and she took a sip of hot coffee from the thermos Murray had prepared for her. Everything was quiet, as if the cold itself muffled each and every little sound.

She clumsily began to assemble the easel. It had been years since she painted, and this easel was a bit different from her old one. After a few attempts, she finally figured out the mechanisms for the easel's legs and height adjustments. Her fingers morphed into icicles, mostly numb except for the less-than-delightful sensation of sharp needles poking at the tips.

More jumping in place. More sips of hot coffee.

Moments later, the sun emerged from behind the mountaintop, its rays tentatively embracing the tips of the tallest trees. Katherine felt as if her bones were actually shaking in anxious anticipation of the glorious arrival of its warmth. She watched the golden light creep slowly downward, from the tips of the trees to the rooftops of the sleepy cabins around the lake then further downward until it gently poured onto the surface of the water, awakening the frozen darkness and igniting a vibrant glow. The steam danced above the lake, swirling around in the light, slowly vanishing into the thawing air.

The warmth crept into the gazebo and surrounded Katherine and her easel. The sunlight peeled the cold away from her skin and slowly began to thaw her fingers and toes. She breathed it in and smiled as she began squeezing paint onto the palette. Then, with brushes in hand and her easel fully prepped, she stared at the white canvas, utterly terrified.

"How do I do this?" she whispered to herself as panic took over.

Yes, she had painted those silly watercolors just days ago. But those were fun—anyone could mess around with watercolors, paper, and water. Oils were a different beast altogether, and Katherine was drawing a blank. What if it had been too long? What if she had lost it completely? Would she have to start from scratch, a ripe beginner, as if she had never painted at all?

She closed her eyes and imagined herself back in the studio in Florence. She could smell the old building, the oil paints, and the espresso brewing. She could hear her Italian painting professor with an accent so thick even his English sounded like Italian, "Be-ah free. Feel, don't-ah think." He always smiled. Maybe it was because he always had a glass of wine in his hand, regardless of the hour of day. She also suspected he had many affairs with his art students. But she'd been far too shy and reserved to ever personally entertain the possibility.

The time she spent in Italy felt so far away from now. Maybe it had all been an elaborate daydream after all. *Maybe she never really was a painter . . .*

Suddenly, Katherine was mixing a beautiful golden color on her palette. She wasn't thinking at all, but her newly thawed hand seemed to know what to do. Trying not to ruin the moment with overthought, she gave into the luscious allure of the paint and began to cover the canvas in wide, bold strokes.

~*~

"Wow. That's beautiful."

Katherine jumped about five feet into the air and dropped the brushes from her hand. She spun around to see Will standing at the entrance of the gazebo.

She had no idea how much time had passed, but her painting was nearly finished. She had been lost in a delightful trance, completely engulfed in the world of creation. Each color she'd mixed was a pathway to new discoveries on the canvas. She was elated. *She was back!* Her gift in art school had been her ability to lose herself in her work, oblivious to any distraction. She never spent more than a day on one painting, but she was able to dive deep and capture so much in those intense and precious hours.

"I'm sorry. We've got to stop meeting like this." Will laughed as he helped her collect the scattered brushes.

Katherine was covered in paint. She had never been a tidy artist. She could only imagine what she must look like at the moment. Did she even put mascara on this morning? Oh God, did she brush her teeth? She had been in such a hurry . . .

"Hi! Thank you." Out of breath, she felt as though she had just run a marathon, not that she actually knew what that would feel like. But she had poured herself into the painting and probably forgot to breathe normally in the midst of all the excitement. Will's unexpected presence also did not help her breathing situation. Why was it that he could wear flannel every day and never brush his hair, and yet look better every time she saw him?

They both stood in front of the painting. Katherine really hadn't stepped back to look at the work as a whole until this very moment. The result took her by surprise—it *was* beautiful! She wasn't expecting to achieve much during this first attempt. She had just hoped to create *something* and eventually she would progress in the right direction. But this painting . . . it was absolutely *beautiful*. She had captured the moment the sunlight first kissed the lake that morning, hours before. Her colors were subtle but evocative, and her brushstrokes were deliberate but unrestrained. Her eyes filled with tears. She just couldn't believe it.

"So, you're an artist?" Will was still admiring the painting. He had no idea what this small achievement meant for Katherine, nor was he aware of the tidal wave of emotions currently washing over her.

Katherine coughed a bit and nonchalantly wiped the tears from the corners of her eyes.

"No. Well, I was . . . I want to be. It's been a while." She couldn't peel her eyes away from the painting, not even to look at Will.

"It's pretty clear that you *are* an artist. This is really incredible," he said quietly. Then he cleared his throat. "Would you like to join me for dinner tonight?"

CHAPTER 13

"Well helloooooo, lovely lady!" Murray whistled and bounced his eyebrows up and down, ogling Katherine as she wandered down the stairs and into the lobby.

"Oh, stop it." Katherine blushed and smiled. She had spent an hour trying to figure out what to wear. *What does one wear to dinner in a place like Bluewater?* In New York, she would have slipped on a little black dress and stilettos with no thought required. But here, she was at a complete loss. Finally, she settled on a pair of skinny jeans, tall brown boots, and her fitted gray cardigan. She curled her hair and wore it down again (it seemed to work for her the other night at the pub) and applied her favorite rose-colored lip-gloss.

Mr. Trust was standing in the lobby, admiring Katherine's painting. When she had returned to the inn that afternoon, he insisted she leave it displayed on the easel, safely placed in the corner of the lobby where everyone could see it. Katherine tried to object; she wasn't ready for an audience. But Mr. Trust wouldn't let her sneak it back into the privacy of her room.

"Miss Ross! This is exquisite! You didn't tell us you were an artiste!" He had gasped when she haphazardly carried the easel through the front door.

111

"I am mesmerized. You would make Monsieur Monet extremely proud!"

Now in the evening light, the warmth of the painting took on an entirely new glow, and Mr. Trust stared at it, shaking his head in disbelief.

"Ah, there is the beautiful artist. Come over here, dear. I want a picture of you by this masterpiece for the wall! I want proof that the famous artist, Katherine Ross, painted our very own Bluewater Lake and lived right here in my inn!"

Katherine laughed and reluctantly walked over to the easel, cheeks red with embarrassment. She was proud of her work, but she was still trying to digest the day: the intense cold, the panic, the painting, and Will . . .

Really, it had been a great day. The best day she could remember in a long time.

Fortunately, Mr. Trust released her from the photo shoot just moments before Will walked through the lobby.

"Will! How are you, son?" Mr. Trust embraced Will in a warm hug and an affectionate pat on the shoulder.

To Katherine's surprise, Will was not wearing flannel. He had shaved, and his hair appeared to be combed. He wore a plain white button down shirt and clean dark jeans. He cleaned up quite nicely.

"Hello, Eli. I'm sorry I haven't been around to visit. Busy, you know." He smiled warmly at Mr. Trust, and Katherine sensed an earnest love and comfort between them. Ginger had said they were close, but it was nice to see Will in this gentle light.

"Oh you don't have to apologize to me. I'm just glad to see you. And how lucky you are to be dining with a master artist this evening!" Mr. Trust beamed and winked at Katherine, as she felt the temperature rise in her cheeks and chest.

"Oh, Mr. Trust, stop. You are too much." She smiled and tried to breathe the blushing away.

"Are you ready to go?" Will asked. At this moment, Katherine realized that he looked as nervous as she felt. He smiled, but fidgeted with his hands, and cleared his throat as he spoke. "You look beautiful."

Yep, the blushing was back and probably here to stay. "Thank you. Yes, let's." She spoke just above a whisper—it was all she could manage. *WHY did he make her so uneasy?*

Will held the door for her as they walked out into the cold evening. She glanced back over her shoulder to see Mr. Trust and Murray waving at her with giant silly smiles.

As they made their way down the street, they were quiet. Katherine felt as though her stomach was on a Tilt-a-Whirl, and she concentrated on breathing slowly and calmly. She couldn't remember the last time she felt so nervous. Even when she had first started seeing Michael, she had been excited nervous, but in the lighthearted way that usually goes along with dating. With Will, she felt nervous in a different way: cautious, terrified, but intensely curious at the same time. Katherine was broken, and she knew she wasn't ready to date. But she'd accepted his offer for dinner without any hesitation, before she had time to think about it.

"That painting really is something." Will broke the silence. He didn't hold her hand or offer his arm. He put his hands in his pockets, but he walked close to her so that their arms brushed together with each step.

"Thank you. I'm glad you think so." Katherine wanted to add more. She wanted to tell him everything she felt and experienced that day in the gazebo. She wanted to explain the huge breakthrough achieved through that one little painting, and how incredibly inspired she had become. But she decided that with Will, at least for now, she would tread lightly and divulge information according to his pace. He was hard to read, and she would have to play it safe. It was too soon for her to get hurt again.

Will stopped in front of a quaint Italian bistro, *Marcello's*, and held the door open.

"I hope you like Italian food?" he asked nervously as they walked to the host stand.

"Yes, I love it." Katherine smiled and removed her coat. "It's my favorite."

"*Buona sera*, Signore Will! I've got your table ready for you!" A rotund and jolly Italian man greeted them. Marcello, Katherine assumed.

"Hello, Marcello, good to see you." Will smiled warmly—another old friend.

"And who is your beautiful guest?" Marcello raised Katherine's hand to his lips.

"Marcello, this is Katherine. She just moved here from New York."

"Ah, belissima! Piacere, amore!"

"*Piacere, Signore. Grazie*." Katherine's Italian was rusty, but she was surprised at how easily it rolled off her tongue.

"Ahhhh! *Parla Italiano! Bravissima*!" Marcello clapped and embraced her, smothering her in his big hairy arms. "Come, come. I doubt Signore Will brought you here to talk to me all night!" Marcello winked and laughed loudly, as he grabbed two menus and led them through the crowded intimate restaurant. Old Italian music was playing in the background, and the walls, painted in deep earthy colors, were adorned with old photographs and framed prints of famous Italian paintings and landmarks.

"Wow, you speak Italian." Will was impressed, quietly impressed, but impressed nonetheless.

She smiled and felt a wave of nostalgia. She missed speaking Italian. To Katherine, it was the most beautiful language in the world—romantic and daring, seductive and elegant. When she had become fluent, she felt more beautiful than ever when she spoke it.

Marcello led them to a quaint table by the front window. It was perfect in its simplicity: a red and white checkered tablecloth with a small burning candle and a bottle of olive oil in the center. Will pulled out a chair for Katherine before sitting across from her. He smiled, but before their eyes connected for too long, he diverted his attention to his menu.

"Thank you for bringing me here," Katherine said, hoping to break the ice again.

"It's the best restaurant in Bluewater. Which isn't saying a whole lot . . . when you're used to the restaurants in New York." He smiled and Katherine laughed. Marcello delivered a bottle of his special house Chianti to the table and winked at Will.

"Welcome to Bluewater." Will held up his glass. The Chianti was delicious—it tasted just like the hundreds of bottles she must have sipped during her time in Florence.

"So, how do you know Italian?" Will asked after they ordered.

"I lived in Italy—Florence—for about a year. Art school . . ."

"Ah, so that explains the painting. I knew you were an artist." Will smiled.

"I guess so. I haven't painted in a very long time, at least eight or nine years probably. You witnessed my very clumsy reunion with the practice today in the gazebo." Katherine laughed.

"Your practice may be clumsy, but the result was far from it." Will's face was calm and serious. He wasn't flattering her; he was just being honest. "Why such a long hiatus?" he asked, somewhat tentatively. Katherine decided to answer lightly.

"Oh, you know. Life. Responsibility got in the way. But a lot has changed, obviously. I mean . . . I'm here . . . in Bluewater." She blushed. *Stop rambling.*

Will nodded. He seemed to deeply consider her words, becoming lost in thought—almost as if he heard what she said, but could see the more complex truths hiding behind her surface-level response.

She decided to shift the focus to Will for a while. "Have you always lived here in Bluewater?"

"No, actually, I'm from LA. I moved here about ten years ago."

Katherine could not picture the flannel-wearing, mountain-man Will in sunny, cheery LA.

"LA, really? Wow. Another world. What do you do?" She realized that she knew what everyone else did in Bluewater—Ginger had her café, Tony and Matt ran the Marina, and Lolo had the Bookstore—but she had no idea what Will did, other than fish and make outsider city girls nervous.

Will seemed to struggle with the question. Clearing his throat, he mumbled, "Um, well, a little bit of everything, I guess. I fix things, build things—really just help people out when they need it." His answer was vague, and he appeared uncomfortable with his words. Lucky for Will, Marcello walked out that moment with two heaping plates of heavenly pasta.

CHAPTER 14

"Hey! How was dinner last night?" Ginger had a smirk on her face and looked very pleased with herself for knowing about the date.

"How did you know?" Katherine hadn't had time to tell Ginger of her plans between the painting and dinner.

"Will. He was in earlier." Ginger winked.

"Oh! Um . . . It was good. Great, I think. Why? Did Will say anything?" Katherine asked anxiously, realizing she sounded like she was gossiping by the lockers in high school.

She did have a wonderful time. Marcello's pasta was rich and delightful, and Will had been very kind. They spent the evening talking mostly about Katherine. She told him about her time in Italy and about her transition into the world of real estate in New York. She told him about her family and her childhood trips to Colorado. She decided to leave Michael out of her story, at least for now. She wasn't ready to open that door just yet.

Will had been interested and engaged, asking her questions and smiling warmly as he watched Katherine converse in broken Italian with Marcello. But every time she tried to ask Will a question about himself, he would stealthily avoid answering with any substance and divert the attention back to her.

At the end of the night, Will had walked her back to the inn. It was late and freezing outside, but the several glasses of Chianti kept them warm as they walked. Again, Will tucked his hands tightly into his pockets, but walked very close to Katherine, their breath visible in the cold air. When they approached the lobby door, he smiled and thanked her for joining him. His eyes revealed a moment of longing, a desire . . . *to kiss her perhaps?* But hesitation quickly clouded over his gaze, and he became unreachable, again.

"Thank you. It was really lovely." Katherine smiled, hoping to find the truth in his eyes, behind the fear. Something was there. She could feel it. She couldn't explain it, but she could feel it. She was afraid too. She didn't even know this man. He refused to tell her anything about himself, and even if he did, she was fairly certain he was completely wrong for her.

She had to blink away visions of Michael's angry glare throughout the evening, shuddering at the thought of his drunken touch—she wasn't ready for this. Doubtful thoughts consumed the back of her mind during dinner and then on the walk home: *What was she doing? Already out with another man?* But there was a strange energy between her and Will, an undeniable force pulling them together in this little town in the middle of nowhere, whether they wanted to be pulled or not.

Will had stood still for a moment, looking at Katherine. His lips parted slightly, as if he wanted to say something else. But the cloud of hesitation grew darker, more powerful, and he began to step back.

"Good night, Katherine," Will had said quietly, as he turned and walked away into the dark.

"He just said you guys went to Marcello's and that it was nice." Ginger smiled as she went on, "He's a man of few words, always has been for as long as I've known him."

"Yeah, I'm beginning to see that." Katherine sipped on her latte.

"I think he likes you." Ginger grinned, sensing Katherine's uncertainty. "Just give him time."

"Well, time is something I seem to have plenty of here." Katherine smiled and decided she would let Will approach her again when he was ready. Until then, she would paint.

~*~

Over the next few weeks, Katherine painted on every canvas she had ordered. Then she ordered more canvases, of all shapes and sizes. She painted several pieces at the gazebo. She loved the view and the atmosphere from that special site at all times of day, and she was able to achieve a sort of time-lapse recording through her paintings. Some had the warm morning light glazed upon the lake's steamy façade, and others had the intense deep blue of the night sky reflecting on the glasslike surface. As Katherine worked, she became more daring with her approach, freer. She painted bigger and bolder, until she was painting on four-foot canvases. Her entire body moved as she swept heaping brushes full of carefully mixed colors. Sometimes she appeared to be dancing, as she swayed from side to side, bending her knees to reach the lower parts of the painting and bouncing up to her tiptoes to cover the top edges.

Each day brought new light, new air to the world around her, and she felt like she was on some sort of high—crazed and energized by her creative mind. She barely slept, and Murray often had to bring her a sandwich as she painted; otherwise she would forget to eat.

One thing Katherine did not forget was her daily latte at *Le Café Bleu*. She had never been able to function very well without a heavy dose of caffeine in the morning, and she loved starting her days talking with Ginger in the buzzing café. Ginger became a bright and positive presence in her life. They talked about many things, but mostly about their favorite places in New York and what they missed most.

From time to time, Ginger would vaguely allude to her former life as the crazy party girl Katherine had known of, but she would quickly change the topic. Katherine suspected her new friend wanted to forget some of the darker parts of her past and focus on the present, just as she herself was trying to erase years of her own sadness and disillusionment with her paintings.

On occasion, she would run into Will. Sometimes, he'd be leaving the café just as she arrived, and sometimes she'd see him on the street as she walked with her easel to and from the inn. Each time they ran into each other, Will would smile shyly and simply say hello. Once or twice, he'd politely ask how the painting was going.

Katherine was beyond confused, and with each encounter, she became a little more hurt. They had shared a connection, she was sure of it. Or at least, she thought she was sure of it. But then, why hadn't he asked her out again? And why was he barely speaking to her? She thought they had made progress with dinner at Marcello's, but now it felt like they had taken several steps backward—back to the time they first met, when all she felt around him was awkward and uncomfortable. What happened? Maybe he was just being nice because she had become a friend of Ginger's. Maybe it was simply a polite "Welcome to Bluewater" dinner and nothing more.

Grateful to have her art as a distraction, Katherine did her best to push thoughts of Will and their apparently nonexistent connection to the back of her mind. She was thrilled with her paintings, and she had even sold a few to patrons staying at the inn. Mr. Trust had been adamant on displaying each finished work throughout the lobby and the dining room, and Katherine would often come back from a day of painting to catch him beaming with pride as he showed the pieces to his guests.

When the first buyers had approached her about one of the paintings, Katherine didn't know what to say. She was so focused on relearning her craft and exploring the process that she had never once considered selling anything. But the man and his wife were enthusiastic art collectors visiting from Texas, and while they hadn't come to Bluewater Lake specifically in search of art, they were thrilled to encounter the original paintings, and they insisted on adding one to their personal collection.

Katherine was tongue-tied when they inquired about pricing, and so when they selected a larger, abstracted interpretation of the calm lake at night, they simply offered her $1500 for the work. "We don't want to offend you. Please let us know if you want more for it," the man said graciously as Katherine stood paralyzed in disbelief.

"No! No, that is plenty. Thank you. Thank you so much!" she finally sputtered as the couple happily carried the painting out to their car, leaving a check in her hands.

Unlike Katherine, Mr. Trust was not at all surprised that the guests were buying the paintings. "They're exquisite, dear. Of course people want to buy them." He winked at her and sat down to play a jazzy tune at the piano. *Simple as that.*

After the first painting sold to the couple in Texas, Katherine decided to pay a generous commission to Mr. Trust and the inn, for any painting sold there, from that point on. Of course, Mr. Trust tried to refuse, but she put her foot down. "They wouldn't sell at all if you didn't insist on displaying them everywhere for the world to see—whether I like it or not!" She smiled and hugged the inn proprietor. "You are like my manager. My agent!" she said, while thinking to herself, *"Or really, my guardian angel."*

~*~

Early one morning, Katherine looked out her window to see a thick blanket of fresh snow covering everything in sight. She had always loved the snow and its power to silence the world beneath it. Even in New York, the tireless noise miraculously quieted when it snowed.

She closed her eyes and thought about the Monet painting back at the Met, with its peaceful valley and beautiful stream, and the snowy mountains in the distance. That painting had saved Katherine when it seemed her entire life had collapsed and when she no longer knew who she was. It had inspired her to change her path or, rather, to build a new path. And now here she was, standing in those distant snow-covered mountains, breathing in the beautiful silence.

Feeling emotional and invigorated, she decided to bundle up and walk around the lake in search of a new painting spot. It had been weeks since she arrived in Bluewater, but she had not yet ventured beyond the end of the street. She dressed in her warmest layers and grabbed her easel then prepared a thermos of coffee down in the lobby and packed a couple of apples in her pockets. The inn was quiet—most of the guests were still asleep, and Murray was tucked away in the kitchen, preparing for the breakfast crowd. Mr. Trust was nowhere to be seen. Katherine figured he was still asleep as well.

When she stepped outside, the cold air crept into her lungs and made her cough. Her exposed face tingled and stung, and she pulled her scarf up to just below her squinting eyes. The town was motionless, resting in a peaceful slumber, waiting for the sun to rise. Its streets were all but empty, and only a few dim lights speckled the formidable white landscape.

As she walked, Katherine marveled at the beauty around her. The snow up on the mountains blended seamlessly into the low-lying clouds, and the earth was no longer separate from the sky. When she looked down to the lake, she stopped in her tracks. It was more breathtaking today than any other day. The cold air and surrounding whiteness framed the blue water, so icy and pure, making it nearly fluorescent in its glow. As much as Katherine wanted to drop everything and paint that very moment, she stuck to her plan and continued onward. The sun would be up soon, and she wanted to find the perfect spot to capture its sparkling effect on the snow.

When she neared the end of the street, she glanced down at the gazebo. There was someone inside. She took a few steps closer. *Who would be sitting out in the freezing cold this early in the morning?*

"Mr. Trust? Is that you?" Katherine asked quietly as she approached the man. His back was turned to her, and he was looking out over the lake. She noticed a bouquet of fresh flowers gently draped over the plaque she had discovered the first time she visited the gazebo.

Mr. Trust turned around, startled by her presence.

"Oh, hello, dear! What are you doing out in the cold so early this morning?" Mr. Trust smiled, but Katherine could see tears in the corners of his eyes.

"I was going to ask you the same thing." She smiled. "Mind if I join you for a moment?"

"Of course." Mr. Trust nodded invitingly, his nose red from the biting cold.

Katherine did not want to impose. She realized that, until this moment, she had never seen him outside of the inn, and she had never seen him unhappy. His sadness broke her heart, and she sat close to him, putting her head on his shoulder.

"I visit this little gazebo from time to time." Mr. Trust spoke quietly. "I married the love of my life in this gazebo." He smiled at Katherine.

"Jacqueline?" she asked delicately. Mr. Trust responded with a look of surprise.

"I read that beautiful plaque over there when I first got into town." She smiled.

Mr. Trust sighed. "She was so beautiful. And she loved this lake and this town. She died a few years ago." Tears started falling down his soft, wrinkled cheeks. "I miss her every day. But when I look at the lake, I'm reminded of her beauty. So, I know she is with me here; she is still with me." He smiled and nodded as he spoke and then winked at Katherine as she gave him a hug. "Would you like some unsolicited advice from an old man?"

Katherine laughed. "Any advice from you is more than welcome, Mr. Trust."

"If you're lucky enough to find your true love, hang on tight. Breathe it in every single day. There is nothing more important in the world." He looked out over the vibrant blue water as he spoke.

"Thank you. I will . . if I ever get that lucky," she replied with a sigh.

"Oh, you will. A heart as good as yours is meant to be shared with another." He stood up and shivered. "Boy, it is quite cold this morning, isn't it? You stay warm, young lady. Happy painting!" He tipped his hat and hobbled out of the gazebo, kissing his hand and gently touching the plaque on his way out.

Katherine sat for a moment, absorbing his words. There had been a time when she thought Michael was her true love. She really believed he was the one. But as time went on, she did not feel compelled to "hang on tight." She felt compelled to dig a deep dark hole so that she could crawl inside of it.

Things really had begun to change when Michael's firm partnered with a European firm. Michael flew to London regularly and was gone for a week at a time. Katherine loved having the apartment to herself. She would cook her favorite dinners, and she would go out to walk around the art galleries when she had any free time. Yet even though Michael was an ocean away, she could feel his condescension hanging above her. "Really, Kate, when are you going to grow out of this art stuff? It's pointless. Your time is too valuable—you need to focus on your business, on my business." Sometimes these thoughts would take over, convincing Katherine that she was wasting her time. She'd sigh, leave the art gallery, and go home to work on contracts late into the night.

When Michael was home, he was but a ghost of his former self, walking around in a dazed, liquored stupor, glued to his phone and computer, screaming obscenities at emails, and calling his secretary to bark orders at all hours. He barely spoke to Katherine unless he had to, and he never touched her again.

~*~

And now, sitting at the gazebo, she realized that, as their marriage slowly dissolved, Katherine had loosened her grip more and more. *He couldn't possibly be my one true love . . . my only shot . . .*

She felt sad. Sad for Mr. Trust. Sad for herself. Sad for Michael. But she also felt liberated. It wasn't right—her life in New York, her marriage. This was right. Bluewater was right.

CHAPTER 15

Katherine walked to the end of Main Street and continued onto the dirt road that veered left, along the lake. Her easel was heavy, strapped upon her shoulder. But she had become used to it; it offered her a sense of companionship. As she walked, she listened to the snow crunch beneath each step. The sound echoed between the tall pine trees lining the road, bouncing off their wise old trunks. Her warm breath swirled around in front of her face and then disappeared into the cold still air.

She felt as though she was in a dream, walking through an enchanted forest. As a child, she often escaped into imaginary lands full of beauty and magic. And this place, this snowy dirt road along a glowing lake, was exactly like something she would have created in her childhood mind.

Occasionally, Katherine passed by small cabins resting between the road and the lake, quietly puffing smoke from their old chimneys as the warm lights from within spilled out onto the snow just beyond the windows. She imagined living in one of the cozy cabins, right on the lake, with a yard overlooking the water, where she could paint every morning. It would be a far cry from her modern loft in the city. But she seemed to be adapting quite easily to this strange new life, worlds away from the life she had known so well before. It was almost too easy.

The road narrowed as it curved around the southern edge of the lake. There were fewer cabins here, and the forest grew more abundant. Robust trees commanded every square foot with their sprawling branches, heavily weighted with the fresh snow. Only at the touch of a slight breeze or gentle vibration of a bird's landing, would the snow release its heavy hold and sift downward, shimmering like glitter in the subtle morning light.

Katherine tiptoed onward, afraid her loud crunching footsteps were an unwelcome disruption to the tranquility of the nature surrounding her. She breathed in the invigorating pine scent wafting through the air as she crept along. The sun would be rising over the mountain any minute now, and she had to make her way down to the water to set up.

The road was situated above the edge of the lake, and the slope down to the water was steep and covered in snow. At last, she spotted a rocky area ahead, where the boulders staggered downward from the road. Nature's version of a staircase . . .

Carefully stepping out onto the first rock, Katherine felt around with her boot, seeking a spot with less ice and more grip. The uneven weight of the easel worked against her, and she adjusted the strap so that the easel rested more in the center of her back as she climbed down. She had about twenty feet of rock to descend before she would reach the small frozen beach below. Each tentative step became a bit easier, and Katherine moved with more confidence as the sun's rays crept out from behind the outline of the mountain.

Just as she neared the bottom, her foot slipped out from under her and she fell backward. Fortunately, her devoted easel broke her fall and prevented her head from smacking against the boulder above.

"Uggghh!" She gasped. The easel saved her head, but its sturdy wood frame did a number on her back, and it knocked the wind out of her. She lay still for a moment, coughing and catching her breath. As she sat up, she was relieved to realize that her back was probably just slightly bruised. *War wounds, earned by a real painter* . . . Katherine smiled. She thought of the young artist in Prague, painting by the river. He'd probably be proud of her die-hard efforts to catch the capricious morning light.

She stepped onto the beach just as the sun illuminated the world around her. The water was frozen along the edges of the lake, and the smooth ice reflected the light like a freshly cleaned mirror. She hurriedly assembled her easel and supplies, blew on her frozen hands, and began painting.

Once again, Katherine disappeared into a world of moving color. Pale yellows evolved into golds and oranges, caressing patches of the commanding fluorescent blue water. She never really had the opportunity to paint snow before. Its glowing presence had an incredible effect on her palette. Not only had the morning colors arrived, beautiful and vivid as always, but they also reflected in the snow, amplifying to an unimaginable degree. Katherine couldn't stand still. She was exhilarated. She danced and bounced and laughed like a crazy person as she smeared on layer after layer of rich scrumptious paint.

While painting the final touches, Katherine thought she heard music. At first, she just brushed it off as part of the mental insanity that typically consumed her when she painted. Yet, as minutes passed, the music remained: faint, but consistent. She paused, straining to hear it more clearly. It was a symphony of some kind. She could hear a piano, strings, and horns. It was beautiful, and it sounded like a story—dramatic and sad.

Where was it coming from?

She took a step back from her painting and examined her work. It was her favorite piece yet, dripping with thick uninhibited color and vibrancy. Katherine closed her eyes, took some deep breaths, and listened to the music. Maybe it was travelling across the lake, coming from somewhere in town, perhaps one of the lodges? But it didn't sound like it was coming from that direction. It sounded like it was behind her.

She decided to find the source. Her painting needed to settle for a while anyway before she could pack up and make the journey back to the inn. Turning around, she began to climb the rock wall that had nearly killed her on the way down. *I'm going to have to climb down this thing again if I go up now . . .* Too curious not to, Katherine decided it was worth the risk and continued to climb.

When she reached the road at the top, she turned around to see the icy lake shining magnificently in full sunlight. And the town of Bluewater, her town, seemed to smile back at her from the other side. She looked down the hill at her painting. Even from a distance, the piece was a striking success.

Katherine listened for the music.

Silence.

She sighed. *Of course . . .*

Just as she turned to head back down, the faint sound of a solo piano drifted lightly through the trees. Katherine walked up the road, following the sound farther into the forest. This part of the road was less traveled, rockier under the melting snow, and she struggled to find her balance with each step. She considered turning around and going back to the beach many times, as she shivered and cursed her lack of coordination. But then the beguiling music would call out to her, and with each clumsy step forward, it became louder, clearer, more intriguing.

After what felt like hours, Katherine spotted a small cabin through the trees in the distance. She hadn't passed a single home since the beach, and she was surprised to see the structure, casually puffing smoke from its chimney. The music must be coming from this tiny home. It was loud and powerful, and it sounded like an entire orchestra sat within the cabin and played just as grandly as they would in Central Park. Perhaps whoever lived there really liked to listen to symphonies at full volume. It seemed strange though, and the music continued, beckoning to Katherine—its sad song telling a tale of loss and loneliness, of love and hope, all at the same time.

The snow became heavier as she followed the winding road, making it difficult to navigate where to step. The slope downward on her left was even steeper than it was back by the beach, and she did her best to walk along the uphill side. She continued to move forward; though she didn't know what she would do upon arriving at the cabin. She certainly didn't plan to knock on the door, disturbing whoever lived inside; she was simply not that bold. But she hoped perhaps she could get close enough to discover the mystery behind the music.

As she neared the entrance to the driveway, Katherine heard a loud, echoing crack. She turned to see a massive tree falling quickly, just above where she stood. It was headed right for her. Instinctively, she jumped back to get out of the way, but she jumped too far.

Her body bounced and twisted as it tumbled down the snow-covered hill. She couldn't stop the fall—the slope was too steep and icy. She kept falling, rolling, unable to grab hold of anything. It lasted forever, her body bending and crushing, seemingly in slow motion.

Until everything went black.

CHAPTER 16

"Katherine? Katherine, can you hear me?"

She began to detect hints of foggy light. Every bone in her body ached, and she was so cold she couldn't move. She was soaking wet.

Did she fall in the lake?

Her head throbbed. The pain was unbearable. She thought she might be sick.

"You're going to be okay. Hang in there."

Someone was carrying her.

Katherine struggled to focus. Everything was blurry. The more she strained, the more her head pulsed in agony. She felt warm, labored breaths fall upon her face.

"I've got you. Can you hear me?"

She closed her eyes tightly and then opened them again. The intense glare of the sun made everything white, and then slowly, things began to take form. She saw the blue sky and the outline of the tops of the tallest pine trees. Then she saw him.

Will.

It was his warm breath on her face.

He was carrying her.

"Will?" Katherine tried to talk, but the pain in her chest was so extreme that she couldn't even muster a whisper.

"Hang on. We're almost there." Will breathed heavily, grunting as he carried Katherine's cold limp body up through the prohibitive snow.

Katherine moved in and out of consciousness. Each time she opened her eyes, she tried to focus on Will's face.

When they reached the road at the top, Will held her more tightly and walked faster, toward the small cabin.

"Okay, we made it. Katherine? Are you with me?"

Will kicked the front door open with unrestrained force. Inside, he laid Katherine gently onto a soft couch next to a fireplace and covered her with blankets. He rushed around, feeding the fire with fresh logs and gathering towels and hot water.

Katherine didn't know exactly what was happening, but she felt her body slowly begin to thaw. She didn't move or talk, but she knew she was safe, and she surrendered to a deep sleep.

An hour later, her eyes fluttered open. Her head still throbbed, but it had recessed from its former intensity. Too scared to move, she slowly assessed her surroundings. A fire crackled in front of her, draping her face in heat. She was wrapped in a fleece blanket, on a worn flannel couch. Stunned, Katherine realized she no longer had any clothes on—only her bra and underwear.

"You're awake." Will walked around the corner, holding a coffee mug.

Katherine jumped, startled. Then she groaned in pain.

"I'm sorry. I didn't mean to scare you. How do you feel?"

"Um, okay, I think. Everything hurts." She had regained her voice. It was raspy and rough, but at least she could talk. "What happened? Why don't I have clothes on?" She was fairly certain Will wasn't the kind of guy to take advantage of a girl in distress, but she was disoriented and she had no idea what happened.

"Sorry about that. You were soaking wet after falling into the lake. I had to get those clothes off you so you wouldn't freeze to death. Really." Will was blushing and stuttered a bit as he talked. "I, um . . . I didn't look or anything. It was all a bit frantic actually."

"I fell in the lake?" Katherine panicked. She remembered the tree falling towards her, and she remembered jumping out of the way. Bits and pieces of her tumble down the hill flashed through her mind. A sharp pain pounded in her head, just behind her ear. She raised her hand to it and felt a bandage.

"I think you hit your head during the fall. That was bleeding pretty badly." Will pointed to her head. "It's slowed down, but you probably have a concussion." He looked afraid and exhausted. "I'm not sure how you fell, but I found you in the lake. Luckily, you landed in a shallow area of the water. You didn't go completely under."

"How did you find me?" Katherine's eyes were filling with tears. What would have happened if he hadn't found her?

"I stepped outside to get some firewood, and I heard the tree fall. I wanted to make sure it wasn't blocking the road, and when I went to check it out, I saw you down there." Will paused. "I ran as fast as I could." He seemed to be reliving it all, as he rubbed his eyes. "Can you sit up? We should get you to the hospital."

"No, no, that won't be necessary. Really. I just have a headache; that's all," Katherine insisted. She took a mental survey of her body. It was sore, definitely bruised, as was her ego, but she knew she would be okay. Will looked skeptical.

"I will go see a doctor, I promise. If I feel worse, I will go," she reassured him. Will sat down, hesitantly.

"What are you doing way out here anyway?" he asked.

Katherine tried to sit up. "I was painting. Just down the road . . ."

She looked around the room. It was simple, masculine, but cozy. The walls were dark wood, and there was a small window next to the fireplace where she could see the driveway she had been approaching right before she fell.

There was paper everywhere, in piles, crumpled into balls, thrown around the floor. As she looked closer at one disheveled stack near the couch, she realized it was sheet music: pages and pages of music scattered all around the living room.

"The music! Is it yours? Are you a musician?" Katherine ignored her throbbing head. She had found the source!

Will was perplexed at her sudden excitement. "Um, well . . . not technically," he stumbled, struggling to find his words.

"I was painting and I heard the music. It was so . . . enchanting. I didn't know where it was coming from. And for some reason, I decided I had to find out." Katherine blushed. It all sounded so stupid as she said it out loud.

"Oh. So this is all my fault then," Will said quietly and then gave a little half smile. He sighed, "It . . . It is mine. I write music."

Katherine carefully reached down to pick up one of the pages. The physical movement sent waves of pain through her body, and she flinched as she grabbed the sheet.

"May I?" She asked as she slowly sat back up, clutching the blanket close to her nearly naked body.

Will swallowed and nodded.

She couldn't actually read music, but Katherine could appreciate the timeless beauty of the assorted black symbols strategically placed along the lines. This page in particular appeared to consist of a highly complex passage, and Will had scribbled handwritten notes all up and down the margins. At the top of the page, there was a heading: *The Walk— A Time Light Motion Picture*, and below in a slightly smaller font, *Score by William Laurence*.

"William Laurence," Katherine whispered, processing the name in front of her. She recognized it. "*You're* William Laurence? *The* William Laurence? As in, the famous composer?"

Will blushed and cleared his throat.

She couldn't believe it. William Laurence had composed some of the greatest scores of award-winning films over the past twenty years. He had also written some of her favorite symphonies performed by the New York Philharmonic. This man . . . This awkward, flannel-wearing, scruffy, small-town fisherman could not possibly be William Laurence.

"Can I get you some tea? Coffee maybe?" Will asked as he stood nervously and walked out of the room.

CHAPTER 17

Katherine carefully sipped the hot coffee, and Will sat down next to her on the couch. She was able to prop herself up with the blanket wrapped tightly around her bare shoulders.

"Why didn't you tell me who you were?" she asked tentatively. She could sense Will was conflicted.

"I don't know. I guess I try to keep that part of my life separate." He paused, sipping his coffee. "Separate from the rest of my life here in Bluewater."

"But you still write? It's what you do for work?" Katherine pressed. Her curious nature had always gotten her into trouble. This was obviously a very sensitive and private topic for Will, but she couldn't resist digging for answers. Her mother's voice rang in her head, *"Katherine, don't be so nosy! It's rude."*

"Yes, I still write. I write every day." Will trailed off, gazing out the window.

Katherine let him be for a minute. Then she spoke quietly. "I guess we all have things about us, things that we're not ready to share. At least not right away . . ."

Will sat patiently, knowing there more, waiting for her to go on.

She took a deep breath.

"I was married, back in New York. I was married, and now . . . I'm divorced." A tear fell down her cheek. When she said it out loud, it sounded like she was admitting that she was a failure, someone who gives up, someone who does not know how to hold her life together. She felt ugly and unworthy.

Will did not press her for more information. He simply sighed and gently put his hand on hers. Its warmth traveled up her arm and into her chest.

Finally, he said, "I'm sorry I didn't tell you who I am. Before Bluewater, my life was a mess: It was chaotic and shallow. I was a different man when I lived in LA."

There was more. Katherine could sense there was more that he wanted to say. But she sat patiently, waiting for him to sort his thoughts, his hand still wrapped around hers. As the seconds passed, she wasn't sure she wanted to know whatever it was he wasn't telling her.

What if he was like Michael?

After a moment, Will continued, "When I came to Bluewater, I got a fresh start. My priorities changed and I got my act together." He paused. "But the music is a part of me. I just . . . I can't *not* write." Will shook his head as he spoke; he appeared to be deeply ashamed—like he was admitting to a heroin addiction or something.

Katherine couldn't understand why he would feel this way. Will's music was world-renowned; it was brilliant and highly coveted. His shame didn't make any sense. There had to be something else.

"Will," she started. A heavy lump formed in her throat, making it difficult to continue. "Thank you.

Thank you for saving me. I can't imagine what would've happened . . . if you hadn't found me . . ."

Tears poured down her cheeks.

Will took her coffee mug, setting it down next to his on the table, and wrapped his strong arms around her. Katherine tucked her face into his warm neck and cried. The reality of what had happened to her struck with sudden force, and she shook, overwhelmed with feelings of fear, humiliation, and gratitude.

As her tears slowed, she slowly looked up at Will. He took a breath and carefully rested his hand on her bruised, wet cheek. His astonishing blue eyes glowed as he looked back at her.

Will leaned in slowly, gently kissing her cheekbone. Katherine closed her eyes and abandoned all sense of pain, surrendering to the sensation of his lips on her skin. His face was soft against hers, not prickly as she imagined it might be. Will moved from her cheek to her mouth, barely brushing his lips briefly against hers. He held her face delicately in his hands and kissed her again. This time, he lingered a bit longer.

It felt so wonderfully foreign. For a moment, she felt bad, like she was doing something wrong, like she should feel guilty. But the moment was fleeting. She was a world away from Michael. That time had passed . . .

Will's lips were soft and warm. He was so gentle, so careful, and he tasted of coffee and cinnamon. The kiss was tender at first, polite. But as they connected, it grew stronger, impassioned, almost ravenous. Will wrapped her tighter in his arms, as they let their mouths explore and communicate.

Katherine's breath quickened, and she could feel the blood pulsing through her veins. She had never experienced this desperate sort of longing with Michael or anyone, ever. They were only kissing, but so much was being said in the kiss. There was a grave hunger and fiery physical desire, but there were also moments of tentative vulnerability.

After a while, Will let go of his tight hold on Katherine. He pulled back just enough to look into her eyes and brush some of the hair back from her face. In his eyes, she saw sadness, hope, and maybe even love. So complex and beautiful, just like the song that had lured her to his cabin.

Will raised his hand to her shoulder and slowly peeled back the blanket. His fingers lightly grazed her arm, as the blanket fell to the couch. Katherine could hardly stand the intensity of the sensation. Her heart pounded, and heat radiated through her entire body, as she sat before him. Her bra and panties were still damp from the lake, but her skin was warm from the fire. Will kissed her again, gently, and then moved his lips down to her neck. He took his time, cherishing each gentle encounter. Katherine lay back on the couch, her fingers running through his thick hair.

Will gently removed her lacy bra and then her underwear. She had never before been confident enough to sit naked, in full view, in broad daylight, not even with Michael, not at any point in their marriage. She had always been reserved and extremely shy—*a total prude* in Andi's opinion.

But today, with Will, she felt different. Despite her badly bruised body and her damp hair, Katherine felt beautiful. She wanted Will to see her. She did not want to shield herself; she no longer wanted to hide behind the wall she hid behind for so many years.

Will was a gamble. He was mysterious and distant, but he was also somehow very present. Katherine decided to take the risk. Something about him made her feel truer to herself than she had ever been before. The thought of him hurting her frightened her, but not as much as the thought of not letting him in.

When Will kissed the soft part of her tummy just below her belly button, Katherine shuddered. She couldn't remember a time she felt so alive, so full of extreme desire.

When she groaned, Will thought he had hurt her, and he looked up to make sure she was okay. Katherine grabbed his face with her hands and pulled him to her mouth. She unbuttoned his shirt and ran her fingers over his chest and down to his abdomen, unbuttoning his jeans. His muscles flexed and twitched as her hands moved around his body.

Will carefully picked her up from the couch, and she wrapped her legs around his waist. He held her for a moment and kissed her passionately before laying her gently on the rug by the fireplace. He kissed her toes and then her knees and then the inner part of her thighs. Katherine's legs trembled. She feared she might scream; she could barely contain herself. It was as if she no longer had any control of her own body, and she wanted the feeling to last forever.

"Will . . ." Katherine gasped, wrapping her arms around his back. They held each other tightly and moved together slowly, in harmony—both savoring every moment.

~*~

When she awoke, it was dark outside. Her sweaty naked body was wrapped up against Will's, and they were still on the floor under the blanket. Will breathed deeply in her ear, and she lay still, soaking in the feeling of his bare skin against hers.

How long had they been sleeping?

Katherine's head throbbed, and every part of her body hurt, but she didn't care. She smiled as she remembered each little detail from the hours before. She carefully turned to face Will. He was so handsome and strong. His eyebrows furrowed slightly; he was always wrestling with his thoughts, even in sleep. Katherine softly kissed his lips, and he slowly opened his eyes.

"Hi," she said.

He looked startled. "How do you feel?"

It only took a moment for Will to snap back into protector mode, as he began examining Katherine's wounds.

"I'm sore. But I feel okay, really," she assured him, putting her hand on his cheek.

Will put his hand on hers and closed his eyes. A look of shame crept slowly over his face.

"Katherine. I . . . I'm so sorry," he said as he stood and began to dress.

"Sorry?" She wrapped the blanket around her shoulders once again and slowly sat up.

"Yeah. I'm . . . I shouldn't . . ." He struggled with his words, avoiding eye contact with her. He seemed upset and was suddenly in a hurry.

"As soon as you're dressed, I'll take you back to the inn." Will spoke now without emotion and walked away into the kitchen.

Katherine felt humiliated and uncomfortable. She put her clothes on as fast as she could, flinching at the pain induced by each minor movement. She didn't understand what was happening. He had looked into her eyes as they made love, and he was there—he was with her. They had shared so much. They had opened up to one another. It all meant something to Katherine. Had it meant nothing to Will? A flood of self-doubt poured over her. Here I go again. I should never have gotten involved with him. With anyone . . .

As much as she wanted to demand answers, Katherine was too afraid. Will's behavior was unexpected and hurtful, and it was apparent they were not going to discuss anything right now. She put on her jacket and wiped a tear from her eye as she followed Will out to his truck.

The snow had started to fall again, and Katherine stared resolutely out her window, trying not to cry. Will looked straight ahead at the road, his jaw clenched tightly. Neither of them said a word.

When he parked in front of the inn, Katherine willed herself to face him, and Will turned to look at her. His eyes were deeply sad, regretful even, but he did not falter.

"I'm so sorry, Katherine." He could barely speak.

Tears now flowed freely down her cheeks, as she sat for a moment, hoping he'd say more, hoping he would explain.

"Sorry for what? Will, I don't understand."

But Will simply turned his face forward again, and he silently waited for her to get out of the truck.

CHAPTER 18

"Oh my God. Do you think he's gay?"

"Andi, be serious." Katherine sniffled. She hadn't yet walked back into the inn. Her feet felt as if they were frozen to the ground where she stood, where she watched Will drive away, down the street and out of sight.

In New York, she would call Andi after a terrible day, and within an hour, Andi would be at her door with wine and pizza. It was a reflex for her to call her dear friend as her heart broke there on the sidewalk in Bluewater.

"I still can't believe you fell into the frozen lake. Thank God he was there, Katherine." Andi's voice became softer. "I'm so glad you're okay. What would I do without you?"

"Oh, I'm sure you'd find some way to survive." Katherine sighed. "You're the strongest person I know."

"Oh, buddy, that's what I always say about you!" Andi replied. Katherine could tell from the sound of her voice that she was choked up.

"What am I going to do, Andi? I'm so confused." She relived the conversation with Will in her mind. It all had happened so abruptly, and none of it made sense.

"Hang in there, sweetheart. He'll come around. And if he doesn't, it's his loss." Andi had always viewed men as objects: objects to consider, objects to entertain, and objects to casually discard if she was done with them or if they failed to fulfill their purpose.

Katherine sighed. "I don't think it's that simple. He *wanted* to let me in. I know it. I could feel it. But then he completely shut down out of nowhere. It was all so wonderful . . . before it was interrupted by this . . . this agony, this battle he seems to be fighting in his head. I don't know. I wish he would just tell me . . ." Katherine shivered as her voice trailed off. Her hair was still slightly damp, and the temperature outside had gone down with the sun.

"I don't think you're going to get any answers tonight. Let him sleep on it," Andi replied. "And you, you need to get your booty inside, take a hot shower, and get warm. No more diving into the lake, Missy!" Andi scolded then laughed. "I miss ya, kid."

Dismayed, Katherine could barely respond, "I miss you too."

She took a deep, cold breath. Her body ached, and her cheeks tightened under her frozen tears. She suddenly felt very alone—alone in the middle of nowhere. For a moment, she wanted to pack up her things and catch the first flight back to New York. Back to Andi, back to where things weren't perfect, but at least they made sense.

Everything had been going so well. She rarely thought about Michael anymore. When his contemptuous voice tried to creep its way back into her head as she painted, she silenced it immediately with her own thoughts. *I am creating beauty. It is worthy. I am worthy.*

Word about Katherine's paintings had spread around town, making the lobby of the Bluewater Inn a local fine art attraction. She had sold over half of the pieces she created since she arrived.

Andi was right. Nothing was going to be resolved tonight, and a hot shower sounded amazing. Katherine wiped the remaining tears from her eyes, cleared her throat, and made her way through the door at the inn.

Inside, Ginger sat with Mr. Trust on the couch. They were laughing and sipping wine.

"Oh my gosh! What happened to you?!" Ginger looked horrified, as if she was face-to-face with a ghost. Mr. Trust sprang up and hustled over. He took Katherine's hand and guided her to the couch, draping a warm blanket over her shoulders.

"Is it really that bad?" Katherine asked with a grin, trying to ease their concern.

"Murray! Murray! Call the doc!" Mr. Trust yelled toward the kitchen.

"No! No, really. That's not necessary. I'm okay. Just a bit banged up, that's all." Katherine tried not to burst into tears. She smiled and patted Mr. Trust's hand on her knee. "Really, Mr. Trust, I'm okay."

Ginger poured a glass of wine and handed it to her friend. "So, what happened?"

"It was silly, really. I'm so embarrassed." Katherine decided it was best to leave Will out of it. "I was painting on the other side of the lake. It was slippery, of course, and I fell. I should have been more careful . . . but I'm okay."

"Who put that bandage on your head? Do you carry a first-aid kit in that easel of yours?" Ginger's eyes squinted. She looked skeptical. Katherine returned her glance, silently begging her not to press the matter any further. Ginger received the girl-code message and changed the subject.

"Well, let's go upstairs and get you cleaned up, shall we?" She winked and reached for Katherine's hand.

Mr. Trust and Murray stood with them, offering anything they could to help. Katherine thanked them, giving them hugs, holding her breath so she wouldn't flinch, when Murray squeezed her tightly. She didn't want them to waste another second, worrying about her.

When she and Ginger made it upstairs and into her room, Katherine shut the door and willed herself to look in the mirror. It was no wonder they had all reacted the way they did when they saw her. She looked like something straight out of a horror film. Her hair was damp and disheveled, and the bandage Will had applied to her head was bulky and stained with her blood. Her mascara ran down her cheeks, and her left cheekbone was badly bruised in an array of dark blues and purples.

"Okay, spill it," Ginger said, as she sat in the chair by the window.

Katherine sighed and surrendered. "I was wandering, exploring, on that road across the lake. A tree fell, and I jumped out of the way, and then I fell. I think I fell pretty far. I blacked out."

Ginger sat patiently. She seemed to know what was coming next.

Katherine continued, her voice shaking, "Will heard it happen. He ran down to the lake and carried me up to his place. I was in and out of consciousness and soaking wet. I didn't even know he lived there."

Ginger leaned back and took a sip of her wine. "Thank goodness he was home, Katherine."

"Yes." Her tears returned.

Ginger smiled gently. Her eyes spoke for her; she already knew there was more. Even though they were new friends, something about Ginger made Katherine feel like they had known each other their entire lives.

"Did something happen between you two?" Ginger asked carefully.

Katherine nodded, unable to speak. She sat down on the edge of the bed, facing Ginger. Her relentless tears said it all.

Ginger put her hands around Katherine's, comforting her, waiting for her to go on.

"It was amazing. He was wonderful. It was like we finally gave in; we let go of everything that has been holding us back. It was *our* time and it was so right, until . . ." Katherine couldn't go on. She couldn't even swallow.

Ginger sighed knowingly and slowly shook her head. "Oh, Will," she whispered.

"When we woke up, something had changed. It was like a switch flipped inside of him. He couldn't even look at me." She stopped to blow her nose and sip her wine. "We got dressed and he drove me back here. He barely said a word to me. He just kept apologizing." Her tears began to dry, and anger started boiling deep inside. "I don't even know what he was apologizing for. There we were. I thought we had made this huge breakthrough, and then it was like he took twenty steps back, for no reason!"

Ginger had looked down at her hands fidgeting with her wine glass, and avoided eye contact with Katherine as she spoke.

"Ginger, do you know something?" Katherine asked tentatively.

"Yes," Ginger replied quietly as she gazed out the window. "Yes. I do."

Katherine stared at Ginger, waiting for her to continue. But as Ginger inhaled deeply and opened her mouth to speak, there was a knock at the door.

"Hello, darlings. Murray made you girls some soup. You must be starving." Mr. Trust smiled gently, holding a beautiful silver tray with two bowls of steaming hot soup and a basket of French rolls.

Katherine took the tray and smiled back at Mr. Trust. "Thank you so much. I didn't realize it until just now, but I *am* starving. Please thank Murray for me." She looked over her shoulder in time to see Ginger nod and wink at her grandfather, silently assuring him that the situation was under control.

"If there is anything else you need, just holler." Mr. Trust tipped his invisible hat and blew a kiss as he slowly turned to walk back down the hall.

Katherine set the tray down on the small table and pulled up another chair. They sipped the hot soup in silence.

Clearing her throat, she looked expectantly at Ginger, who was obviously procrastinating the inevitable conversation, as she shoveled spoonful after spoonful into her mouth, filling all remaining space with bites of bread.

Finally, she swallowed her food, took a big drink of her wine, and sighed deeply. "Katherine, Will was engaged."

Katherine sat back, speechless. Ginger's words felt like a punch to the gut.

Why wouldn't he tell me that? Especially after I told him about Michael?

Ginger continued, "It was a long time ago, before he moved to Bluewater." She paused, looking down at her hands again. "Will and I knew each other, you know, through the film industry. We met at the premiere of his first big project." Ginger looked away, appearing to get her thoughts in order. "He was a different person back then. You wouldn't believe it, knowing him now. But like myself, he got caught up in that crazy scene. I'd sometimes see him at wild parties in New York or while I was on set in LA."

Katherine tried to imagine Will in that kind of environment. Ginger was right—it was impossible to picture. She knew all about Ginger's crazy past with drinking and drugs and men. It had been all over the tabloids and online on a regular basis. But Will just didn't fit into that visual.

Ginger went on, "When I first met Will, he was this shy musical genius who had just been discovered, an innocent who was engaged to his high-school sweetheart." She sighed. "I remember them at the premiere party. She was an elementary-school teacher, and they were both so nervous and out of place at such a major event." Ginger paused, smiling nostalgically as she remembered more. "She was sweet, soft-spoken, beautiful. Her name was Julee."

Ginger paused and refilled their glasses of wine.

"So . . . what happened?" Katherine asked, unsure if she really wanted to know the answer.

"Well, Will's first film score was a huge success. He became one of the most in-demand score writers, literally overnight. And, unfortunately, he lost himself in the fame over time." She shook her head and continued, "He traveled all over the world for events and premieres. And he fell deeper into that crazy world, full of parties and women—a world where everyone offers you everything, and you let yourself indulge because it's all part of the package."

"Are you saying Will cheated on his fiancée?" Katherine asked carefully. She knew that, if the answer was "yes," it would likely change everything; it would change the way she thought about Will, the way she felt about him. She vowed she would never again be with someone she couldn't trust.

"No. He didn't. He really didn't. He loved her so much." Ginger's eyes filled with tears. "The chaos involved in the world of fame is a kind of beast—the kind that swallows you whole. Sometimes you don't even realize it's happening until it's too late."

Katherine shook her head. She didn't follow what Ginger was trying to say. "So, if he didn't cheat on her, what happened?"

Ginger sniffled. "As time went on, Will became consumed with his role in the film world. He would often tell Julee to quit her job and travel with him, to accompany him at the parties and premieres, to live a life of fame and luxury. But that wasn't Julee. She loved her job, and she loved her family. So she would often stay back in Los Angeles, awaiting his return.

"I remember one night, at a party in Manhattan, I ran into Will, and he was drunk and so sad. He said that he had begged Julee to come with him, and she wouldn't. They had a big fight, and she told him that maybe they should take a break, that she didn't want to marry him if she was always going to be second place to his career. He was so scared, so devastated. He said he never thought she would leave him and that he felt completely lost. He didn't know what to do."

Katherine nodded, assuming the story ended with a sad breakup. But Ginger went on, her voice now cautious and fragile, "What he didn't know was that Julee had a change of heart after he left. She decided she loved him too much to let him go and that she would compromise her life so that she could be with him, so that they could be together. She told her parents everything, got in the car, and began to drive across the country. She planned to surprise Will at a premiere we were attending in the city a few days later."

Tears ran down Ginger's face, and Katherine handed her the box of tissues. Ginger cleared her throat and continued, "Somewhere in Oklahoma, I think, there was a drunk driver . . ." She took a shaky breath. "It was a narrow, two-way road, and it was late at night. He swerved across the line . . . and Julee . . . it was a freak accident. No other cars for miles and miles, but she was there—right there, right at that second." Ginger exhaled. "They were both killed, instantly."

Katherine felt sick to her stomach. "Oh, my God," she whispered.

After a few moments, Ginger continued, "Will has never forgiven himself. He blames himself for her death and for her family's pain." She shook her head as she spoke, "He called me shortly after the accident, asking for help. And so I made arrangements with Gramps for Will to come here— to mourn, to recover. He hasn't left Bluewater since."

She paused before adding, "And he hasn't been with anyone since Julee."

CHAPTER 19

There was a knock at the door.

And then another knock.

Katherine's head pounded, and her body felt like it weighed a thousand pounds under the quilt on her bed.

What time was it?

Knock, knock, knock.

She slowly moved toward the edge of the bed, grimacing as she sat up. It was morning—the sun was already making its journey over the lake.

"Be right there!" she called out, her voice hoarse after such a deep sleep.

Ginger had stayed with her late into the night. After learning the truth about Will and his past, Katherine needed time to process, and so they finished the bottle of wine and switched topics, sharing stories from their lives back in New York.

Ginger admitted to spiraling out of control when she was at the prime of her stardom, something Katherine had read about, but in entertainment news, it was difficult to know what was actually true. She told Katherine how she ended up back in Bluewater after being hospitalized for an accidental drug overdose that nearly killed her.

"Gramps came all the way out to Manhattan to get me. My parents had died when I was young; he was my emergency contact. That little man got on a plane for the first time in decades and flew to New York. He refused to leave unless I came home with him. And so, here I am." Ginger laughed and cried as she told Katherine her story.

"Do you miss it?" Katherine asked.

"I miss the work: the movie sets, the shows. But I don't miss life beyond the set. I clearly wasn't built for all that. Neither was Will." She smiled and continued, "Life here in Bluewater Lake has so much more to offer. I made the right choice." She laughed. "Well, actually, *Gramps* made the right choice for me."

Knock, knock, knock.

Katherine wrapped her robe around her silk nightgown and tiptoed to the door. Every step sent waves of pain through her bruised body.

When she opened the door, she nearly fell over when she saw Will standing there patiently, holding her easel and the painting she had finished down by the frozen lake.

"Will . . ." She gasped, staring at him with wide eyes. She couldn't move; she couldn't think. Once again, the quiet blue-eyed man rendered her speechless.

"I'm sorry. Did I wake you?" Will looked concerned and embarrassed. He obviously did not expect to find her half-asleep.

Suddenly, Katherine panicked at the thought of what she must look like. She had seen the damage from the fall on her face last night, and she took a shower after Ginger left. But she went to bed with wet hair and had not an ounce of makeup on.

"No! I was up. I just got up," she lied. "Come in."

She stepped back, trying to look comfortable, nonchalant, cool—all of the things she was furthest from at that very moment.

Will cleared his throat and carefully maneuvered the painting and easel through the doorway.

"Make yourself comfortable. I just need a minute," Katherine said as she excused herself into the bathroom.

When she closed the door behind her and looked in the mirror, she had to cover her mouth with her hands when she shrieked at the sight of her reflection. Her hair was plastered to her head on one side and puffed up like cotton candy on the other. The bruise on her face had evolved beyond the initial monochromatic ensemble of blues, and now incorporated some delightful swampy greens and earthy yellows around its border.

Katherine worked quickly, brushing her teeth and pulling her hair up into the ever-faithful bun she had resorted to so many times before. Then she carefully brushed foundation onto her face, biting her lip as the brush swept over the tender bruise. Finally, with a touch of mascara and lip-gloss, she was ready. It wasn't perfect, but at least she resembled something remotely human again.

When she opened the bathroom door, she found Will standing by the window with his hands in his pockets, looking out at the lake. He turned to her and smiled shyly, before looking away again.

"Thank you," Katherine said quietly, "for bringing my painting. You didn't have to do that."

She was nervous, but she felt a strange sense of ease. Knowing the truth about him somehow offered her a bit of comfort; it had explained so much. Butterflies still danced in her stomach just at the sight of him, but there was less of the unknown haunting the air around them.

"Glad to do it. I saw it from the road. I can't believe you climbed down those rocks to get to the beach." He looked at the canvas. "This painting . . . It's extraordinary. I think it's my new favorite." He kept studying the work, avoiding eye contact with Katherine.

"Mine too," she replied, as she stood closely next to him.

After a moment, Will took a deep breath and turned to face her. "Katherine, I'm so sorry about yesterday." He clenched his jaw tightly, struggling to go on. "It's just that . . ."

"I know." Katherine saved him from having to say it out loud, understanding the pain it must cause him.

"You know?" Will looked confused.

"Ginger was here when I got back last night. She told me everything."

Will kept his head down, staring at the floor. Katherine raised her hand to his cheek. He slowly lifted his chin and looked intensely into her eyes, tears slowly beginning to fill his.

"Will, I'm so sorry. I had no idea," she began, but Will raised his hand gently to her lips and shook his head.

"No," he said. "You couldn't have known. I should have told you. It's just not something I talk about . . . with anyone."

Katherine looked out the window. She thought she was more than just *anyone* to Will.

"Then you came along"—he sighed— "and I started feeling things, things I hadn't felt in a long time." He put his hands gently on her arms. "I wasn't ready. I didn't think I was ever going to be ready again—to feel that way." He paused. "When I found you yesterday, in the lake, after you fell, I was so damn scared. Scared that I'd lost you . . . when I hadn't even let myself have you. But then . . ."

"I understand." Katherine didn't want him to feel guilty. She didn't want him to feel obligated to explain.

"Wait. Let me finish, please," Will interrupted before she could go on. "I was mad at myself for feeling that way about you. I felt like a traitor . . . to Julee." Tears crept along the creases at the outer corners of his eyes. "But when I got back last night, after I drove you home, I swear I could feel my heart dying inside of me. Thinking of losing you . . . It actually hurt; everything inside of me hurt."

Katherine waited, trying to sort his words in her mind. It was all so overwhelming and terrifying. She wasn't planning on falling for someone, especially so soon after ending things with Michael.

It was too soon. Wasn't it?

Will went on, "When I woke up this morning, I had to see you. I had to tell you." He paused and took some breaths. Katherine could feel her pulse in her neck. *What? Tell me what?*

165

"Katherine, with you, everything is different. I loved Julee, with all of my being. When I lost her, I thought I would die too. And part of me did, for many years. I never thought I would really live again." He coughed and spoke slowly, "I loved Julee then. But I'm here now and I'm a different man now. And I think I,"—he hesitated— "I think I love you, Katherine. I know that's crazy . . . but I love you, here and now. I feel alive again. And it scares me to death."

Katherine put her hands on the back of Will's neck and kissed him softly. "I'm scared too," she whispered. She felt the same way. She thought she would have to be whole again before she could give her heart to another man. But somehow, her brokenness made her feel more alive, more aware, than she had ever felt before. Maybe that was the wholeness she had missed. She felt pain, and she desperately feared losing Will, but at least she was *feeling* again.

Will picked her up and carried her to the bed. At his cabin, they had been fiery and passionate, surrendering to adrenaline, the excitement, and the sorrow they held deep within trying to escape through their bodies. But now, in Katherine's sun-soaked room, they took their time. As Katherine lay on the bed, Will ran his lips over her entire body: her ankles, behind her ears, the soft inner part of her arms, her palms. He paid extra attention to the bruises on her side and on her lower back, kissing them gently.

They made love and talked and slept all day. Katherine told Will more about her marriage, about

Michael's gradual disinterest. She talked about Andi and about visiting Bluewater Lake as a girl. But mostly she talked about art school, and she talked about painting.

Will told stories about Bluewater, funny stories about Matt and Tony and Ginger. He talked about his music, noting his favorite scores, and he talked a little about Julee. When a subject became too difficult to discuss further, they just held one another, letting their bodies take over the conversation.

At one point, Mr. Trust knocked on the door to check on Katherine. When Will answered with a towel wrapped around his waist, Mr. Trust smiled, put his hand on Will's shoulder, nodded once, and walked away, whistling as he meandered down the hall.

CHAPTER 20

Though it lasted for several months, the winter
season seemed to pass by quickly in Bluewater.
Katherine and Will split their time between the inn
and his cabin—never spending a night apart. During
the day, Will would work on his music and help
neighbors with car or home repairs, and Katherine
would help with reservations at the inn when she
wasn't out painting.

The snow created calmness within the town, and
the smell of wood lingered steadily in the air. Main
Street looked like something straight out of a Thomas
Kinkade painting, with fresh wreaths hanging on
every shop door and pinecone-ornamented garlands
wrapped around the street lamps. Mr. Trust had
decorated the inn with lights and red bows, putting
candles in the windowsills and hanging stockings
from the fireplace. Aromas of baked apples and
nutmeg and cinnamon wafted out of the kitchen and
dining room, and Murray concocted an assortment of
traditional holiday treats. The children in town
bundled up in their heavy coats and hats and scarves
and went ice-skating on the lake after school, and hot
chocolate was readily available at every Bluewater
establishment. It was a magical time, a time designed
for new love.

When Will and Katherine had first walked into Ginger's café together, the day after they reconciled, Ginger slammed a pot of coffee down on the counter and ran over to them. "Oh my gosh! I'm so happy for you guys!" She hugged Will tightly and grabbed Katherine's hands, smiling at her friend. "You really do deserve one another."

~*~

As the warm spring air moved into town, melting the snow off the trees and thawing the ice on the lake, visitors returned to Bluewater, and the town was busy again. The lake was more radiant than ever, and Katherine found it difficult to want to paint anything else. She worked on a new series, where she focused on the colors in the water—just as she had the first day she met Will by his favorite fishing spot so many months ago, with only the flimsy watercolor set and cheap pad of paper.

Only this time, the series consisted of massive canvases and rich, vibrant oil paint. Mixing an array of delicious blues on her palette; Katherine squinted at the water and let her brushes do the work. Each completed painting was uniquely different; though they all represented the same subject. Delightful variations occurred due to weather, the time of day, and her own thoughts and emotions while she worked. Even the artist herself was amazed to see the steadfast Bluewater Lake adopt so many visual personalities.

One morning at the inn, while she was savoring one of Murray's warm homemade chocolate croissants, a gentleman approached her in the lobby.

"Excuse me, are you the artist?" he asked. His voice was confident and professional.

Katherine, caught off guard with a mouthful, looked around nervously, wondering what gave her away.

"Your shoes." He laughed, acknowledging her confusion. "Your cover's blown."

She looked down at her boots. Once a beautiful caramel brown, they were now covered in dry splatters of blue and green paint. She laughed and felt her cheeks warm. "Ah, yes, I must work on my disguise."

The man smiled. He was young, probably around Katherine's age, and preppy. He wore smart-looking glasses and carried a stylish shoulder bag. His hair had started to recede from his forehead, but he had the face of a little boy. He held out his hand. "I'm Pete Steinberg, Arts & Entertainment reporter for the *Denver Post*."

Katherine put down her croissant and checked her palms for chocolate before reaching out to shake his hand.

"Hi, I'm Katherine, Katherine Ross," she said, still trying to figure out why the reporter was talking to her.

"I'm staying here at the inn. My editor wanted me to do a story about Bluewater Lake. There are rumors floating around that this town is some sort of magical artists' colony—a place where talented and well-known actors and artists and writers flock to escape stardom and work in peace . . . like Paris in the 20s." Pete smirked. "Ring any bells?"

Suddenly this preppy young reporter seemed more like a preppy young prosecutor cross-examining her on the stand. Katherine could feel the red in her cheeks and chest betray any chance she had at coolly dismissing his suspicions, and she froze. She didn't want to answer him.

Bluewater had become her home, and the people in Bluewater had become her family. She felt extremely protective, and she didn't want some nosy little reporter sniffing around, attracting unwanted attention. She knew Will would not want the world to know where he was, and Ginger had worked so hard to create a better life for herself here. Katherine cringed at the thought of the media finding out that Ginger Mayrose was now serving coffee at her own café deep in the Rocky Mountains. No one would believe it, and they'd all come running to see for themselves. It would be total chaos.

"I'm not sure what you've heard, but this is just a small town like any other, with families who've been here for generations." She tried to speak nonchalantly, returning to her croissant so that she could avoid eye contact with the prosecutor, er, reporter.

"That certainly would appear to be the case, but *you're* not from Bluewater originally, are you, Miss Ross?" Pete pulled out the chair next to her, making himself comfortable.

Katherine ignored him and looked out the window. Maybe if she pretended he wasn't there, he'd get the hint and go away.

"Look," Pete started, speaking more frankly, "I was going to do research for the story my editor wanted, but when I checked into the inn, I was completely blown away by these paintings. I haven't seen works like these, ever . . . and I've spent a lot of time in the art world."

Katherine rolled her eyes. He seemed sincere, but she had been caught off guard, and she was still suspicious.

Pete cleared his throat and leaned forward. "I'd be willing to forget the other story, about Bluewater being a secret retreat for world-famous talents, if you agree to talk to me a bit more about your art. I find that more interesting anyway."

She sat quietly, considering his offer. Katherine had never expected to gain attention for her paintings beyond the borders of Bluewater, and she was fine with that. But she would be lying to herself if she didn't admit she was quite flattered to have the arts reporter from a major paper showing interest in her work.

"Okay." she said in her best business-like tone. She looked at Pete with a straight face and said, "Besides, your other story would have been a bust anyhow. You guys better check your sources. Someone is feeding you false rumors." She looked away, hoping she was convincing.

"Great. Well, thanks for saving me from wasting my time, then." Pete smiled and winked. "Dinner here? Let's say eight o'clock? I'll prepare some questions, and I'll have my photographer take a few pictures if that's okay."

"Sure," Katherine said with a dazed nod.

As Pete walked away, Katherine went to take another bite of her now less-warm croissant, but paused. She had been so wrapped up in her defensive mindset she failed to realize the significance of what had just transpired. A writer for the *Denver Post* wanted to do a story about *her*, about *her paintings*! It was something she had dreamed of as an art student suffering through long nights in the studio and eating peanut butter out of the jar, thinking, *Maybe one day, someone will love my work, and share it with the world . . .*

Was that day today?

She called Will and asked him to meet her at Ginger's café.

~*~

"What's up, lady? You look a little pale," Ginger teased, handing her a steaming latte.

"A reporter from the *Denver Post* wants to do a story about my work," Katherine said. For a moment, she thought she might be sick. But as she sipped the latte, the hot liquid calmed her, and she looked nervously at her friend.

"What? That's great! Katherine, that's amazing!" Ginger ran around the counter to give her a hug. "Why do you look like you ate a bad oyster? This is *good* news."

"I don't know. I'm so nervous. What if it's a trick? What if he really just wants to mock me? What if I say something stupid? It's been known to happen once or twice." Katherine rambled on. But when Will walked into the café, she immediately felt better. Seeing him made her feel safe again, quite the contrast to the host of emotions she used to experience upon encountering him when they first met.

"A reporter is going to do a story about her paintings!" Ginger blurted out. "Oh! Sorry. You probably wanted to tell him yourself. I'm just so excited for you!" She blushed and hugged Katherine again, before returning to her place behind the counter, helping other customers.

"Well, at least someone's excited," Katherine murmured. Will removed his jacket and kissed her. He pulled away only an inch or so, smiling as he held her glance just for a moment.

"You're not?" he asked, confused. He sat down next to her and sipped on the cup of black coffee Ginger set in front of him.

"I don't know. I'm too nervous to be excited," Katherine said, sighing. "I've never been very good at controlling my nerves. That's why Andi used to deal personally with all of our most intimidating clients and with the press. I tend to freeze up or ramble uncontrollably."

"Katherine. It's what you've wanted your whole life. You deserve this. You're amazing." He grinned and reached out for her hand.

"Thanks." She blushed. Sometimes it felt like they were still brand new. They had been together for months, but the excitement and curiosity was stronger than ever. And the butterflies still danced around in Katherine's stomach every time he touched her.

"Let's go out to celebrate at Dale's tonight after the interview! I'll call Lolo and the boys!" Ginger said as she brought a plate of her famous mini muffins over.

"That's a great idea. It'll give you something to look forward to." Will winked and kissed her forehead. "Don't worry. You'll be great."

~*~

Much to Katherine's surprise, the interview was a lot of fun. Pete Steinberg turned out to be a genuinely nice guy. He was funny and honest and easy to talk to.

"When my editor isn't sending me out on a wild goose chase"—he rolled his eyes— "I like to look for stories that I feel will contribute some good to our crazy world, maybe some beauty if I'm lucky." He sipped the complimentary wine brought to their table by Mr. Trust. "When I found out that the artist of these fantastic paintings lived right here in town, I couldn't wait to meet you. I'm a serious art lover. I have an addiction problem when it comes to great art. It's bad. It's an illness." He laughed, and Katherine laughed, and they enjoyed some bites of their delicious dinner.

As the buzz about the interview had traveled throughout the small inn that afternoon, Murray decided he would make his famous smoked trout with crispy potatoes and *hericot vert*.

"This is so *good*. Wow. This town really does have some magic, doesn't it?" Pete was blown away by the meal. He paid his personal compliments to the chef before diving into the interview questions with Katherine.

"Okay, let's get down to business," he said as he finished and savored his last bite.

When he asked how she became an artist, Katherine let her story unravel. The words flowed freely and eloquently, and to her surprise, she didn't stutter or ramble. Perhaps she spoke with ease because she was speaking about something she truly loved, or perhaps it was because of the wine.

She told him about discovering her talent at a young age and about the college oil painting class she attended as a twelve-year-old. She talked mostly about art school and shared colorful memories from the art studios in Italy. Then she went on to describe her less-colorful time in the gallery industry in New York.

"Wow, it sounds like you found your calling early on and you were smart enough to pursue it. It took me many wrong turns before I succumbed to my inevitable destiny as a writer. It was something I knew a long time ago, but I didn't accept it until recently."

"I wish it were that simple." Katherine continued, sharing with Pete the darker, less enchanting aspects of pursuing art as a career. She told him about the competitive gallery world, the corruption, and her years of financial and emotional struggle.

Pete was shocked to hear that she had turned instead to real estate, and that she had been the "K" in K&A Manhattan Realty. "You're kidding. I know you girls! My buddy bought his place in Battery Park from you!"

Katherine smiled and blushed. "Yeah. We were very lucky with our business. And we had a lot of fun. Andi still rocks it. I wish success had come to me that easily with my painting."

"So, how *did* you get here? How does one of the top young realtors in Manhattan end up in tiny Bluewater Lake, Colorado?" Pete asked, perplexed. He was no longer the "conniving reporter-guy" trying to dig up a juicy scandal story. In fact, he seemed like the kind of person Katherine would be friends with. He was smart, and he knew a ton about art.

"Well, as much as I loved K&A, it wasn't my 'calling' as you mentioned before. And things have a way of working themselves out, I guess." Katherine paused and sipped her wine, hoping Pete would move onto another question. But he just smiled with his eyebrows raised, waiting for her to continue.

She sighed. "Honestly? I got a divorce. And strangely, it opened up the possibility for a new life. It was like I got a second chance, a do-over." Pete nodded as he took some notes. Katherine went on, "I was at the Met. I love the Met. It was my special sanctuary in the city. Anyway, I saw a little Monet painting of a valley in the mountains, and it grabbed me. I wanted everything I saw in that painting. I wanted the fresh air and the peace and quiet; I wanted the mountains instead of skyscrapers. I wanted to be Monet standing out there, painting it." She shook her head and laughed. "I guess it goes to show the power one piece of art can have over a person, especially if that person is vulnerable or in search of hope."

After dinner, Pete and his photographer had Katherine pose by the few paintings that had not yet been sold. Pete would say, "Oh, get this one. This one is so fierce and wild! But it's peaceful too. It's remarkable!"

Katherine was flattered and amused by Pete's enthusiasm. It was all very surreal. She hoped her blushing skin wouldn't translate too dramatically in the pictures if the article went to print.

As they finished up the last few shots, Pete gave her a hug. "Thank you for chatting with me, Katherine. I'm so glad I came up here and found a story that I am actually proud to write."

He smiled at her. "Oh, by the way, I bought that one today, for my personal collection." He gestured toward one of the largest works from her recent series. Mr. Trust stood next to it with a huge grin, giving her a "thumbs up."

The canvas was covered in brilliant blues, each layer of color whispering through the next. If one stood in front of the painting long enough, the effect of the combined colors and textures gave the illusion of swimming underwater. It was one of Katherine's personal favorites. When she painted it, she was looking at the lake, but when she finished it, it reminded her of Will's eyes.

CHAPTER 21

"There she is!" Ginger yelled from the back of Dale's when Katherine walked in the door. Lolo and Tony and Matt were there, and they all cheered and applauded loudly as she made her way back through the crowd. Her face turned bright red and she laughed.

Will walked over from the bar, handing her a glass of chardonnay and a flower he had picked from one of the spring planters outside. "Hey, you." He kissed her cheek then grabbed her hand and guided her back to their friends.

"Guys, stop!" she pleaded, putting her hands on her cheeks, as Matt and Tony began to chant and pump their fists in the air, "Katherine! Katherine! Katherine!" The other timider bar customers at Dale's kept looking back at the noisy group, wondering what all the commotion was about.

"Hey, Katherine, could I get your autograph before it's too late?" Tony held out a dirty napkin and a pen, and they all laughed. "No, really . . . can I?" Tony said, handing her the napkin as they all calmed down and situated themselves around the table.

"So?" Ginger asked anxiously. "How did it go?"

All eyes fell on Katherine, and she suddenly felt nervous. She had never liked being the center of attention.

"Actually, it was pretty great." She smiled and breathed a sigh of relief. "He asked a lot of good questions, and he knows a ton about art." But as she relived the interview, Katherine began to second-guess herself. "I don't know. He was probably hoping for some great dramatic story. I must have bored him to death."

"Not possible," Matt said firmly and then gave her a wink.

"Yeah, you're like the most interesting person to come to Bluewater in years!" Tony chimed in.

"Hey!" Ginger teased, pretending to be offended. They all laughed.

Lolo squeezed Katherine's hand. "I'm sure you were fabulous, doll. You need to give yourself more credit. It's about time you just accept how wonderful and talented you are!"

"She's right," Will added quietly, winking at Katherine and squeezing her knee under the table.

She was glad when the conversation finally transitioned away from her and back to the normal topics: fishing, poker, funny stories about tourists in town, the marina, fishing . . .

Will barely spoke as usual, but his hand remained on Katherine's leg and would rub her thigh tenderly when she spoke. Once in a while, he'd lean over and kiss her cheek.

Did he know the effect he had on her?

Her legs trembled with desire even now, even after so many months had passed since that fateful day at the cabin. Katherine was on such a rush from the interview, and she became giddy from the drinks. It took every bone in her body not to drag Will out of the bar and take him home where she could have her way with him and release some of the crazy energy stirring around inside her.

As the night went on, the energy Katherine felt inside seemed to be in the air at Dale's. For the first time, there was something different between Ginger and Matt. They always ended up playing poker and having cigars, but tonight they sat closer together as Matt dealt the cards. Ginger was a bit more reserved than usual, and she actually appeared to blush once or twice while he talked quietly to her. He wrapped his massive arm around her shoulder, and he pulled her close.

Oddly enough, Katherine realized, they would make an adorable couple. Matt was like the big, protective bodyguard Ginger would have had back in Manhattan. But they made each other laugh, and tonight Katherine detected some serious sparks.

At one point, Katherine locked eyes with Ginger and raised her eyebrows, asking in girl-code, *"What's going on over there?"* Ginger just smiled and shrugged, as she put her hand in Matt's hanging over her shoulder, prompting him to kiss her forehead as if they had been together for years. Ginger blushed and snuggled into him.

Once again, they closed down Dale's in the early hours of the morning, and Matt had to carry Tony over his shoulder as they all walked out onto the sidewalk. Will and Katherine walked hand-in-hand, and Ginger walked next to Matt, giggling as Tony snored loudly.

As they passed her apartment, Lolo hugged everyone good-bye. When she squeezed Katherine tightly into her soft billowy blouse, she whispered into Katherine's ear, "I've never seen Will so happy." She pulled away and winked, before leaving a dark pink lipstick mark on Will's cheek.

Bluewater was like a dream at two in the morning. The only lights were the stars in the dark indigo sky, and there were millions to be seen on the crisp cloudless night. Some of the larger stars twinkled lustrously, calling out for attention. Others huddled together in quieter congregations, swirling gracefully along the dark backdrop. Katherine thought of Vincent van Gogh's *Starry Night*. She had memorized every detail of the painting in college, and now she could see the same colors in the rich night sky above Bluewater. She smiled at the silly notion of looking at the same sky as Van Gogh himself, but, in a way, she was.

Ginger nonchalantly bid goodnight, following Matt down the road toward the marina with Tony still hanging over his shoulder like a ragdoll. As they walked away into the dark, Katherine could see Matt reach out for Ginger's hand.

Will appeared to notice it too. He looked down at Katherine with a goofy expression on his face, but didn't say a word. Instead, he smiled and leaned down to kiss her. His lips were warm in the cool night, and she melted into him. They crept quietly back into the inn like a couple of teenagers sneaking in after curfew, trying not to wake Mr. Trust or the other guests.

As soon as Katherine shut the door to her room, Will took her passionately into his arms. They were both mentally exhausted from the long day and late night, but their bodies were electric.

The *Denver Post* article was published a few days later, and the town was buzzing. Katherine's picture alongside two of her largest, most expressive works claimed the front page of the paper with the article headline *"The Artist Within."* She couldn't walk a block down the street before someone would stop to congratulate her.

Pete Steinberg had taken what she felt was an anti-climactic jumble of an excuse for a story, and extrapolated profound points of beauty and depth, infusing them into inspirational and elegant prose. As she read, she could hardly believe the eloquent and insightful words were written about *her*:

> "Miss Ross is a beacon of hope for those souls who wander the streets, hungry and lost, desperately searching for fuel and purpose. Her story is quiet, but mighty, triumphing in long-awaited riches of self-actualization. After questionable leaps of blind faith, a little bit of hope, and complete abandonment of all logic and reason, Katherine

```
Ross      discovered     the
artist within. And, thank
God she let her out!"
```

Pete continued on with a review of her paintings and technique, likening her work to great masters of artistic achievement: Monet, Chagall, and Rothko. Katherine shook her head in disbelief. Never once had she thought of herself on that caliber. She was thrilled enough to be painting, and yes, she was happy with her work. But for her, it was not about the achievement; it was about the process. It was about letting go; it was about the surrender.

Pete's words brought tears to her eyes. It was one thing to love what you're doing; it was something else entirely to witness such a profound and positive reaction to what you have created.

"Girl, just wait. The floodgates will open now," Ginger said casually as she bustled about behind the counter at the café.

"What do you mean?" Katherine asked, feeling like a naïve child.

"If a major paper publishes a story like that, it's just a matter of time before you are bombarded with agents, dealers, and other media machines itching to get their hands on the latest thing." Ginger went on as she refilled coffees along the bar.

"No way. I mean maybe that happened with you . . . because, well, you're *you*. But this is different. It's just art. People don't get excited about art, not the way they do about movies and rock stars." Katherine shook her head as she rambled on. She realized she sounded self-deprecating, but really she hoped that Ginger was wrong. As much as the article boosted her confidence about her skill, she didn't want to fall into a world that Ginger and Will had worked so hard to avoid. She was finally happy in Bluewater, and she didn't want her life to change again so soon.

CHAPTER 22

In the weeks that followed, Katherine was approached by a handful of art dealers and agents from all around the country—just as Ginger had prophesied. And while she entertained a few conversations with those who pursued her, she respectfully declined the various offers for representation. She was surprised to encounter some big-name players with international reputations for bringing their artists to the top of the chain. One dealer outwardly admitted that he only represented artists if he was certain they would make him millions, *and he wanted to represent Katherine!*

"Listen, kid. You're young, you're attractive, and you're likeable. It's hard to find that in an artist these days. Your paintings aren't half-bad either," he said coolly over the phone, sounding a lot like a savvy New York agent from the 1920s. Katherine could picture him leaning back in his chair with his feet up on the desk, smoking a big cigar.

The offers were intriguing and flattering. She still couldn't believe it was happening. But each proposal required that she move to LA or back to New York so that she could establish a big-time studio and be more accessible.

Leaving Bluewater Lake was simply not an option for Katherine, and so she was content to turn them down. After all, she had found what she was looking for in Bluewater, and she was already making a decent income off her paintings. She didn't want or need the fame and fortune.

Girl, you are HOT right now! That art and fashion blogger guy we love so much is writing about you! Everyone is talking about your fabulous paintings. Mwah Mwah! Xo

Andi's text made Katherine's jaw drop. The blogger was Vincent Valley. They had followed his blog for years in New York: Andi for the fashion and Katherine for the art. Vincent Valley was flamboyant, hilarious, and unforgiving. He was brutally honest in his opinions, but he generally had great taste.

Oh gosh. What did he say? Does he hate my paintings?

Katherine knew it shouldn't matter what some blogger on the other side of the country was writing about her work. Especially Vincent Valley. He was a self-proclaimed expert in art and fashion, but he was non-academic and held no certifiable accolades. Nevertheless, he had tens of thousands of followers in Manhattan and beyond, because he was witty and funny and he often said the things other critics were too reserved to say.

He LOVES them! He says he wants to swim in your colors and that you are "the best thing to come along since properly mixed patterns"! ☺ I couldn't agree more by the way. ;)

Katherine let out a sigh of relief. If Vincent Valley liked her work, then all was well in the world. She laughed to herself. She had never imagined a day when she'd be biting her nails over a Vincent Valley review.

One balmy night, Katherine and Will were sipping wine out of plastic cups and walking around the lake. The stars were out again, and live music echoed from the lodge. Sweetness drifted through the air, floating from the purple blossoms that scattered across the wild sage bushes lining the shore.

"You're quiet tonight," Katherine said softly, taking Will's hand. "Is something on your mind?"

Will shook his head and smiled, looking down at his feet. "No, not really."

But she could tell something was up. They had grown so close. Will knew her better than anyone: better than her family and childhood friends, better than Michael, even better than Andi. She had let Will in, completely. And over the past few months, she had let him see the good, the bad, and the ugly. Will too had finally opened himself to Katherine. He talked about his past, and he let her watch him when he worked on his music—an incredibly private process he had never shared with anyone before, not even Julce.

She stopped on the path and put her hand on Will's chest. "What is it?"

Will sighed. "I just, um . . . I wonder if you're doing the right thing." Katherine looked at him, perplexed.

191

"I mean with your art. I mean keeping it here and not sharing it with the world." He cleared his throat. "Don't you feel like you are abandoning your dream or something?"

Katherine was taken aback. *Was he disappointed in her? Did he find her foolish?*

Will continued, "What I mean is you're not turning down all those offers because of me, right? I love you, but I don't want to stand in your way. I don't want to hold you back." He looked intensely into her eyes, the way he did whenever he talked about anything serious.

"Oh, Will." She felt a bit relieved. "You are not standing in my way. My dream is to paint freely and live a life that makes me happy. Bluewater . . . you . . . this is my dream." He didn't appear to be totally convinced, as they began to walk again.

"Listen. I *did* the crazy, glitzy Manhattan life, remember? If I missed it, or if I wanted to play 'famous artist,' I would go back. But I don't. I love it here. I don't want to be anywhere else."

"I'm just so proud of you. I don't want you to pass up anything you deserve," Will said as he squeezed her hand.

"If the right opportunity comes along, you'll be the first to know." She winked at him and sipped her wine.

Will began to lead her away from the main path.

"Where are we going?" Katherine asked, looking around, trying to get her bearings, while attempting not to trip over fallen branches and rocks.

"Hang on." Will held her hand tightly and carefully guided her through the dark.

As they made their way through some thick bushes, Katherine caught the glimmer of the lake peering through just ahead. Then she saw it: the rock on the beach where she sat and painted those silly watercolors after her first night in Bluewater, the spot where she and Will first met, in the autumn.

"Remember?" Will said as he walked her down to the water?

Katherine laughed. "Remember? How could I forget? You were so put out to find a strange girl at your secret fishing spot." She snickered at him, pretending to be sassy.

"Yes. Now, just who did she think she was?" Will played along, tossing their cups to the ground and putting his hands on her hips.

Katherine hadn't returned to the rock since that day so long ago. At first, she was scared to go back—afraid she'd upset Will or another fisherman. But after a while, she just forgot to go back. She had spent most of her time in the gazebo or plummeting down steep rocky slopes on the other side of the lake.

They stood for a moment, staring at the gleaming cerulean water near their feet. At the far end of the lake, the water was black, and the millions of stars in the sky reflected perfectly on its silky surface. It was after midnight, and there wasn't a soul around.

Will leaned in close, kissing Katherine softly. As he moved his lips down her neck, he slowly unbuttoned her shirt and then her jeans. Katherine shivered, not because she was cold, but because she felt exhilarated. She had never made love in a public place before. It wasn't something she had ever been interested in doing, not with anyone—until now. Her body pulsed with excitement and nervousness, and her hands trembled as she removed Will's clothes. For a moment, they stood facing one another. The light from the glowing water fell handsomely on Will's chiseled body.

"You are so beautiful," he whispered, lifting her up so her legs wrapped around his waist.

He held her tightly, with his hands strongly pressed on her back, as he carried her into the water. To Katherine's surprise, the water wasn't cold at all. It was nearly warm, and it felt amazing on her skin. She wrapped her arms tightly around Will's neck as he carried her in deep enough so that the water was just below their chins. Will spun her around, making her dizzy, and then effortlessly tossed her into the air. Katherine screamed and laughed, pushing her wet hair back from her face and splashing water back at him. When Will swam over to her, he picked her up again and made love to her in the water under the stars.

Summer in Bluewater was more beautiful than Katherine could have imagined. The lake assumed a warmer shade of turquoise, inviting locals and visitors to swim daily in its sun-soaked water. The trees radiated in verdant greens, and the air smelled of sweet pine and wildflowers. Silky indigo columbines, white daisies, and fiery red Indian paintbrush speckled the tall grass along the shore.

A variety of colorful town events occurred every weekend: concerts in the park, art fairs, boat races, chocolate festivals. The long sunny days bustled with activity. Kids ran up and down the streets, their faces covered in ice cream. Families posed for pictures by the lake and rented bright colored paddleboats from the marina. The shops kept their doors open from sunrise to sunset, and the sidewalk along Main Street was heavily lined with giant pots of fresh flowers.

Katherine loved every minute. She couldn't believe how lucky she was. Each morning she would have breakfast with Will, and then she would head to Ginger's Café to sit outside and enjoy a latte while she watched visitors meander by, before going off to paint for the rest of the day.

The buzz from the *Denver Post* article had eventually dwindled. Although, Katherine still received occasional letters and emails from art dealers around the world. One morning, she and Will giggled over a letter petitioning her to do a yearlong professional residency program in Tokyo.

Her paintings had become one of the major Bluewater Lake attractions. Art collectors in Denver and beyond booked trips to the little town just to see her work, and she sold nearly every painting she completed.

Every Friday night Mr. Trust hosted a *Gallery and Dinner* event at the inn. Murray would cook one of his most exquisite dinners, and attendees would eat and drink fine wine while enjoying an exclusive private viewing of Katherine's latest pieces.

One hot day in July, Katherine was painting in the gazebo, when her phone rang.

"Helloooooooooo, lovely! Guess who's finally coming to visit?" Andi squealed on the other end, her voice muffled by sirens and car horns blaring in the background. Sounds that now seemed so foreign to Katherine.

"Shut up. Seriously?!" She was so excited; she nearly knocked her painting into the lake.

"Yes ma'am! Annnnd, I have a surprise!!" Andi announced.

"You're pregnant?" Katherine joked.

"Yep. Twins." Andi answered bluntly. "Just kidding. My God, can you imagine?" They both laughed.

"So, when are you coming?!" Katherine jumped up and down. She felt like a little kid who had just planned her first sleepover party.

"I'll be there by the weekend. Do I need to arrange, like, a horse and buggy to get me up to that place? Or do they have cars in Colorado?"

"Hilarious. I can't wait to see you, Andi. I'll make sure you get our best room at the inn!"

"Sounds wonderfully charming. Can't wait to meet the sexy William and all of your new mountain friends!" Andi paused and then went on before Katherine could reply, "Don't worry. I'll be on my best behavior, of course." She giggled coyly.

~*~

"What do you think the surprise is?" Will asked as he repaired the bathroom door hinge in the room Katherine selected for Andi. It was a larger room than her own, just down the hall. It had a Juliet balcony and the most breathtaking view of the lake.

"Who knows? With Andi, a surprise could simply mean she's bringing fresh bagels from

196

Zabar's, or it could mean she recently discovered she was the heir of a French king and has inherited a forbidden treasure of rare diamonds and jewels." Katherine rolled her eyes and laughed.

"She sounds like quite the character." Will smiled.

"She is. But I love her. You will too," she said as Will stood up and walked over to her. He wiped the grease off his hands and removed his tool belt while he leaned in to kiss Katherine.

"No, no, no, Mister. We've got work to do." She ran her hands lightly down his chest and slowly turned away, dragging her fingers across the lower part of his abdomen. Will groaned as she wandered over to a table by the window and arranged a bouquet of wildflowers. Andi would be arriving the next day, and Katherine wanted everything to be perfect.

CHAPTER 23

Katherine paced back and forth in the lobby the following evening, anxiously waiting for Andi to arrive. She had told Will they would all meet the next morning at Ginger's for breakfast, after Andi had time to get settled. She wanted her friend all to herself first so they could catch up and talk late into the night, the way they had on so many occasions back in New York.

"Okay, you girls have fun." Will kissed her good-bye after they put the final touches on Andi's room. "Not too much fun." He squinted his eyes playfully.

Katherine laughed and pushed him out the door. Andi had texted to let her know she landed safely in Denver and she would be arriving shortly. Earlier that morning, Katherine requested that Murray cook his famed Halibut Confit for dinner, and now the entire inn smelled of heavenly lemon and coriander.

"Well, isn't this just the sweetest little slice of wonderful?!" Andi exclaimed as she barged through the lobby door, her arms weighted down by numerous pieces of Louis Vuitton luggage.

Katherine had been standing with her back to the door, looking out over the lake.

"You made it!" she shrieked and ran over to hug her friend.

Andi looked more fabulous than ever. Her hair was perfect, even after a long day of travel—one of her many annoying attributes Katherine had always envied. She wore a perfectly unwrinkled Michael Kors summer dress and thigh-high Prada boots. She looked like a supermodel. Katherine suddenly felt frumpy in her white shorts and lace tank.

"Oh, my Gawd, look at you—all tan and rustic and gorgeous!" Andi gasped. "I guess this rugged mountain life suits you after all." She winked and squeezed her again. Katherine wrapped her arms around her friend, and they jumped up and down, giddy with excitement.

"Well, this must be the famous Katherine." A man's calm deep voice came from behind Andi. As they pulled away, Katherine noticed a studious-looking gentleman standing in the doorway, holding two more bags. He was tall and thin, very well dressed, and slightly balding. His eyes were gentle, hiding behind chic glasses, and he had a kind smile.

Katherine was confused. Did Andi hire a personal butler for her trip?

"Katherine, this is Sebastian . . . my boyfriend." Andi said smiling ear-to-ear with wide eyes, her hands clasped together in front of her chin.

"Boyfriend?" Katherine couldn't believe it. In all the years they'd known each other, Andi had never been in anything remotely resembling a serious relationship, and Katherine had never heard her utter the term *boyfriend.* Of course, Katherine had always hoped Andi might find someone, but Katherine also suspected her dear friend might very well be a lifelong bachelorette.

"I told you I had a surprise! And here he is . . . SURPRISE!" Andi laughed and went over to the man, who comfortably put his arm around her waist and lovingly kissed her forehead.

Sebastian was not like any other man Andi had ever dated. For starters, he was significantly older than Andi. He looked to be in his forties, like Will. And unlike the meaty gym-obsessed hunks she usually pursued, Sebastian was quite gangly. There was a charm about him, though, an earnestness. And it didn't take long for Katherine to realize he completely adored Andi. But what was perhaps most surprising, was the fact that Andi obviously adored him as well.

"So nice to meet you, Sebastian." Katherine shook his hand slowly, dumbfounded. "Well, let me show you two to your room so you can get settled. Our chef Murray has prepared an amazing dinner for tonight!"

"It smells unbelievable! I may never leave!" Andi gushed and then winked at Sebastian. Katherine grabbed a smaller bag, but Sebastian insisted on carrying the rest. As they walked by the piano and up the stairs, Andi hooked her arm through Katherine's.

"I'm sorry I didn't tell you about Sebastian sooner. I didn't want to jinx it or anything. Then I figured you wouldn't believe me anyway, unless you could see him for yourself." She giggled, looking back at Sebastian over her shoulder.

"He seems really nice, Andi. I'm so happy for you!" Katherine squeezed Andi's hand and then unlocked the door to their room. "I'll see you down in the lobby for dinner. Say around seven?"

"Sounds great. I'm starved!"

Murray prepared the best table in the dining room for Katherine and her friends, and Mr. Trust opened a bottle of their finest chardonnay. Katherine sipped on a glass in the lobby, examining one of her recent paintings.

"This place is positively incredible! I feel like I've stepped back in time!" Andi exclaimed as she and Sebastian walked hand-in-hand into the room.

"I know. I've fallen in love with it. Mr. Trust is one in a million, and just *wait* until you taste Murray's food," Katherine said, leading them to the dining room. Sebastian lingered in front of her paintings along the way. He didn't say anything, but he studied them closely, nodding and smiling to himself. Katherine looked at Andi quizzically, but Andi just smiled and raised her shoulders as if to say, "No idea!"

After introducing Andi and Sebastian to Mr. Trust and Murray, they settled into the wine and French breadbasket.

"Okay, so how did you two meet?" Katherine wasted no time.

"At the Met, just after Christmas," Sebastian said casually as he buttered a roll. He smiled at Andi, who blushed.

"The Met?" Katherine was intrigued. Andi never went to the Met.

"Yes. I'm the—" Sebastian began to answer, but Andi interrupted.

"Yes. At the Children's Hospital Benefit, just after Christmas. I had to go for work," she said abruptly, locking eyes with Sebastian.

"That's right." Sebastian grinned. "She walked into the room and my heart stopped. It took me two hours to work up the courage to introduce myself."

"Two hours and a heck of a lot of champagne!" Andi teased. "We got to talking, and the hours just flew by. He took me to dinner the next night and the rest is history!" Andi was giddy, like a sixteen-year-old girl who just got asked to the prom. Sebastian lovingly kissed her cheek.

"Wow. That's wonderful! You must be a wizard or something, Sebastian. No one has ever been able to win her over. And I mean *no one*." Katherine winked at Andi, who playfully stuck her tongue out at Katherine.

"I'm sad to admit that wizardry is not my specialty. I'm just unbelievably lucky," he replied and raised his glass toward Andi.

Murray walked over with their entrees, and everyone paused to inhale the scrumptious aroma. Each plate looked like a masterpiece, carefully composed and bursting with color.

"Murray, you've outdone yourself!" Katherine couldn't tear her eyes away from the food. "It's too pretty to eat!"

"I assure you, darling, the taste will far exceed your visual pleasure tonight." He winked and strutted confidently back into the kitchen.

For a few moments, they ate in silence, closing their eyes with each bite, savoring every nuanced flavor. Sebastian even groaned at one point.

Once they recovered from their trance, Katherine wanted to hear more about Andi's new beau.

"What do you do in the city, Sebastian?" she asked, sipping the chardonnay and anticipating her next wonderful bite.

Sebastian looked at Andi, who was shoving her mouth full of halibut. She smiled and gave a little nod. Katherine wondered what the big deal was.

"Well"—he cleared his throat— "I am the Curator of Contemporary Exhibitions at the Met." He smiled and waited for a reaction. Katherine sat up straight and looked immediately at Andi, mystified.

Sebastian continued, "In fact, I've been looking forward to meeting you for quite some time, Katherine Ross." He said with a grin.

~*~

After dinner, Mr. Trust invited everyone into the lobby for nightcaps. Andi stood by the piano and sang along while Mr. Trust played "The Way You Look Tonight" and Sebastian talked with Katherine by her paintings.

"I enjoyed reading about you in that fella's blog. Vincent . . . something?" Sebastian started. "He's not always a credible source, but I've discovered some great artists through him." He smiled and turned to look at a large painting covered in rich blue texture with hints of gold and cream. "And then, of course, Andi talks about you all the time. She's your biggest fan."

"Andi's the best." Katherine blushed. It was nice of Andi to promote her work to her new boyfriend.

"Aside from Andi, that *Denver Post* article circulated quite a bit in the art world. Pete Steinberg is a great writer, and he found a great subject." Sebastian grinned. "Katherine, you've got something really exceptional going on here." He nodded toward the painting and then stood quietly, studying her brushstrokes.

Katherine didn't know if she should speak, and so she stood next to him, pretending to study the work as well, even though she knew every brushstroke by heart.

Sebastian walked on to the next painting: the winter scene she had painted down by the lake, the day when Will had saved her life. "This one . . . It's so distinctive. Powerful. It's almost seductive: the way the light teasingly creeps across the ice there."

"Thank you. I think that one is my favorite, actually." Katherine stared at the painting, reliving the monumental events that had taken place that very day. It felt like it had all been a dream: the music in the woods, the tree crashing toward her, the fall. And then Will, the cabin, the fireplace . . .

"Katherine? Are you alright?" Sebastian's voice brought her back to reality.

"Yes. I'm sorry, too much wine. What were you saying?" Katherine felt her cheeks burning. *If only this man knew what I was thinking about . . .* She cleared her throat and looked back at the painting, too embarrassed to make eye contact with Sebastian.

"I asked if you might consider doing a solo show? At the Met?" Sebastian asked so casually, as if his question pertained to something habitual and mundane like, *"I wonder if you might like coffee with your breakfast?"*

"Th-the Met? *Me*?" Katherine looked as if she had seen a ghost. "As in, the Metropolitan Museum of Art? In New York?"

Sebastian laughed. "Yes. That's the one."

Katherine continued to stare at him with wide eyes. Her skin went pale, her mouth went dry, and she was speechless.

Mr. Trust and Andi, along with Murray and the other guests, were happily consumed with song, completely oblivious to Katherine and Sebastian and the potentially life-changing conversation they were sharing.

Sebastian continued, "Katherine, I'm quite particular when it comes to my shows. I will only curate an event if it is truly unique. The work must be groundbreaking, but it must also hold a certain level of beauty and integrity. The Contemporary Exhibition circuit is a fairly new concept at the Met, but the shows have been very well received thus far." Sebastian paused and sipped his scotch.

"Your work truly exemplifies the merit I seek for the exhibitions. You're daring, uninhibited. But your inhibition is not offensive. Rather, it is pure and refreshing, almost spiritual. You paint nature— water, air, and light—but you present nature through idealistic perspectives and interpretations. It's mesmerizing. It's hopeful." He looked at the painting and then reached out to shake her hand. "Brava, Katherine. Brava."

Katherine was finally able to nod as Sebastian gently held her hand in his, but words continued to elude her. *Say something, you moron!*

"Tell you what. Why don't you sleep on it? Give it some thought? We can talk more in the morning." Sebastian smiled and put his hand on her shoulder. Then he walked over to Andi and the others and joined in on the group's rendition of "The Best Is Yet to Come."

Standing immobile by her painting, Katherine sipped her wine and gazed numbly at the joyous gathering. Mr. Trust craned his neck around the guests gathered around him so as to catch her eyes. When she smiled at him nervously, still processing her conversation with Sebastian, Mr. Trust winked at her and gave her a single confident nod. *A nudge, perhaps?*

What was it she had said to Will the night they walked by the lake? The night she convinced him that none of the offers were worth leaving Bluewater? *"If the right opportunity comes along, you'll be the first to know,"* she had assured him before they went swimming under the stars.

CHAPTER 24

As Katherine dressed the next morning, her heart raced. She had barely slept a wink all night while Sebastian's words tumbled around in her restless head. Maybe she had had too much wine. Maybe she misinterpreted. Surely, he didn't offer her, Katherine Ross, a solo exhibition at the Met! *Her Met . . .*

There was a knock at the door. Expecting Andi, Katherine was surprised to find Will.

"Will! I thought we were meeting at the café?" She was suddenly flustered. She still hadn't figured out a way to tell Will about Sebastian's offer. She knew Will didn't want to stand in the way of her pursuing her dream; he had made that clear. But she also knew how he felt about New York. If she decided to accept, would he be upset?

"Good morning, gorgeous." Will pulled her close and kissed her sweetly. "I hated being away from you last night."

"Me too," Katherine whispered, holding Will's hands in her own. "Will, I need to . . ."

"Good moooooorning, lovebirds!" Andi's chipper voice traveled from down the hall. She was wrapped in a red silk robe and had obviously just gotten up, but she was flawless nevertheless. "You must be Will!" She wrapped her arms tightly around Will's neck as if they had known each other for years. Will looked wide-eyed at Katherine, stunned by Andi's forwardness, his hands open and awkward, afraid to hug her back.

"And you must be Andi," Will said quietly with a nervous smile. "It's a pleasure to meet you."

"Oh gosh, Katherine. You said he was handsome, but I was not expecting *this*!" Andi gestured toward Will and spoke as if he were not standing right there. "He's a total knockout!"

Will looked at Katherine skeptically then winked at her.

"Oh, stop it, you stinker. He's taken." Katherine blushed and hugged Andi. "Did you sleep okay? Is the room alright?"

"Are you kidding? I haven't slept that well in ages. I didn't even need to take an Ambien! It's all perfectly glorious, dawwwling!" Andi gushed. "Sebastian is in the shower. I think I'll join him." She smirked naughtily. "Are we still on for breakfast?"

"Of course! We'll meet you there. It's just down the street, *Le Café Bleu*. You can't miss it." Katherine felt anxious. She knew she would have to talk to Will about Sebastian's proposition right away.

"Great! Hey, Will, did you hear the big news?" Andi asked.

Will looked at Katherine curiously. "No, I didn't. What's the big news?"

Katherine glared at her friend, pursing her lips, silently begging her not to go on. Andi received the message loud and clear. She cleared her throat and attempted a diversion, "Uh, um . . . you know, the news? That I've finally landed myself a proper Mister?" She giggled and awkwardly sauntered back into her room, silently mouthing the word "Sorry!" to Katherine before she shut the door.

"She's exactly how you described her." Will said with a laugh. "And she brought a guy?" He was as surprised as Katherine had been. She had told him all about Andi, and Will was well aware of her commitment-free lifestyle.

"Yeah. It's crazy." Her mouth dried up again. She stalled. "He's wonderful though—so not what I would expect. He seems really good for her." She grabbed her purse, and they walked downstairs.

When they stepped outside, the sun was already high in the sky, and the town was at its best for Andi and Sebastian. Children were lining up at the candy store as if on cue, and the flowerpots exploded with bouquets of pansies and daisies and poppies in every color. A local bluegrass trio played cheery songs in the town park while townspeople assembled tents for the weekend's craft fair. It was nearly utopian: the kind of sight one only witnesses in sappy movies, a perfect Bluewater day. And it was completely clouded by the nervous pressure rapidly mounting in Katherine's chest.

"Will," she started. *Just spit it out!*

"Yeah, babe?" he asked casually as they walked hand-in-hand by Lolo's bookstore. Lolo was putting some of the latest bestsellers out on display. She waved at them and blew a kiss.

"Sebastian, Andi's boyfriend . . . Well, he works for the Met, in New York. He's the Curator of Contemporary Exhibitions."

"Wow. Impressive," Will replied. "Isn't the Met your favorite museum?"

Katherine loved him for that. Will remembered everything she ever told him. He was so different from Michael in that way. It wasn't that Michael had intentionally ignored her, really, at least, not at first; it was just that he didn't allow his busy mind to grab hold of the things she said.

"It *is* my favorite, always has been." She took a deep breath. "Anyway, as it turns out, Sebastian is familiar with my work." She stopped and looked up at Will. She had his undivided attention. "And last night after dinner, Sebastian offered me a solo exhibition."

Katherine tried to gauge Will's reaction. He was quiet for a moment and seemed to be processing what she told him. Then he suddenly grabbed her hands and looked deeply into her eyes.

"A solo show? At the Met?" he asked, still holding her gaze.

She nodded nervously.

"Katherine. That's amazing!" He picked her up and spun her around. Then he kissed her for a long time and slowly set her back down. "I'm so proud of you." He stood with his hands still on her waist.

"Really? You think I should accept?" Katherine's nerves began to melt into excitement. *Why had she been so nervous? Of course Will would support her. It was Will.*

"Katherine, it's your dream. When someone offers you your dream, you don't say no." For a moment, she thought she saw a wave of sadness wash through his eyes. But Will smiled and kissed her cheek. "Let's go meet your friends."

The café was packed. But Ginger had put a handmade "Reserved" sign on a table for four near the front window. Andi and Sebastian arrived just as Will and Katherine walked over from across the street. Andi was literally bouncing with anticipation.

"I can't believe I'm about to meet Ginger Mayrose!" She gasped, looking around nervously and touching up her lip gloss.

"She's Ginger Trust, here." Katherine smiled and squeezed Andi's hand.

Ginger spotted the group from inside and ran out to greet them. Before she could say anything, Andi assaulted her with a huge hug, nearly knocking her over. "You are even more beautiful in person! I adore you!"

Sebastian laughed, and Katherine winced, mouthing, *"Sorry!"* to Ginger behind Andi's back.

Ginger waved her off and laughed. "Well, if you are the famous Andi whom I hear so much about, then I adore you too!" Ginger hugged her right back. "Welcome to my café!"

After everyone was introduced, the foursome sat down at the table, and Ginger went back to the counter. Sebastian had been a classical music major in college and was a longtime admirer of Will's work, so they quickly fell into a deep conversation about some of his recent film scores. Andi leaned over to Katherine and whispered, "So? Did you talk to Will about the show?" Katherine smiled and nodded.

Ginger brought specialty lattes and warm croissants to the table. Andi and Sebastian gushed over the flavors and the atmosphere of the place, and

Will told them a bit about the history of Bluewater and his ties to Ginger and Mr. Trust. Katherine tried her best to pay attention and remain engaged in the conversation, but her thoughts tumbled over one another in a chaotic rapid spiral.

"So, Katherine, did you give my offer some thought last night?" Sebastian casually segued as he sipped his latte.

Katherine looked at Will, who nodded once and gave her a wink as he squeezed her hand.

"I did," she replied. She took a breath and went on, "I'm definitely interested in hearing more." She smiled.

"Oh, yay!" Andi squealed and hugged her friend.

"I'm delighted to hear you say so." Sebastian looked sincerely pleased. "I feel it could be one of the greatest exhibitions of the year."

Will raised his eyebrows at Katherine and kissed her forehead. Sebastian continued, "Ideally, you would prepare a body of work—maybe fifteen or twenty larger paintings. I'd like to have your show premiere in November, just before the holidays. It's our busiest time. I anticipate many successful sales for you."

Katherine glanced over at Will. He gazed out the window, appearing to detach from the conversation. She suspected his concerns.

"And what would *my* commitment look like? In New York, I mean?" she asked, reading Will's mind.

"Andi has made it clear to me that you have no intention of moving back to Manhattan, and I can respect that. This place, Bluewater, is obviously an excellent muse for your work." Sebastian looked around, smiling. "So, really, your only commitment in New York would be installation and the opening reception. I'd say a week. Tops."

Katherine looked over at Will. He turned to look at her, and she put her hand on his knee. He smiled and put his hand on hers.

"I think I can make that happen." She tried to sound calm and professional, but adrenaline raced through her limbs, and she had a hard time sitting still.

"You bet your ass you'll make that happen!" Andi chimed in and held up her latte. "To Katherine, the next big thing to hit the Manhattan art world!"

Sebastian and Katherine laughed and held up their mugs. Will smiled and joined in the salute, but Katherine noted something other than joy in his eyes. She took a deep breath and figured he might just need time to process everything. After all, he himself told her she should accept.

It was settled. Sebastian excused himself to make some calls to secure the show dates at the Met and to pitch the initial announcement with his PR team. Katherine's mind raced with ideas for the paintings. But she knew she had a few months to complete the work, and for now, she wanted to enjoy the weekend with Andi.

The following evening Will and Katherine took Andi and Sebastian to Dale's to meet the rest of the crew. Lolo flirted relentlessly with Sebastian. "Sebastian darling, where do you buy your trousers? They are perfectly tailored for you. So long and lean," she said in a low velvety voice.

"Why, Lolo? You in the market for some trousers? Or just hoping to get *in* some?" a cheerful and sweaty Tony teased over his shoulder as he twirled Andi around the dance floor. "Sorry, Sebastian, but I'm going to steal your girlfriend. I think I'm in looooove!"

Everyone laughed, including Sebastian. "Just return her to me before midnight, my good man," he responded, sipping on a glass of fine whiskey.

Ginger and Matt had become an official item, and they snuggled in the booth, talking with Will and Katherine.

"Katherine, I'm so excited for you. And I'm definitely coming to the show!" Ginger exclaimed.

"Yeah, kid. You deserve it. Your paintings are so kick-ass. Watch out, New York. Here she comes!" Matt chimed in. His art vocabulary was limited, but his words were full of sincerity.

Will sat quietly with his arm draped on the back of Katherine's chair. He still seemed distracted.

"You okay?" she leaned in to ask him discreetly.

"Me? Yeah. I'm fine. Just a little tired, that's all." He kissed her softly and turned to watch Tony and Andi attempt what looked to be some form of swing dancing.

Katherine felt strange in the pit of her stomach. She sensed something was bothering Will, but she didn't want to get into it tonight. Everyone was having such a good time, and Andi and Sebastian would be leaving the next morning to head back to New York.

CHAPTER 25

Early the next morning Will left the inn while it was still dark outside. Katherine opened her eyes sleepily as he dressed, waiting for an explanation. Will buttoned his jeans and bent over to kiss her forehead. He told her he had a deadline with one of the studios and wouldn't be able to stay to bid Andi and Sebastian farewell.

"Please tell them good-bye for me. It was great to meet them both," he said casually as he pulled his shirt on over his head.

"Okay. Call me later?" Katherine was still half-asleep, but awake enough to find his departure peculiar. Will had never before mentioned any kind of deadline. When he composed, it always seemed to Katherine to be on his terms, according to his time and inspiration. From what she could tell, the studios gave Will free rein over his schedule, as if they knew that his best work could not be rushed.

But before she could give it any more thought, Katherine fell back into a deep sleep. It had been a late night, as all nights spent at Dale's tended to be. But she had laughed, she had danced, and she had loved every moment watching her two worlds collide—old friends meeting new friends, sharing memories, and celebrating new possibilities. It was the past, the present, and the future all dancing and laughing along with her. It wasn't just fun. It was elevating; it was hopeful.

Murray made a decadent send-off breakfast for Andi and Sebastian, and Mr. Trust gifted them a framed photograph of Bluewater Lake.

"It was so lovely to meet you both. You come back and visit us soon. It's good for Bluewater to get a dose of the big city once in a while." He winked and kissed Andi's cheek and tipped his invisible hat to Sebastian, who shook his hand appreciatively.

"Oh, Andi, I can't believe you're leaving already," Katherine said sadly as she squeezed her friend in a tight embrace.

"I know. It's far too soon. I can see why you'd never want to leave this place. It's simply wonderful." Andi smiled and put her hands on Katherine's shoulders. "I'm so, so happy for you. You made the right choice, coming here. Just promise me that you'll continue to shave your legs and wear deodorant." She winked and Sebastian laughed behind her.

"Katherine, it has been a tremendous pleasure. I look forward to working with you, and I'll be in touch." He gave her a hug and picked up their luggage. As he walked out the door, Katherine took hold of Andi's hand.

"Sebastian is . . . I mean you seem . . ." She couldn't find the right words.

"Happy? I am. I truly am." Andi responded so confidently and sincerely Katherine almost didn't recognize her formerly untamable friend.

"And Will, he is also . . ." Andi started.

Katherine nodded. "Yes, he is. I'm . . ."

"Happy," they said simultaneously and then laughed as Katherine linked her arm through Andi's and walked her out to Sebastian waiting by the rental car.

"Happy painting!" Sebastian called out the window as they drove away.

Katherine stood on the sidewalk and waved until they were out of sight. It was an especially warm day, and the sun caressed her cheeks. She closed her eyes and breathed in the air, fragrant in fresh-cut grass, wood, and coffee.

It had been a few hours since Will left. She pulled her phone from her pocket to check for any messages, but there were none. For a moment, she thought she'd borrow Murray's car and go check on Will at the cabin. But then she thought better of it. Maybe he truly did have a deadline. She didn't want to interrupt his work. Instead, Katherine decided to paint at the gazebo. The heat in the air seemed to lend a golden glow to the already vibrant summer colors, and she couldn't wait to complete her first piece for the big show.

As the sun began to set behind her that evening, Katherine finished the painting. It was her boldest work yet, bursting with light and energy. She clearly channeled her elation and anticipation for the show into her every move. But between strokes of brightness, there were underlying shadows and contrasting darks. As thrilled as she was, Katherine couldn't help but think of Will and his distant behavior. He still hadn't called, and he hadn't even sent her a text all day.

Katherine decided enough was enough. She packed away her supplies and carefully carried her painting back to the inn. She was covered in paint and sweat, and she was edgy from hunger. Murray had packed her a sandwich for lunch, but when she got caught up in painting, she rarely stopped to eat or rest until the work was complete.

She knew she should shower, but Katherine suddenly felt a sense of urgency. It was not like Will to go an entire day without seeing her, let alone without talking to her. She simply washed her hands, and went into the kitchen to ask Murray for his car keys, which he handed over to her without question.

As she approached the cabin, the sun had set and the stars were starting to pop up all over the dark blue sky. Smoke swirled from the chimney, and the lights were on inside. Katherine climbed out of the car and stood quietly outside the front door for a few moments to listen to the music within; it was beautifully haunting and suspenseful. She heard mostly piano, the keys telling a story of loss and fear, followed by a serene, almost calming resolution.

She hated to interrupt, but she figured she'd just say hello, give him a kiss, and let him get back to it. She knocked loudly, knowing it would be hard for him to hear. No answer. She knocked again, more loudly.

When Will answered the door, his hair was wildly disheveled, and he didn't have a shirt on. Katherine smiled. After watching him work the past few months, she knew he was probably doing pushups when he needed a break—it was something he did to reenergize while he wrote. He also would uncaringly comb his fingers violently through his hair while he scrutinized the notes he madly sketched onto the paper.

She started to speak, "Hi! I just wanted—"

Before she could finish, Will grabbed her and pulled her to him, kissing her passionately. He picked her up and held her tightly against him, shutting the door behind her.

After they made love among the scattered sheets of music, they lay facing one another on the rug by the fire, as they now had done so many times. Katherine looked up at Will, beckoning him to look back at her. He hesitated for a moment, but then let his eyes lock with hers.

"Something is bothering you," she whispered, lightly tracing Will's jaw with her finger. The warmth of the fire fell like a blanket upon their skin.

"It's stupid," Will said, looking down at the floor. "That's why I wanted to keep my distance today. So I could be an idiot by myself."

Katherine laughed. "What are you talking about?"

Will still struggled to look her in the eye.

"Is it about the show? Because I thought you wanted me to do it."

"No. I did. I mean . . . I do."

"So what is it?" She was confused.

"It took me so long to find you," he started and then looked away out the window. She waited, wondering if she was supposed to read his mind for the rest of it. But then he continued, "It took me so long to let myself move on . . . from Julee."

Katherine whispered, "I know." She knew how painful it was for Will to say Julee's name.

"Look. I want you to do this show. I'm so damn proud of you." He hesitated. "But I know that world. It's powerful and seductive. I don't know. What if . . .? What if it rips you away from me?"

Katherine sat up and looked into his eyes, holding his face in her hands. "Are you kidding me? I thought I've made it perfectly clear that *nothing* is going to take me away from Bluewater or from you."

"I know. I know you think that," Will said as he sat up with her. "But I also know what that beast can do. Fame, it *is* a beast, and it can render you powerless in its claws. Before you know it, you won't recognize yourself."

"Will, I have no interest in fame. I don't want fortune. And I certainly don't want New York." Katherine tried to assure him that she knew what she was doing. "This is different. The Met was my heart when I lived there. It was the one place I could go and feel alive—where I could breathe. I am here. I met you because of the Met." She looked at him and took a breath. "This show is something I need to do for me and only for me. It's not for the critics or for the collectors. But it is something I have to do."

"Yes, it is." Will pulled her down to lie on his chest. "I just don't want to lose you. I don't think I could take it."

"You won't lose me. I promise." Katherine yawned and wrapped her arms tightly around him. "I'm yours, all yours."

Will kissed her forehead and cleared his throat, "You'd understand if I don't go. . . to the show?"

She sat up quickly and turned to look at him, her expression a mixture of bewilderment and sadness. "Why not?"

"I vowed never to return to New York. After . . . . after everything happened . . . I just . . . I can't go back there." Will's voice became hoarse, and his fierce blue eyes searched Katherine's for forgiveness.

"Of course . . . Okay. I understand," she said weakly. She was stunned and heartbroken. She knew the heartache Will associated with Manhattan, but she had hoped his love for her would overpower his pain from the past.

"Thank you." Will looked genuinely relieved. "I love you, Katherine." He kissed her lips and pulled her body against his as he dozed off to sleep. Her mind raced as the fire burned in front of her.

Was Will right? Would she find fame at the show? Would it consume her before she could realize it? And now Will wouldn't even be there to stop it from happening. He wouldn't be there to keep her grounded.

The long summer days gradually shortened, and a soft cool breeze danced through the air. Seemingly overnight, flecks of yellow emerged among the fluttering green aspen trees, and rather than fragrant flowers, Main Street began to smell of pecans and pumpkin. As fall crept its way through Bluewater, the town quieted. Children went back to school, and summer visitors had mostly returned to their busy lives elsewhere. There were fewer boats out on the lake, and there were no longer weekend events in the town park.

It was a magical time for Katherine. The smells, the colors, the calm and quiet—it was all so enchanting, so comforting. It had been one year since she arrived in Bluewater, and so much had happened in that short amount of time. Her path had taken many unexpected turns, but each turn seemed to guide her closer and closer to the kind of contentment she had been missing her entire life.

After Andi and Sebastian had left, Katherine spent several weeks painting feverishly, with reckless abandon as she had never painted before. She woke up early every day, grabbed a quick latte at Ginger's, and then painted until the sun set every night. Sometimes she worked outside of Will's cabin, drawing inspiration from the music he created inside. Other days were spent painting at the gazebo or along the shore.

Sebastian kept in touch with updates about the show. He'd email her to notify her about big names and press outlets RSVP'ing to the event. *This is looking to be the most highly attended exhibition we've hosted in the Contemporary Wing. The New York Times wants rights to the first onsite interview. I've just received a request from the mayor, hoping to secure VIP tickets."* Katherine kept most of Sebastian's emails to herself. She did not want to worry Will with the hype. His words about the dangers of fame resonated deeply with her, and she did not want to lose sight of why she was doing the show. While each message from Sebastian delivered a jolt of nervous excitement, she did her best to maintain clarity and focus, and she redirected that energy into her work.

She became known around town as the "mad artist," a nickname she likely earned due to her inattention to personal appearance and lack of interaction with others. She carelessly tossed her hair up on top of her head in messy bundles, rarely remembering to brush it. She had no time for makeup, and she wore what became her "painter's outfit" every day: stained jeans, a baggy white tee shirt, and the paint-blotched boots Pete Steinberg had noticed when he approached her for the article. Katherine's adrenaline felt like it was on overdrive ever since she agreed to do the show. A victim of total physical exhaustion, she would submit to deep sleep at night. But the sleep would only last for a few hours before she was wide awake and anxious to paint early each morning.

Katherine and Will did not speak again of his not coming to New York. But Will was happy for her, and he held a genuine reverence for her work. He always asked questions and studied her completed paintings with profound interest. Will himself had a massive new film score to work on, and they fed off one another's creative dynamisms. Katherine taught Will more about painting, about some of the techniques and movements, discussing her favorite artists of the past. And Will showed her how he approached music, explaining how he heard a song in his head before he even wrote a single note. Sometimes he'd finish a passage, and he would be so elated that he'd run outside and grab Katherine, pulling her away from her painting so they could make love and celebrate the rush of achievement.

"Will! I can't! I have to finish this!" She'd halfheartedly try to resist.

"Oh come on, *Mad Artist*. Let me be your muse!" Will would tease, and Katherine would toss her brushes aside and let him have his way with her.

They would shower and drink wine late at night, snacking on grilled cheese sandwiches or leftovers. Mr. Trust and Murray rarely saw Katherine around the inn. She was either painting, or sleeping, or at Will's, and she missed most of the meals in the dining room.

~*~

"Perhaps you can join us for dinner this evening, Miss Ross? I'm sure Murray would happily whip up one of your favorites," Mr. Trust said cheerily one morning, catching Katherine on her way out.

Katherine paused to consider. She was nearly finished with all of the paintings for the show, and she missed having dinner with Mr. Trust and Murray as well.

"Okay, that would be wonderful! I'll ask Will if he can make it. I know he's down to the wire on his latest project. But you can count me in!" She smiled at Mr. Trust as she hauled her easel out the door.

After another successful day of painting, Katherine decided to dress up for dinner at the inn. She showered, curled her hair, applied some makeup, and even picked out a few pieces of jewelry to wear for the occasion.

She'd called Will earlier, but he was deep into his process with the film project, and so he regretfully declined the invitation to dinner.

"They're used to my work binges. I've disappeared for a lot longer than this before. Besides, it sounds like *you're* the one they're missing."

"Are you sure you can't sneak away for a quick bite?" Katherine pressed.

"Nah. It's never quick with Eli and me. But I'll make it up to them soon. I'm nearly finished with this."

"Okay. I'll see you tomorrow then. Don't miss me too much." She made kissing noises through the phone.

Will laughed. "See ya tomorrow."

~*~

Katherine walked down the hall, lightly touching the old photos as she passed. She heard Ginger and Murray laughing downstairs, and when she walked into the room, they all applauded and whistled.

"Well, well, well! Look who remembers how to shower?!" Ginger teased as she handed Katherine a glass of chardonnay.

"Hey! I *shower* . . . most days." She giggled and clinked her glass against Ginger's. "I didn't know you were coming to dinner. What a treat!"

"Yeah. Gramps said Will couldn't make it, so I figured it would be my only chance to actually see you before you become all 'Mad Artist' again tomorrow," Ginger said as she elbowed Katherine lightly and added, "And I think I'm beginning to resent William for taking up all of your free time."

227

Everyone laughed.

"I'm sorry I've been so MIA." Katherine blushed. "I can't believe how carried away I've become with this project. But I'm almost done, so you all better get ready to bid the Mad Artist adieu!" she insisted, as they walked into the beautifully prepared dining room. Candles were burning softly, and each table was covered in a pristine white cloth. The entire room smelled of herbs and spices, and lemon, and something tantalizingly sweet.

Katherine's mouth began to water as they sat down. "I can't remember the last time I had a proper meal," she said, folding her napkin on her lap and trying to comprehend how much time had passed since Andi and Sebastian's visit.

"Who needs food when you have looooooove?" Ginger jested.

Mr. Trust raised his glass. "Indeed! I'll drink to that."

The dinner was exceptional, and Murray surprised everyone with a molten chocolate cake for dessert. Katherine savored every bite as though it may be her last.

"If I'm ever on death row, this meal . . . This is what I want," she joked.

"Oh my, what an uplifting topic." Murray chuckled as he cleared their plates. When they stood up to move into the lobby, Mr. Trust paused for a moment, putting his hands down on the table.

"Mr. Trust? Are you okay? Katherine asked, standing next to him.

"I'm fine, dear. I think I just stood up too fast." He smiled and patted her forearm. "Any song requests?" He turned and walked slowly toward the piano.

Late into the night, they sang and sipped champagne. Ginger was so tipsy she had to stay with Katherine, and Murray fell asleep, snoring loudly on the couch in the lobby. Fortunately, there were only a few guests staying at the inn this time of year, and they were all tucked away in their rooms, safely distanced from the musical debauchery.

The next morning Katherine and Ginger winced in pain when there was a knock at the door. They both lay sprawled across Katherine's bed, fully dressed in their clothes and jewelry from the night before.

"Man, Mr. Trust and Murray throw quite a party." Katherine groaned as she struggled to sit up.

"Who do you think I get it from?" Ginger spoke into the mattress, refusing to move from her face plant position.

There was another knock and then Mr. Trust's voice through the door, "Good morning, girls! Miss Ross, you have a visitor waiting downstairs." His voice sounded strange, like he was nervous or something.

"A visitor?" Ginger mumbled. "Is that what Will calls himself these days?" Even in her painfully hungover state, Ginger was still witty.

"It can't be. He always just comes upstairs." Katherine quickly checked her face in the bathroom mirror and tied her hair up in a bun. Who could it possibly be?

"I'm right behind you." Ginger moaned, but remained motionless on the bed while Katherine opened the door.

Mr. Trust had gone, and Katherine tiptoed by the other rooms and down the stairs. As she entered the lobby, she looked right, toward the door and the front desk, but saw no one. Then she turned and looked toward the window behind the couch. There he stood, his back to Katherine, hands in his pockets. He was looking out over the lake.

Katherine's heart leapt into her throat. She thought she might pass out. She crept quietly past the piano, hanging onto it for support, blinking her heavy eyes against the bright morning light.

"Michael?"

CHAPTER 26

"Hi ya, Kate." Michael slowly turned to face her and flashed his killer smile that had won her over so many years ago. He walked toward Katherine and wrapped his arms around her tightly. Katherine awkwardly hugged him back, still stunned by his presence. Paralyzed by his touch.

"What . . .? What are you doing here?" Katherine let go and stepped back, bumping into the piano. Michael was clean-shaven, and it was obvious he had just gotten a haircut. He wore a gray Brooks Brothers suit and Italian leather shoes. He looked younger, somehow, than the last time Katherine had seen him—the night when he left. It felt like so long ago.

"I, um, well . . . can we sit?" Michael put his hand on the lower part of her back as they walked over to the couch, a gesture so familiar to Katherine from their time together at work parties and social gatherings.

When they sat down, Katherine swallowed, still trying to comprehend the fact that the man who sat in front of her was Michael: Michael, her ex-husband, Michael here in Bluewater. She stared at him silently with wide eyes, trying to breathe away the wave of nausea that had suddenly washed over her.

"This place suits you, Kate. It's beautiful here." Michael looked around, stalling.

"Michael. What are you doing here?" Katherine became increasingly irritated. How dare he show up here? After everything he did? After all the pain he caused? How dare he interrupt her life with no warning? The life she worked so hard to build on her own . . .

"Look. I made a mistake, a huge mistake. I was an ass," he said, reaching for Katherine's hand. But she pulled away and put one of the couch pillows on her lap as a barrier. Michael went on, "I was confused, drunk. I was working too much; I lost sight of . . . of everything. Kate, life is just not *life*, without you." His eyes saddened and his voice became shaky.

"I'm confused. I thought you met someone in London." Katherine shook her head, hoping the right words would come to her in the midst of the shock.

"I did. It wasn't right. *She* wasn't right," Michael whined. "Kate, I'm an idiot. A shmuck. You're the one for me, I *know* it now." He shifted closer to Katherine on the couch while she sat completely frozen, unblinking, processing.

"I've read the articles and reviews about your work. I'm so proud of you, Kate! And the show at the Met next month? I mean, wow! You're a star!" Michael gushed.

"Michael . . ." Katherine's throat felt hot and tight, and his name came out in an inaudible whisper. Her heart began to beat faster, the adrenaline building up inside her. But the words wouldn't come.

"You inspired me, Kate. I left my father's firm! I'm done with corporate law. I'm following my dreams and working for a non-profit. I got a new place in Brooklyn; you'd love it. And I've been sober for ninety days!" Michael seemed to be unable to stop. "It's all because of *you*, Kate." He leaned in toward Katherine. She felt paralyzed, terrified. She knew she should jump off the couch, that she should slap him, that she should run away, but she couldn't move a single muscle. *Was this a bad dream? Some kind of champagne-and-chocolate-cake-induced nightmare?*

"Ahem!"

Katherine jumped just as Michael moved within inches of her lips. Ginger stood by the piano with her arms crossed.

Katherine shot up from the couch, and Michael stood casually, adjusting his suit jacket.

"Ginger! Oh, thank God. This is . . . Michael, my ex." Katherine could feel the blood pump through her face. She didn't need a mirror to know that her cheeks and chest were a deep crimson by now. "Michael, this is Ginger Tr—"

"Ginger Mayrose! Wow. I know exactly who you are," Michael announced suavely.

"Ginger Trust, actually," Ginger said dryly, scowling at him. "Katherine, may I speak to you for a moment?" Ginger had pulled her hair up into a ponytail, and while Katherine knew she was painfully hung over, she somehow still looked refreshed and beautiful.

They walked down the hall, by the foot of the stairs, stopping near the old picture of Ginger and Mr. Trust. Ginger took Katherine's hands into her own. "What is he doing here, Katherine?" Her eyes were wide and serious.

"I honestly don't know! I haven't even spoken to him since I left New York!" Katherine panicked. She was trembling, her chest began to burn inside, and tears rushed to her eyes.

"Okay, okay. Calm down." Ginger rubbed Katherine's arms. "What do you want to do?"

"I'll talk to him." Katherine swallowed heavily and closed her eyes.

Ginger looked concerned and opened her mouth to say something, but shut it again and looked down at the ground.

"What?" Katherine begged.

"It's just . . . If Will knew Michael was here, he wouldn't like it, Katherine. He wouldn't like it one bit." Ginger looked at Katherine nervously.

"I know." Katherine shook her head. "But he has nothing to worry about. *You* have nothing to worry about. I'm just going to get some closure. Things need to be said. And then I will send him on his way. Please don't call Will, Ginger. I don't want to freak him out for no reason."

Ginger nodded and gave Katherine a hug. "I'm going to go up and shower. Call me if you need anything." She gave Katherine one more cautious glance, before returning upstairs to the room.

Katherine walked back into the lobby and took a deep breath. Michael was standing by the fireplace. "Michael, I'm sorry but—"

"Wait. Just, please. I'm staying down the street at the Fallen Leaf Lodge. Can you just have dinner with me tonight? So we can talk?" Michael pleaded.

"I've made the trip and everything. Please, just one dinner, Kate." His dark brown eyes searched hers with such anxious intensity. The last time he looked at her so forcefully he was drunk and on top of her. She had to look away.

"Fine. One dinner," Katherine said shortly. "Meet me at the restaurant in the lodge. Eight o'clock."

"Thank you, Katie bear. Thank you!" Michael kissed her cheek and strolled confidently out of the inn. Katherine put her hand to where he had kissed her. For a moment, her heart felt as though it was made of lead, and when she closed her eyes, all she could see were Michael's two black suitcases standing by the door at their New York apartment.

When she went back upstairs, she found Ginger lying on the bed.

"So? Is he gone?" Ginger asked.

"Not yet. I'm going to meet him for dinner tonight at the lodge," Katherine replied nervously, avoiding eye contact with her friend.

"What! Why?" Ginger stood up from the bed and walked over to Katherine. "Katherine, what are you doing?"

"Look. I need to make my peace with this. With my past. I want a clean slate."

"He *cheated* on you!"

"I know. But that wasn't entirely his fault. We both failed in our own ways." Katherine looked out the window. The lake was a sharp sapphire blue—a dark seductive temptress among the red and yellow leaves that surrounded it.

Ginger stood in front of Katherine, forcing her to look her in the eye. "What about Will, Katherine?"

"I love Will, more than anything. Ginger, *nothing* is going to happen. I just want to have a conversation with the man—get some closure." Katherine walked over to make the bed. "We both deserve that."

Ginger left the inn a while later, after promising again that she wouldn't tell Will about Michael. Katherine took the day off from painting and went for a walk around the lake, attempting to sort through her thoughts before dinner. She knew she loved Will and that she would never go back to Michael, ever. But something about seeing Michael again made her feel vulnerable and weak. His smile, his familiar body language—they transported Katherine to the years they had spent together, and it confused her. Even after all this time, Michael's touch had felt familiar.

As she walked along the dirt path, through the tall pine trees, Katherine breathed deeply, hoping the crisp fall air would give her clarity. She didn't want to hurt Michael; though he had deeply hurt her. Instead, she wanted to thank him for taking the step she had been too scared to take. They had been contented and natural together for a while, yes, but in a way that roommates or friends should be. And then, he fell into his dark phase, and they were both ruined. Their marriage lacked the rawness, the vulnerability that forces two people to find completion in one another: the way she had with Will. Perhaps, if she explained her feelings to Michael, he would understand that they were not meant to be, and perhaps, he would be able to find closure too.

Before long, Katherine had made it to the far side of the lake, and she was only minutes from Will's house. She paused on the path, unsure of what to do. Glancing back at the lake, Katherine watched as two ducks swirled effortlessly around each other like stunt planes in the air before gliding gracefully upon the silky surface of the water. A pair of butterflies mimicked the playful dance above the glistening blades of tall grass along the shore.

Should she go on and see Will? Kiss him fiercely and then tell him about Michael?

But instead, she turned around to head back to town. She pulled her cell from her pocket and called Will.

"Hey gorgeous," Will answered, symphony music playing in the background.

"Hey, you, I miss you," Katherine said as she walked.

"I miss you too. Can you come over for a while?" Will asked.

"Actually, I think I'm going to stay in town today. I have a lot to take care of." She clenched her teeth, awaiting his reply.

"Yeah. I need to finish this anyway. Come over tonight if you want, okay?" Will sounded slightly distracted. Katherine could picture him leaning over his paper, scribbling madly with his crazy disheveled hair bouncing atop his head, half-empty coffee mugs and papers strewn all over the cabin in a beautiful chaotic mess.

"Okay. Love you," Katherine said, a lump forming in her throat. She felt like a liar, like she was betraying him. *Was she?*

"Love you too." He hung up, remaining blissfully unaware of anything beyond his music.

~*~

Katherine stood in the lobby of the lodge, nervously fiddling with the bracelet on her wrist. She went casual, in skinny jeans and a sweater, and wore her hair down and loosely curled.

"You look beautiful." Michael's voice came from behind her, sending chills down her arms. He had changed into slacks and a collared shirt, and he smelled of the Armani cologne he had worn for as long as she'd known him. "I like your hair like that." He smiled and kissed her cheek.

They walked into the restaurant, and the host sat them at a quiet booth near a window looking out onto Main Street. Michael ordered a club soda for himself and an elk carpaccio appetizer for them to share. The restaurant was quiet and dark, with its walls and ceilings built entirely of massive logs. Old-fashioned wall sconces and half-burned candles provided the only light in the place. Katherine looked around nervously, not ready to speak.

"This town, Bluewater Lake, it's really something!" Michael said casually as he browsed the menu. He behaved as though they were on a first date—as though nothing had ever happened between them.

After the waiter brought her wine, Katherine chugged half the glass and forced a smile. "Michael, I'm really flattered you came all the way out here."

"For you? Anything," he said smoothly, raising his glass. "Here's to you, my Katie."

Katherine cringed, resenting his signature smile, which had always helped charm his way through anything. "That's the thing though, Michael. I'm . . . I'm not yours anymore. I haven't been for a long time." She looked down at her menu. She couldn't stand to look him in the eye.

"Well, I figured you would date and whatnot. But I'm here to win you back, Kate," Michael said matter-of-factly.

"You can't. I . . . I met someone, Michael." Katherine swallowed another big gulp of wine. "I fell in love."

Michael laughed out loud. "*Love*? Already?"

Katherine looked away, waiting for him to process. *Yes, love. A love like you would never know.*

"You mean to tell me you met someone *here*? In a shabby little town like this?" Michael looked around pretentiously. "Who is he? Some kind of fish bait salesman or something?" Michael smiled jokingly. "A canoe designer maybe?"

"That's really none of your business," a man's voice suddenly chimed in behind Katherine.

"Will?" She gasped as she spun around. "What? How? I mean . . . What are you doing here?" She panicked and stood up.

Michael stood as well and calmly placed his napkin on the table.

"I could ask you the same thing," Will said quietly to Katherine, before looking sternly at Michael.

"You've got to be kidding me," Michael chimed in obnoxiously. "This guy? This *lumberjack* is your new love? Oh, that's fresh."

Will stepped toward Michael, who stood firm with his chin up and chest sticking out.

"I suggest you leave," Will said through clenched teeth.

"Me? I believe you, sir, are the unwelcome guest at *our* dinner," Michael said arrogantly and looked confidently at Katherine. Katherine put her hand to Will's chest and looked back at Michael.

"Michael, you should go. There's nothing left to say. This is done." She gestured between Michael and herself. "It was done years ago." She spoke firmly, hoping he'd receive the message.

"No way. I flew all the way out here to see you, to take you back. New York is where you belong, Kate, and you know it!" Michael smiled and calculated his next words carefully. "You don't belong with this *trash*." He turned to face Will but had no time to react before Will punched him hard across the left eye, sending Michael crashing violently into the next table.

"Will! Are you crazy?!" Katherine screamed, helping Michael up from the floor. His nose bled profusely, and his left eye was swollen shut.

Michael stumbled to his feet and stared at Will, silently daring him to punch him again.

"Michael. Go. Please go now!" Katherine's voice trembled as tears poured down her face.

"Some winner you got yourself, Kate. I wish you and Old Man River here a lifetime of happiness." Michael muttered sourly as he limped over the broken glass and out of the restaurant. The servers and other customers remained unmoving, jaws on the floor, staring at Katherine and Will.

"Will . . . I . . ." Katherine reached for his arm, but he was already turning to go.

"Don't," he said coldly. She searched his eyes for forgiveness, but all she could see was a dangerously fragile and terrifying mix of anger and fear.

"What am I going to do?" Katherine asked Ginger as she somberly sipped her latte the next morning. Will had stormed out of the lodge in a quiet rage, and he hadn't answered her calls.

"He'll come around, girl. Just let him cool off for a day or two," Ginger said as she wiped the counter. "And again, I am so, *so* sorry for spilling the beans, Katherine. He was worried when he couldn't find you at the inn, and he said you wouldn't answer your phone." Ginger put her head down in shame. "And he just didn't give me time to explain before he ran out of here. I feel terrible." She tossed the rag in a bin behind the counter.

"I know. I'm sorry too. I shouldn't have put you in that position." Katherine looked down at her latte. "I just hope he forgives me. I don't know what I'd do if, if he . . ." She let her words fall into silence and looked despondently out the window. Dark gray clouds concealed the sky, and a cold breeze carried

241

fallen leaves up and down the street, spinning them around in a haunting sort of dance.

Michael had left town late in the night, without another word. In a way, Katherine felt sorry for him, but she was also glad to be rid of him once and for all. Yes, he had played a major role in her life, but that destructive chapter was long over, and she vowed she would not look back. She refused to make that mistake, no matter how handsome or charming or enticing it may be. Michael was her past. Will was her future. Bluewater was her future. She was sure of it.

As tempted as she was to drive over to Will's cabin and force him to forgive her, Katherine decided to heed Ginger's advice and give him some space. The show at the Met was only weeks away, and she had at least two more paintings to produce for the big event. She finished her latte, hugged Ginger good-bye, and headed home to pack up her supplies.

Back at the inn, Murray was in the lobby, helping some guests check out.

"Where's Mr. Trust?" she asked, wondering why Murray was at the desk and not in the kitchen. Murray just shrugged and turned his attention back to the guests.

Katherine wandered around the dining room and checked the kitchen. Both were empty. She made her way upstairs and lightly knocked on Mr. Trust's bedroom door on the way back to her own. There was no answer, and the door was locked—not unusual, because they all kept their doors locked when they were out and about during the day. The inn guests appeared to be respectable people for the most part, but better safe than sorry.

She sighed and shrugged, figuring Mr. Trust must be out for a walk or running errands. She desperately wanted to talk to him about Will, but figured it could wait a few hours. For now, she would gather her things and head over to the gazebo to paint.

The breeze from the morning had grown in speed and strength, and Katherine struggled against it as she made her way up the street, carrying a large canvas under one arm and her heavy easel over the other shoulder. The sidewalks were mostly empty, and the town was strangely quiet. The candy shop was closed, there were no children out playing on a day like this, and Lolo had moved all the books back into her shop, safely inside with the door closed.

Some would undoubtedly find the overcast day dreary and depressing, an excuse to stay in bed. But Katherine felt a strange energy in the air, swirling around her as she walked. She felt unsettled. Her skin tingled. Rather than retreat, she resolved to embrace the darkness of the clouds, the foreboding smell of dirt and rain in the air, and the surreal silence in the usually bustling street. She would use the intensity, the strangeness of the day. She would use the pain in her heart, the longing for Will's forgiveness. She would use it all to fuel her painting.

Katherine finally made it to the path that led down to the gazebo. She smiled, remembering the first time she clumsily made her way down to the charming little structure—how unfamiliar it had all been. Now, she knew every step, every rock, like the back of her hand, and she navigated the steep path easily, supplies and all. As she shifted the canvas from one arm to the other, she noticed someone sitting in the gazebo.

"Mr. Trust? Is that you?" she asked as she stepped closer. The man sat motionless with his head hanging down and did not respond.

"Mr. Trust? It's me, Katherine." Her heart began to pound violently when he did not reply. Katherine threw the canvas and her easel to the ground and ran over the small bridge, noticing a fresh new bouquet of red roses draped gracefully across the plaque for Jacqueline, their dark green leaves shuddering in the wind.

As she approached him, Katherine saw that his eyes were closed. "Mr. Trust? Mr. Trust, can you hear me?" She hoped that perhaps he was in a deep sleep. But when he failed to respond to her raised voice and her hands upon his shoulders, Katherine began to panic. "Mr. Trust! Please! Wake up!"

Her hands shook wildly, and she could barely retrieve her cell phone from her pocket. But she finally grabbed it and held it tightly while she dialed 911 and then called Murray.

The few minutes that passed felt like hours. The wind howled ferociously, and the sky blackened. Thunder roared in the distance, and the lake darkened to a color Katherine had never seen before, its surface shifting tumultuously in uneasy waves. Katherine thought she could feel a faint breath escaping from his nose, but Mr. Trust exhibited no other signs of life, and his lips looked slightly blue. She didn't know how to do CPR, and she didn't want to hurt him. She was terrified and felt entirely useless, and she bawled uncontrollably as she gently laid him on the floor of the gazebo and draped her coat over him to keep his body warm.

"Please, Mr. Trust. Please don't go," she whispered, wrapping his cold lifeless hand within hers, just as the paramedics came sprinting down the path.

~*~

In the hospital waiting room, Murray sat with his arm around Katherine.

"He'll be okay, kid. Eli is a rock." He tried to comfort her, but Katherine could see fear in his eyes. She couldn't speak. Every time she opened her mouth to say something, her voice caught in her throat.

"Where is he?" Ginger demanded frantically as she came barreling through the sliding doors, her face stricken with panic. Her stained café apron was tied around her waist, and she still held a counter rag in her right hand. Behind her, the door opened again, and Will walked in, his face as white as a ghost.

Murray went over to Ginger. "They're doing everything they can, sweetheart. He's in good hands." She sobbed into his giant shoulder.

Katherine looked up at Will, her cheeks stained with tears. Their eyes met, and she stood slowly, her legs trembling and weak. She opened her mouth to speak, but before she could say anything, Will ran over to her and held her tightly in his arms. Katherine collapsed, barely able to breathe.

Will held her tighter, whispering in her ear as they slowly sat down. "Shhhh . . . shhhhhhh . . . It'll be okay." His voice was calm, but when she pulled away to look at him, his jaw was clenched and tears threatened to crawl out from the corners of his beautiful eyes.

"Oh, Will, I-I'm so sorry." Katherine pulled him to her again, refusing to let him go. "I should have told you about Mi—"

"I know. I'm sorry too." He pulled back and put both hands on her cheeks, gently wiping her tears with his thumbs.

Katherine looked into his eyes. "I love you. You are . . . You have to know you are the only one I want." She spoke clearly and intensely. She wanted to be sure he heard her; she wanted to be sure he understood. Will pulled her to his lips and kissed her softly.

Her heart felt as though it may burst. She had nearly lost Will, and now she might lose Mr. Trust, the man who welcomed her to Bluewater with open arms, the man who treated her like a daughter, the man who encouraged her art and her love for Will. She couldn't stand to imagine the inn, or Bluewater, without Mr. Trust—the thought made her sick. She closed her eyes and tucked her head into Will's neck, praying silently for a miracle.

CHAPTER 27

Matt and Tony and Lolo arrived at the hospital shortly after Will and Ginger. The group sat silently in the dated waiting room, under the blinding fluorescent lights, watching nurses and doctors converse by the desk while other visitors walked by casually, smiling and holding bouquets of flowers and stuffed animals.

All anyone could do was sip bad coffee from the hospital cafeteria and wait for news. Matt cradled Ginger in his arms, kissing her head, and rubbing her back. She had cried every tear, and now she sat still as a statue, unmoving and unblinking. Tony sat quietly next to them, his solemn face strange in the absence of all its usual silliness and comedy.

Will held Katherine's head against his chest. She could hear his heart beating wildly, as he tried to breathe deeply and calmly. Katherine felt an unsettling numbness take over her body. Her toes and fingers tingled for a while, until she could no longer feel them at all. Her skin felt strange, as though it was not her own—like she was trapped inside someone else's body, witnessing a devastating and very private moment she should not be witnessing. Whenever she closed her eyes, all she could see was the bouquet of red roses draped across Jacqueline's plaque.

Did Mr. Trust know? Did he know something was wrong? Is that why he went to the gazebo? To be with Jacqueline?

A tall doctor walked slowly over from the registration desk. He was a handsome man, probably in his fifties. He had kind eyes and silver hair, and in his hand, he held a clipboard down by his side.

"Miss Trust?" he asked, reading the paper on the clipboard and searching around the room. Ginger shot up like a bolt of lightning.

"Yes?" she asked, eyes wide with both fear and expectation. The doctor looked around at Ginger's friends, hesitating.

"It's okay. They're family. Whatever you've got to tell me, you can tell them," Ginger said firmly, holding Matt's hand so tightly his knuckles turned white.

"Okay then. I'm Doctor Wilson. I've been working on Mr. Trust, your grandfather?" The doctor looked to Ginger for confirmation. She nodded. "He is stable, right now."

Ginger's knees buckled, and she fell back into her chair. "Oh, thank God." She gasped.

"We still have some tests to run. I'm afraid he suffered a myocardial infarction, an acute heart attack. But we were able to put a stent in, and it seems to be functioning successfully. We will need to keep him here a few days for observation." Doctor Wilson looked at everyone as he spoke. He clearly understood that Ginger was not the only person in the room who regarded Mr. Trust as family.

Ginger's tears returned, and she threw her arms around the tall doctor. "Thank you! Thank you so much, Doctor Wilson!"

He smiled and hugged her back. "Your grandfather is a lucky man. I've never seen someone survive a heart attack of such severity, especially someone of his age. I'd say it's a miracle, really." Doctor Wilson patted Ginger's hand between his. "I'll need to go over some paperwork with you, and I have instructions for his care at home. When you're ready, I'll take you back to see him. But I'm afraid I can only take Miss Trust for now." He smiled again and nodded at everyone else.

"Thanks, Doc!" Tony hollered. He was back to his happy self, dragging Lolo up from her seat to do a do-si-do in celebration. Murray rested his elbows on his knees and held his head in his hands whispering, "Thank you, God. Thank you."

Matt kissed Ginger and picked her up, spinning her around in a tight embrace. She looked over at Katherine.

"Thank goodness you found him, Katherine." She cried and blew a kiss over Matt's shoulder. Then she followed Doctor Wilson behind the desk and down the hall.

Katherine collapsed back in her seat, and tears started to pour down her cheeks.

"Hey, he's going to be okay." Will sat next to her and handed her a tissue.

"I know. I was just so scared. I've never been so scared." Katherine's heart pounded in her chest, and some feeling started to pour back into her limbs and fingers and toes.

"Let's get you home so you can take a hot shower, maybe get some food. We'll come back to see Eli tonight. He probably needs some rest." Will helped her up from her chair. They hugged the others good-bye and climbed into Will's truck.

The hospital was in Graydon, a town about fifteen miles away from Bluewater. As Will drove, Katherine sat quietly, looking out the window. The ambulance ride from town had been nothing but a blur for Katherine, and in hindsight, she couldn't remember anything about the scenery or how long it took. All she could remember was Mr. Trust's cold pale face lying on the gurney, blurred by the tears in her own eyes. The paramedics had allowed her to come along, but she had to sit back and give them space to do their work. Time seemed to stand painfully still in that ambulance, but in a way it also felt like the minutes had passed at warp speed—as though time itself, and light, and the whole world were spinning violently around Katherine, like a terrible ride at the carnival, and there was no way for her to make it stop.

Will drove down the winding road, wet from rain. It traveled alongside a beautiful stream surrounded by radiant orange and yellow aspen trees. Katherine cracked the window so she could smell the wet leaves and wood, and then she looked over at the man she loved.

"Will, I really am so sorry . . . about Michael," she said, her heart full of shame and embarrassment. For a moment, he did not respond. He kept his face forward and his eyes on the road. Katherine could see his jaw tighten.

"Why didn't you tell me he was here?" he asked almost inaudibly, keeping his eyes straight ahead.

"I don't know." Katherine exhaled. "I guess because I knew nothing was going to happen. I wouldn't have *let* anything happen. And so I thought it would be better . . ." She couldn't find the right words—everything sounded like a pathetic excuse in her head. "He caught me off guard. I didn't think I'd ever see him again, and I knew you would want to protect me . . ." Katherine let her voice drift, and she stared at Will. He nodded slightly, but did not say anything. "Things are so good with us. With you and me. I didn't want Michael to steal that away." Katherine sighed and looked outside. There was a vast green field with an old wooden fence along its border. In the distance, Katherine saw dozens of massive black cows congregating and chomping lazily on the wet grass. She made a mental note to return soon and paint the field on a day like today, when the rich colors were saturated and vibrant after a good rain.

Minutes passed, and then Will cleared his throat, "I understand why you didn't tell me." He looked over at Katherine for a second and then back at the road. "Look. I know you, Katherine. I know that you like to handle things on your own, that you've had to do many things in life on your own." He put his hand on her knee and locked eyes with her. "But if we're going to do this—you and me—then you've got to let me in. For all of it—the good, the bad, and the ugly—we've got to be in this together."

Katherine put her hand on his and gave it a squeeze. "Okay. Deal," she said.

When he looked over at her and grinned, Katherine could feel her cheeks turn pink. She bit her lower lip and smiled back. Even after all this time, she could not keep her composure around him. Will slowed the truck and pulled it to the side of the road. "Come here." He unbuckled his seatbelt and pulled Katherine to him, and then he kissed her more passionately than he ever had before.

In the weeks that followed, Mr. Trust was released from the hospital, but received strict orders to rest at home in the inn. Katherine, Murray, Ginger, and the others cared for him each day, bringing him food and tea in bed. Lolo brought over a stack of new bestsellers to help him pass the time, and Will even brought over some music to work on in Mr. Trust's room.

"Had I known this is what I needed to do to finally hear you work, I would have had a heart attack a long time ago, William," Mr. Trust joked one afternoon while Will wrote and played some melodies on his acoustic guitar.

"That's not funny." Katherine walked in, carrying a tray with tea and cookies.

"Ah, there she is. Katherine, my angel, come sit with me." Mr. Trust smiled and patted the bed. "You all needn't wait on me like this. I'm fine, really. I even walked to the end of the hall earlier!" Mr. Trust held up his arms in a symbol of victory and looked at Will for backup. Will smiled and nodded to Katherine to confirm.

"Please, Mr. Trust, you've waited on all of us for so long. Let us spoil you, at least for a little while." She poured him a cup of tea. "Besides, Doctor Wilson was very clear. We've got to take it slow, baby steps."

"Now she's calling me a baby." Mr. Trust frowned and looked at Will, who laughed out loud. "So dear, how are the paintings coming along? Are you ready for the big show next week?"

"Oh, I don't know. I keep thinking maybe I should postpone it. I don't want to leave you here, not now." She looked down at her hands. She had been so worried about Mr. Trust; she hadn't given the show much thought. It was only when Sebastian called her earlier in the week to confirm details that she realized that it was all happening so soon.

"Young lady, don't you dare," Mr. Trust ordered sternly, in a way Katherine had never heard him speak before. His eyes became serious, and his bushy gray brows lowered as he put his hands on hers. "This is your dream. And it has become a dream for everyone in Bluewater as well. We are all so very proud of you, and you will *not* let us down. You hear me?" Mr. Trust spoke to her as though he were her father, reprimanding her for skipping school.

"Yes, sir, I will not let you down." She smiled and kissed his cheek.

"Besides, I've got enough people fussing over me here. It's exhausting." Mr. Trust winked at her and then looked over at Will, who was avoiding the conversation and any eye contact with Katherine. They did not speak much about New York. She knew Will still felt tense about the whole thing, and she really just wanted to get the show over with so she could get back to Bluewater and they could move on with their lives.

"You two go on. Will, take the girl to dinner. I'm going to shut my eyes for a bit." Mr. Trust turned his head toward the window and pulled the covers up to his chin.

Will gathered up his papers and his guitar, and Katherine put the dishes back on the tray.

Out in the hallway, Will cleared his throat. "I can't believe the show is next week. How are you feeling? Are you ready?" He put his hand gently on her back as they walked down the stairs.

"I think so. The paintings are mostly dry and the shipping company is coming for them in a few days." She felt nervous.

"And you're staying with Andi?" Will asked with a smile, his eyebrows raised—a conscious gesture suggesting that Katherine and Andi would be getting into trouble.

"Yes, Andi *and* Sebastian. They live together now, remember?" Katherine couldn't believe it herself. Andi and Sebastian had purchased an apartment in the city together a month earlier, a penthouse—quite close to the Met.

"I think this is it, Katherine! Sebastian, he's the one!" Andi had happily gushed over the phone. "It's crazy though, isn't it? I mean it's *me*—committing, like for real."

Katherine laughed. "It is crazy but in a wonderful sort of way."

"And you? When are you going to make it official and shack up in the cabin with William?

Although, from what I remember, that place is in *desperate* need of a woman's touch before it's livable." Andi teased.

"I don't know. This show and everything that's happened with Mr. Trust . . . It's just a lot. We really haven't had much time for *us*, you know?" As Katherine spoke, she thought about the time that had passed since Mr. Trust's heart attack. It had been weeks, but she had been so busy helping Murray with the inn and finishing her paintings. Each piece had to dry before she could apply a protective shiny varnish to the surface, and then she had to wire each painting so it was ready to hang. *Ready to hang on the walls of the Met . . .*

Will worked feverishly on his film score when he wasn't helping out with everything at the inn. He and Katherine really didn't get to see each other much during the day, and they were both so exhausted at night. They often just collapsed into one another's arms, falling into a deep sleep until the next day and its demands arrived.

As they walked into the lobby, Will stopped Katherine, taking the tray from her hands, and setting it down. "I want you to know I am so proud of you," he said as he held her shoulders in his hands. "Your paintings, they're . . . Well, they *should* be seen by the world. They are incredible."

"Thank you," she whispered. She searched his eyes, hoping he would go on, hoping he would tell her he had a change of heart and that he would join her in New York.

But instead he kissed her and then said, "Marcello's? To celebrate?" He smiled and grabbed their jackets from the old-fashioned coatrack by the front desk.

Katherine sighed. "Yes. Marcello's." Behind her smile, she pushed back tears.

CHAPTER 28

The week flew by in a hurry. Mr. Trust regained more strength each day, testing his physical limits and the patience of those who wanted to look after him. He was determined and stubborn, and before long, against the advice of Katherine and everyone else, he was back behind the desk at the inn, happily taking reservations and accommodating guests.

Will, Matt, and Tony assisted Katherine with the paintings. Each piece had to be meticulously prepared for the journey: delicately wrapped in plastic, protected with foam sheets on all sides, and carefully placed in designated and properly labeled boxes. They set up an assembly-line station in the basement of the inn, where they had plenty of room to work.

"Wow, this is what the basement of that big fancy French museum must look like! The Lou, the Louveh, the Lou . . ." Tony struggled.

"The Louvre," Will finished for him, smiling and slapping his back.

"Yeah. That's what I said." Tony shrugged and kept wrapping.

"They wouldn't even let you in the Louvre." Matt snickered at Tony, who feigned offense and punched him in the arm. Matt didn't even flinch.

"Oh, was that a fly landing on me?" He chuckled, and Tony swung at him again.

"Hey. Take it easy, Stooges. You break it, you bought it," Will warned authoritatively.

Katherine laughed and felt her cheeks flush. She loved that Will felt protective over her paintings.

"Well, now *would* be the time to buy one. After this New York gig, we'll never be able to afford any of these masterpieces." Tony winked at Katherine, as he loaded a five-foot painting carefully into its box.

"Oh stop, you guys." Katherine reddened and shrieked as Matt effortlessly threw her over his shoulder and spun her around playfully.

~*~

The shippers arrived early the day before Katherine's flight. A professional company hired by the Met, they were obviously trained specifically for the transportation of fragile artwork. When the men in matching black pants and gray tee shirts opened the back hatch of the truck, Katherine marveled at the various metal slots, masterfully designed to hold boxed paintings. As the crew loaded their dollies with her work, she stood on the sidewalk, watching anxiously. Will came up behind her and handed her a hot cup of coffee.

"It's weird. I feel nervous about letting them go. Is this what parents feel like when they watch their kids go off to college?" Katherine said quietly, watching her paintings slide perfectly into the protective slots.

Will laughed. "Don't worry. You'll see them again in a couple of days." He kissed her cheek and wrapped his arm around her shoulders as he stood behind her and watched the shippers work precisely and mechanically like clockwork. The air was chilly, and Katherine thought she could smell snow.

"Yeah. I hope so." Katherine was a fatalist by nature, always imagining worst-case-scenarios—one of the many lovable character flaws Andi had always teased her about. Today, as Katherine watched the able-bodied men load the paintings, she imagined the truck getting into a horrible accident, sending her paintings sprawling across a major interstate only to be violently demolished by heavy oncoming traffic. Or perhaps there was a hole in the roof of the truck, and they would encounter a terrible storm in the Midwest, and unbeknownst to the driver, the paintings would be soaked and destroyed. Or maybe the company wasn't as good as it appeared to be, and they would make a huge mistake and deliver the paintings to California instead of New York.

"Miss Ross?" The crew leader stood in front of Katherine with a clipboard. He was in his thirties, a hipster, with a thick dark beard and Vans sneakers.

"I'm sorry?" Katherine snapped out of her paranoia and looked at him blankly.

"I just need your signature here." He handed her a pen and pointed to the form on the clipboard.

"You're done? Already?" Katherine felt like she had blinked and all of the paintings were suddenly locked behind the bolted door of the truck.

"Yes, ma'am. We just need you to sign, and we can hit the road." He replied with a polite smile.

Will gave her shoulders a squeeze.

259

"Okay." Katherine signed on the line with a shaky hand.

"Thank you, Miss Ross. See you in New York." The man said casually, tipping his hat to her, and then whistling at his team to load in. The truck roared to a start and slowly made its way up the street. Katherine took a long, deep breath.

"They'll make it. You'll see," Will whispered in her ear. She turned around and wrapped her arms around him.

"This is all happening so fast," she said into his neck. "I feel like just yesterday the reporter was here."

"I know. Time is a crazy thing." Will kissed her tenderly. His warm lips tasted of coffee.

"What would you like to do today?" he asked her as they walked back toward the inn.

"Well, I'm basically packed. I've been packing for days." Katherine laughed out loud at herself. She had always been compulsive when it came to traveling. "And now that the paintings are gone, I don't know. I need a distraction so I don't just sit around and think about how nervous I am." She looked at him suggestively.

"I'm here to serve, my lady." Will took a bow and they both laughed.

"Actually, are you still working on your score? I'd love to come over and listen to you work." Katherine took him by the hand. "I don't know what it is, but your music always seems to calm me down—it helps me escape."

"Well, let's go then." Will put his arm around her, and they walked out to his truck.

Back at the cabin, Katherine tidied up dirty plates and stray coffee cups while Will worked in the living room. He sat at his old upright piano, his fingers hovering above the keys, but not touching them, his eyes closed.

As she made her way around the tiny cabin, Katherine stopped in the doorway that connected the living room to the kitchen, silently watching Will. His face moved through emotions while his hands danced in the air. At first, his face was calm, relaxed, unwrinkled. His hands looked to be fluttering lightly above the midrange keys. But then, he frowned: eyes closed tightly, brows furrowed, and the corners of his mouth tensed downward. The wrinkle between his eyebrows creased deeply, as it often did when he fell deep into thought or frustration. His fingers crept toward the lower keys, and his hands looked rigid, aggressive, and almost angry.

Katherine had never observed Will so closely while he worked. Usually, she was painting outside or in the other room where the light was better. She had never witnessed this strange impassioned process void of any musical sound at all. For a moment, she thought she should leave the room, that perhaps she was intruding on a fragile or sacred practice, but she simply couldn't tear her eyes away from him.

As Will's hands mimed their way up to the higher notes, his face relaxed once again, and his eyebrows lifted. His beautiful mouth crept into a slight smile, and his fingers loosened as they moved more freely and gracefully above the keys. Katherine couldn't imagine what the music sounded like, but whatever she was witnessing was completely inspired; it was like magic.

"Hey, you." Will looked over at her.

"Oh! Hey. Sorry, I didn't mean to eavesdrop." Katherine had been admiring his strong hands and failed to notice that Will had opened his eyes.

"Busted." He winked. "So, what'd you think? It's beautiful, isn't it?" He was serious, looking back at the black and white keys.

"Well, that's hard to say. Either I was temporarily deaf or you didn't actually play any music." Katherine joined him on the bench.

"Oh, but I did." Will kissed her cheek. "Really, it plays me first. I listen and follow in my mind. The physical music comes later."

"Amazing." Katherine looked down at the keys. She had always wanted to play piano, but never learned.

"Would you like to hear it now?" Will asked.

"Yes. Can you tell me what it's about?" Katherine wanted to visualize the story.

"Okay. So it's a film—Spielberg, I think. Anyway, I guess it's about a ship transporting dangerous prisoners from America to Europe, and there's a terrible storm, and the ship is destroyed. There are only two survivors—a man and a woman—who manage to get themselves into a lifeboat. One of them is an innocent, wrongly convicted of murder, and the other is a guilty and dangerous murderer, but we don't know who is who. Then it turns into a bit of a love and survival story."

Katherine stared at Will with her eyes wide open. She was riveted. Will continued, "Anyway, this passage I'm working on here . . . It's for a scene with the two of them in the boat, just after the fiery ship has sunk. The sun is rising over the ocean's horizon, and they realize they are the only survivors."

Katherine turned to face the piano and closed her eyes. As Will played the actual keys this time, she let her imagination run wild with the scene he had described. It was remarkable. With only his hands, and the row of black and white keys, he was able to powerfully and magnificently communicate fear, desperation, terror and death, survival, and hope.

When he finished, Katherine could barely catch her breath. "Do it again." She smiled at him eagerly. "Please."

Will laughed and played it for her again.

This time when he finished, Katherine kept her eyes closed for a moment, anticipating what might happen next in the story. And before she could open her eyes, she felt Will's hand on her cheek and his lips upon hers.

They spent the rest of the afternoon making love. It was the passionate, strong, desperate kind of love. Katherine was leaving the next day, and neither of them wanted to say good-bye. They didn't speak much; they just reached for one another and held each other tightly. It was Katherine reassuring Will that everything would be okay, that she would come back and they would be together. And it was Will reminding Katherine that she belonged to him and that he would be there, waiting for her return.

~*~

That night at the inn Mr. Trust and Murray hosted a grand farewell dinner for Katherine, and nearly the entire town attended to wish her luck for the show. Mr. Trust decorated the lobby and dining room with elegant candles and fresh flowers, and Murray made an assortment of Katherine's favorite dishes: caprese salad, smoked salmon with capers, filet mignon, and homemade apple tarts for dessert.

"Send me a postcard of the Statue of Liberty!" Tony yelled across the room.

"You doofus. She'll be back in town by the time the card gets here." Matt shook his head.

"I'll try to find one for you, Tony." Katherine smiled and Tony blew her a kiss.

"I'm so excited for you," Ginger said as she hugged Katherine.

"That makes two of us," Matt said as he walked up to Ginger, handing her a fresh glass of champagne. He leaned down and kissed her softly. It would normally seem quite strange to see such a large, tough and tattooed man act so tenderly—but not Matt. He wore his heart on his sleeve, especially when it came to Ginger.

"Have you guys seen Will?" Katherine asked, looking around the crowded room. They had arrived together, but she hadn't seen him since. As she walked around the dining room, townspeople stopped her to shake her hand and congratulate her. It took her forever to make her way into the lobby.

"Hey! There you are." She walked up behind Will. He stood, sipping a glass of whiskey, admiring one of her early paintings she had donated to the inn for permanent display.

"Hey there, cutie." His smile melted her heart, as he put his hand low on her waist and pulled her toward him.

"Where have you been? Aren't you hungry?" Katherine looked up at Will, who continued to stare at the painting.

"I should be. After the day we had . . ." He looked down at her and winked. Then he sighed. "I just can't believe how far you've come. I mean it's the *Met*, Katherine." He shook his head.

"I know," she whispered. She still couldn't believe it herself. She wondered when it would feel real to her, if ever. Would it be when she landed in New York? Or perhaps when she installed the paintings on the walls of the museum? Or would it all feel like a dream to her until the party on opening night? Even then, she would likely have to pinch herself to believe it was happening. Though, the dream would feel incomplete without Will there.

When she tried to imagine the show—with her paintings hanging in the Metropolitan Museum of Art, New York's finest crowding around them—she always stopped at the vision of her standing by herself, all dressed up, at the peak of her artistic career, alone—without the one person she wanted there the most.

A clinking sound echoed from the dining room, someone tapping their spoon against their glass. It was Mr. Trust, "Katherine? Where is the artist?"

Katherine looked up at Will, silently begging him to read her mind, pleading with him to let go of his past and join her in New York. But he just smiled and gently pressed on her lower back, guiding her to the dining room.

Mr. Trust clinked his glass again to quiet down the room. "Ah, there she is—the star of the show. Katherine darling, a few words before you go?" He smiled and held out his hand. Everyone in the room stared at her happily, patiently waiting for her speech.

She cleared her throat, which had become suddenly stiff and hoarse. "I, um . . . I just can't thank you all enough." She felt her cheeks burn as she listened to her voice carry over the roomful of faces smiling at her expectantly. "I mean you opened your arms to me. I was an outsider, a city girl. You welcomed me to your town. You encouraged me and supported me in so many ways. I could never imagine . . ." She felt a lump rising in her throat. "I came to Bluewater Lake to escape. I didn't know what I would find, but . . ." She paused, sipped her champagne, and smiled at Mr. Trust. "But what I found is . . . family. And I hope to make you all very proud." Tears crept out from the corners of her eyes as she lifted her glass. "Thank you!"

Everyone cheered and applauded, and Katherine was instantly surrounded and bombarded with hugs and kisses. The party continued on into the early hours of the morning. Of course, the most resilient of party guests gathered round the piano while Mr. Trust and Ginger led them in their favorite ballads.

By sunrise, not a drop of champagne was to be found, and not a single soul was awake—except for Katherine, who groggily showered and quietly packed the few remaining items she would need for

New York. Will slept peacefully on her bed. She paused and smiled down at him. His hair was tousled and he was naked. But the sheet wrapped around one of his legs and across his hips perfectly—as one might prepare a model for a figure-drawing class. He would be a good model too—lean, but strong. His muscles were carved from physical life in the mountains, but he wasn't bulky. He was perfection.

Katherine sighed and leaned down to kiss his forehead.

"Good morning," she whispered, as he shifted.

Will struggled to open his eyes. When he did, they looked bluer than ever.

"Morning. You ready to go?" he sleepily asked as he held her hand, softly rubbing his thumb along the outsides of her fingers.

CHAPTER 29

As Will's truck rumbled quietly out of town, Katherine cracked the window and tried to calm her fretful mind. She was nervous about flying, and she was nervous about the show, but she was also excited about the show. She was excited to go back to New York, but she was also nervous to go back to New York. *What if the show is a bust? I'll be humiliated. What if I get back to Manhattan and realize how much I miss it?* And of course, perhaps above all else, she was so sad to leave Will.

Neither of them spoke a word as they made their way down the mountain. Katherine's suitcase slid around in the back, and she nervously handled her plane ticket in her lap. The fall colors were at their best, just as they had been when Katherine first arrived in Colorado. *How ironic,* she thought. Everything looked the same as it did when she nervously navigated her way to Bluewater over a year ago. Only this time, as they passed the rolling waves of golden yellow and deep red leaves mingling with the rich green pines and cool blue ponds, Katherine found it all quite familiar and comforting. The expansive wonder of Mother Nature had become her home, and she was careful not to take it for granted. She was thankful for the snow-capped mountains and the quiet streams, which had replaced the skyscrapers and busy streets of Manhattan. Katherine sighed deeply. She knew she would only be gone for a week, but she hoped the rapidly changing leaves would hang on until she returned. She had been so busy getting ready for the show that she hadn't had much time to get outside and enjoy her favorite season.

As Will merged onto the interstate, he glanced over at Katherine and she caught his eye. She tried to smile, but it felt unnatural today. Will reached over and took her hand in his, and then he brought her hand to his lips. He held it there for a moment, breathing in her skin, but still did not say a word.

The Denver airport was a madhouse, and Will struggled to find a spot to pull over alongside the curb. Angry travelers honked at one another, and airport security guards hustled people along. Katherine suddenly felt ill. Her hand trembled as she reached for her door. Will parked the truck and hopped out, grabbing her suitcase from the back. When he met her on the sidewalk, they stood for a moment, looking silently at one another.

"Move it along, folks." A grumpy heavy-set security guard walked by and nodded toward Will's truck.

Katherine looked up at Will. "Come with me. You can still change your mind." She didn't plan to say it, but the words spilled out before she could stop them. Will's eyes saddened. He picked her up and held her tightly so that her face was level with his, their noses touching.

"I can't." His throat tightened. "I wish I could . . . more than you know," he whispered and then kissed her passionately.

"Folks, wrap it up." The same curmudgeonly guard strolled back by them.

"Just a minute." Will glared at the guard, who rolled his eyes, and continued on to harass other travelers.

Katherine's eyes filled with tears, and Will wiped them away with his hands.

"Please don't cry. This is *your* moment, Katherine. I'll be thinking of you every second you're gone." Will kissed her again. She sniffled and nodded.

"Call me when you get to Andi's. I'm so proud of you," Will said through clenched teeth. He was mad at himself, Katherine could tell. But before she could say anything else, he kissed her forehead and walked back to his side of the truck, just as the guard approached them for the final time.

"I love you," Will said through the open window, as he turned on the ignition and then slowly drove away.

"I love you too," Katherine responded too late, standing motionless on the sidewalk, watching his truck drive out of sight.

As she sat at the gate, she sipped a latte and took a Valium. She didn't know who would be sitting next to her on the flight, but she knew for certain that she did not want to be trapped in a small seat alone with her restless thoughts and turbulence for the next four hours.

Fortunately, she had a window seat next to a sweet older lady wearing a floral print dress and droopy stockings with thick lens glasses and tight curly white hair. The lady smiled kindly at Katherine before returning her attention to her book, some kind of dirty romance novel with a very racy cover. Katherine's eyes became heavy as the plane lifted off the ground. She struggled to keep them open long enough to watch the massive mountains become tiny specks on the ground, and then she fell into a deep sleep.

"Excuse me, dear . . ."

Someone was tapping her gently on the shoulder.

"We're there, dear."

Katherine pried her heavy eyes open to see the lady with the romance novel, smiling at her.

"You're quite the sleeper! I don't think you moved a muscle the entire flight." She smiled and patted Katherine's hand, before standing stiffly and shuffling her way out of the row of seats, nervously shoving her dirty book quickly into her handbag as the flight attendant walked by.

Katherine looked out the window and was relieved to see the familiar exterior of the terminal at JFK airport. The Valium had worked wonders.

Outside, the sky was clear, but darker than the afternoon sky in Colorado. The city air seemed to cast a sort of veil over the pureness of its glow. Katherine took a deep breath, willing herself to stand

and walk. She was the last one on the plane. *There's no turning back now.*

"There she is!" Andi jumped up and down and shouted from the other side of the crowded baggage claim carousel. Sebastian stood with her, craning his neck to see.

Katherine waved at her friend lethargically, as Andi came running toward her, in stiletto heels, of course. They hugged for a long moment, and then Sebastian walked over to say hello.

"How was your flight?" Andi asked, looking concerned at Katherine's lack of enthusiasm.

"Fine. Valium." Katherine smiled and nodded.

"Ah, I see. Well done." Andi grabbed Katherine's purse, and the three of them waited for her suitcase. Before they left the airport, Sebastian got a coffee for Katherine, and she began to perk up.

"So, no Will?" Andi asked quietly as Sebastian helped the driver load her bags into the back of the black Mercedes he had hired.

Katherine shook her head dejectedly.

"Don't worry. This will be a fabulous week anyway. I promise!" Andi squeezed her hand and they slid into the back seat.

"Yes. I suspect it will be a week to remember," Sebastian chimed in confidently as he sat down in the front. He continued over his shoulder, "But it won't be all fun and games, of course. Your paintings should be arriving tomorrow morning, Katherine. And we will begin installation immediately. I have assembled a team to assist you. And then we have some meetings arranged the following day—a private preview of the show with the *New York Times* and another viewing with the Curator of Contemporary Art from the Tate Modern."

"Yes, fine. Work tomorrow, blah, blah, blah, but fun tonight!" Andi retorted and then blew Sebastian a kiss, as he smiled and shook his head.

Katherine closed her eyes and breathed deeply. Sebastian spoke so casually about the show, so comfortably. But when she thought about talking with the *New York Times* and the curator from the Tate Modern, her heart began to beat wildly, and her throat tightened.

The Mercedes drove out of the airport and headed into the city. It wasn't long before Andi was on the phone with one of her new brokers, unwaveringly ordering the poor soul to stay at the office late and finish drafting an offer for a top client. Meanwhile, Sebastian worked quietly in the front seat, replying to pressing emails and politely suggesting less congested routes to the driver. Katherine looked out the window at the metropolis she had called home for so many years. But now, as the car slowly made its way across the Queensboro Bridge, the city felt strange to her. Her senses were overwhelmed by the quantity of cars and people and by the density of the tall buildings engulfed in a myriad of sounds and lights. In only a year, Katherine had transformed from city mouse to country mouse, and right now, she longed for the country.

It took over an hour in heavy traffic to arrive at their destination: Andi and Sebastian's new apartment on Park Avenue, situated just two blocks from the Met. Park had always been one of

Katherine's favorite streets in Manhattan. It was wide, with large spacious sidewalks and nice trees, classic awnings, and beautiful high-end retail storefronts. And its proximity to the Met was, of course, an added bonus.

She felt better as she stepped out onto the sidewalk. The sun was setting behind the tallest buildings to the west, and the humid autumn air had a touch of coolness.

"And here we are dawwwwwling!" Andi had just finished her phone call and gestured proudly toward a regal building with an elegant gray and gold awning over the entry.

"Oh, Andi, it's wonderful!" Katherine's energy was slowly returning. Things began to feel familiar, and she detected a sense of ease washing over her. She was possibly even a bit exhilarated, sensing the Met so nearby.

"Just wait until you see the rest!" Andi squealed and took her by the hand. They lived in the penthouse, which had a clear view of the Met and Central Park behind it. Katherine gasped as she stepped out onto the balcony. She stared at the grand entrance of the Met, desperate to walk through those doors again.

"So?" Andi stepped out behind her and handed her a glass of champagne.

"Andi .. it's . . . amazing." She gazed out across the panorama sprawled before her. From this vantage point, she realized there was a part of her that did, in fact, miss New York.

"I knew you'd love it." Andi lifted her glass. "Here's to you, my dear friend."

Katherine clinked her glass against Andi's, "And to *you* . . . and to Sebastian." They giggled and sipped the champagne as dusk faded to night, and only the brightest stars made their presence known above the city lights.

Inside the apartment, Katherine marveled at Sebastian's personal art collection, one that rivaled most museums she had visited. He owned original Rothkos, Braques, and some remarkable works by Russian abstract expressionists, among many other intriguing pieces. She could easily spend hours studying each work, while asking Sebastian a million questions, but she knew Andi was anxious to go out and celebrate, and she was starving.

Sebastian took them to dine at *Daniel*, one of the best French restaurants in the city, and the three of them stayed late into the night, sipping the finest French champagne and sampling heavenly black cod, lamb chops, and lobster salad. The dinner was relaxing and full of laughter—an elegant distraction to the major event that would be commanding Katherine's time and attention over the next few days.

Andi and Sebastian were utterly smitten with one another. They were tender and loving, but they teased each other playfully. They were opposites, but they were equals. Katherine smiled as she watched them; she was so happy for Andi. And then for a moment, she was sad.

She missed Will.

CHAPTER 30

The following morning, Andi had to leave early to meet with clients, and she made plans to meet Katherine and Sebastian at home for dinner. The long trip from Colorado, followed by several glasses of champagne and rich French food, had sent Katherine into a blissful comatose sleep, and she awoke feeling refreshed and invigorated. She dressed in a simple tee shirt, leggings, and sneakers, and she threw her hair up into a bun. It would be a long, physical day at the museum, and she could hardly wait to go.

As she and Sebastian walked across Park Avenue, Sebastian prepped her for the day.

"We will be meeting with my staff in the Contemporary Wing. The installation team will work with you and help you to realize your vision for the show. They are all completely at your disposal for the day, so don't be shy." Sebastian winked and smiled. He could tell that she was a ball of nerves. "It's going to be great, Katherine. My last artist had a sell-out show."

"Wow, that's great. I'm not worried about selling or anything. I just . . . I guess I still can't believe this is happening." Katherine felt like a child approaching the gates at Disney World for the first time. Her heart raced, and her feet dared to sprint well beyond the speed at which they walked. But she refrained from losing her composure. Today was just the first step, and she knew she'd have to pace herself through an unforgettable week of overwhelming experiences.

As they crossed the bustling 5th Avenue and approached the grand staircase she had happily climbed so many times in her life, Katherine thought she might cry. When she'd left New York, she didn't know if she'd ever return, and leaving the Met had been the hardest part. Now, only a year later, she was back! And she was not entering the Met as merely a daytime visitor, but as a participating component of the museum. She tried to wrap her head around the reality of it all, while her eyes drank in the grandeur of the building she loved so much.

"Ma'am?" The impatient security guard held her hand out toward Katherine.

"Huh? Oh, my purse. Sorry!" She was too busy drooling over the lobby that she had forgotten to hand over her personal items for inspection.

Sebastian waited patiently for her to pass through the checkpoint, and then with a quick and habitual swipe of his ID badge, he led her through an unmarked, seemingly insignificant door she had never even noticed before. Katherine followed him through narrow hallways glaring with fluorescent lights, white undecorated walls, and white tile floors. She felt as though she were walking through some kind of maze or a mental asylum. Their footsteps echoed as they walked, and Katherine wondered how Sebastian knew right from left. There were no signs, and yet he easily sauntered straight along, would turn left down one of many indistinct hallways then right down another. She followed quietly, suspecting after a few minutes that he might be playing a joke on her, but then they stopped, and Sebastian opened a door labeled *Contemporary Gallery #4*.

They walked into a spacious square-shaped room. The walls were pristine and white, and the floor was a beautiful natural wood. There were no windows in the room, but it was beautifully illuminated with gallery lighting. On the far side of the room, there was an opening, public access into the gallery and out to the rest of the museum. A group of nine men and women waited to greet Sebastian and Katherine. They were all dressed identically in black tee shirts and black pants, and they smiled and nodded at her as they approached.

"Katherine, I'd like to introduce you to your installation team." Sebastian gestured toward the group. "Everyone, this is the artist, Katherine Ross."

It sounded so official, so important: *"the artist, Katherine Ross."* She felt her cheeks burn as she smiled and waved at the friendly staff.

Sebastian continued, "I have some meetings this morning. Katherine, the team will take care of everything for you. Your paintings are just over there." He pointed to the left side of the room. Katherine's heart jumped. *They had arrived safe and sound!* All twenty-five paintings were unwrapped and resting delicately along the wall.

"If you could hang four along this wall here and then seven paintings on each of the remaining walls, that will leave us room to present your bio here, near the entrance." Sebastian was all business as he gestured toward a large space. Katherine sensed that

279

he was very good at his job. "The rest is up to you. Arrange the works according to your preference." Sebastian turned to walk toward the door that led to the secret white hallway. "And Katherine?" He stopped.

"Yes?" she replied anxiously, her head already spinning with ideas.

"Have fun." Sebastian smiled and winked and then disappeared behind the door.

"So? How did it go today?" Andi sat down next to Katherine on the balcony. It was late, and they had all just returned to the apartment. Sebastian was inside ordering Chinese takeout, and Katherine and Andi had changed into their pajamas and sat with blankets wrapped around their shoulders. As Katherine sipped the delicious red wine Sebastian had poured, she looked out over the city lights.

"It was . . . incredible." She sighed deeply. "And it was exhausting." She laid her head back on the cushion. Every muscle in her body ached. After Sebastian had left her in the gallery, she worked with the installation team to design the perfect exhibition. They all worked enthusiastically through the day, forgetting to break for lunch.

First, they arranged the paintings according to color themes. And while the concept looked great, Katherine found it difficult to connect with emotionally. Then they mixed and matched according to size. She liked the variety and energy in the arrangement, but something was still missing for her—it just didn't feel right. Finally, she decided to organize the paintings according to season. One wall held the paintings she completed during winter, one wall for fall, one for summer, and one for spring.

When the team finished hanging the final piece—the winter painting Katherine completed down on the icy beach, that one fateful day when everything changed for her and Will—she stepped back, took a deep breath, and looked around the gallery. It was perfect. Each wall was a chapter of the story, a story about Bluewater. And as Katherine stood in the center of the gallery and slowly turned around, she breathed a sigh of satisfaction. This was it. This was her show—it was her love letter to Bluewater. The team cheered and applauded when she laughed and nodded. It was all so exciting, and Katherine felt exhilarated. But for just a quick moment, she felt a pain in her heart. *If only Will could see this . . .*

The next morning, she sipped her French press coffee and stared blankly at the clothes laid out on her bed in the guestroom. What does one wear for an interview with the New York Times and the Curator of the Tate?

"I cleared my calendar!" Katherine turned to see Andi standing in the doorway. "I'm all yours today, for moral support." Andi came into the room and looked over the clothes.

"Oh, thank God. I don't think I can do this alone." Katherine didn't know what to expect. Her interview with Pete Steinberg back in Bluewater was nerve-wracking enough, but this was the *New York Times!*

"Don't be silly. You most certainly could do it alone. But I don't want to miss out on the fun." Andi winked and nudged Katherine's side. "That one." She pointed to a fitted black blazer lying on the bed. "With those and . . . those." Then she pointed to ripped skinny jeans and cobalt blue stilettos.

"Really? You're sure?" Katherine asked, thankful for her friend's indisputable fashion sense.

"Definitely. It gives the 'I'm being professional, but I'm still a tormented moody artist on the inside' effect. You'll be a total knockout." Andi gave her a hug and left her to get ready. Katherine laughed as she shut the door. She had encountered many "tormented and moody" artists throughout art school and in the gallery world, but she never thought of herself that way. In fact, she was still so new at this whole artist thing that she really didn't know what kind of artist she was.

"Good morning!" Sebastian sat at the kitchen counter with the paper and a cup of coffee. He was reading the *New York Times Arts* section. "So, I will meet you ladies in the lobby at ten, sharp, and we will head to the gallery for the interview." He casually nibbled on a blueberry scone. "Katherine, you will be talking with Harriet Hughes. She's one of the most celebrated writers at the *Times*, and she is very excited to meet you."

"Wow. She's excited to meet *me*?" She was starving before she walked into the kitchen, but now her stomach was suddenly in knots.

"Of course she is. Who wouldn't be?" Andi answered decisively as she walked around the corner.

"I don't know. I just worry. I don't really have any kind of dramatic, life-altering story. What if . . .? What if she finds me . . . boring?" Katherine picked at a scone. Her heartburn began to flare up.

"Nonsense," Sebastian replied confidently as he packed up his briefcase. "Your art speaks *for* you, Katherine. They don't need another clichéd, overdramatized real-life saga. They find that excitement and thrill, that emotional revolution they seek, right in your paintings." He put on a gorgeous, perfectly pressed navy-colored suit jacket and kissed Andi on the cheek. Before he walked out the door, he turned and smiled at Katherine. "They simply want to meet the face behind the brilliance." And then he left.

"So, what do you say?" Andi had a mouthful of scone and looked at Katherine expectantly. "Shall we go for a walk in the park? Get some fresh air before the interview?"

"Yes, please." Katherine smiled.

The park was just as she had left it a year ago, flawlessly radiating in its timeless autumn splendor. The all-knowing trees watched over those who walked the paths and picnicked on the grass, while their deep red leaves shifted in the sunshine. A gentle breeze plucked some of the leaves from the branches, inviting them to pirouette through the air before falling to the ground. The air was brisk, but the sun kissed her cheeks with its last rays of warmth—a final farewell before the imminent winter would nestle into the city.

"Gosh, I missed this place." Katherine said, much to her own surprise, as they walked under an old stone bridge, sipping lattes.

"It missed you too." Andi smiled. "But not as much as I missed you." She wrapped her arm through Katherine's.

They followed the path through a dense garden covered by a tunnel of branches, and Katherine heard a familiar sound up ahead—music. Her pace quickened, and she followed the path around a narrow bend. And there, in a small grassy clearing, was the harpist! Katherine squinted to be sure. Indeed, it was the same harp player she encountered the day she broke down in the park, after everything fell apart with Michael, the day she decided to change her life. It seemed like years and years had passed since she last stood and watched the peaceful woman sway to the enchanting music echoing outward from her fingers, which danced effortlessly along the strings. She looked the same: still simply and exquisitely content, still blissfully lost in her music.

"Katherine?" Andi asked, wondering why they stopped.

Katherine smiled as tears crept down her cheeks. The last time she stood and listened to this harp, her life was in shambles. Everything was uncertain; she didn't know who she was or where she would go; she was broken and lost. But today, she stood and listened to the music, breathing happiness and hope and love. So much had changed for Katherine, but this harpist looked as though not a day had passed in her life.

Laughing out loud, Katherine wiped her cheeks and hugged a very confused Andi. The harpist looked up and glanced over at them. She caught Katherine's eye, smiled warmly, and nodded once, before returning her gaze to her beloved instrument.

"Oh, hon, we gotta go. We have to be at the Met in twenty," Andi said as she checked her phone. "You good?" she asked as they turned to walk back down the path.

Katherine smiled. "Yeah. I'm good."

CHAPTER 31

"Katherine Ross, I'm pleased to introduce you to Harriet Hughes from the *New York Times*." Sebastian walked Katherine over to a tiny woman, probably in her late thirties, with short jet-black hair and giant red-framed glasses that threatened to swallow her entire face. She wore a jean jacket and green corduroy pants and didn't appear to wear an ounce of makeup. But she had a kindness in her eyes, and she smiled welcomingly at Katherine.

"Miss Ross, it is truly a pleasure," Harriet said as she gently shook Katherine's hand. She gestured toward the large bench perfectly situated in the center of the gallery, surrounded by Katherine's paintings. "Shall we?"

Sebastian and Andi excused themselves from the room, and Katherine took a deep shaky breath as she sat down with Harriet. Harriet retrieved a sleek-looking recorder from her pocket and pulled a pen from her other pocket as she opened her leather-bound notebook to a page of pre-drafted questions.

"Miss Ross . . ." she began.

"Oh, please, call me Katherine."

"Okay, Katherine, I must tell you I'm a huge fan." Harriet smiled, looking around the vibrant room alive with color and light. "And that makes my objective review very difficult to approach."

"Thank you so much," Katherine replied bashfully. Harriet was so warm and approachable. Katherine almost forgot she was speaking to the *New York Times*.

"What strikes me most is your ability to marry contemporary art style with the timeless spirit of traditional master work. Is that something you do intentionally?" Harriet marveled at the paintings along the *Winter* wall as she awaited Katherine's answer.

"Honestly? I'd have to say that nothing about my work is intentional." Katherine thought about the lake and how it held a wonderful power over her when she painted.

"Really? What do you mean by that? I mean . . . how can you achieve this rich uniqueness and mature consistency in your work without intention?" Harriet was baffled and intrigued.

"Well, I leave each morning with my easel and with the *intention* to paint." Katherine thought for a moment. "But beyond that step, I kind of lose myself in the process. I guess it's almost as if I lose consciousness while I paint, and then when the piece is finished, I wake up and see what I've done." She blushed as she heard herself speak. She probably sounded like an idiot or an insane person.

Harriet couldn't write fast enough, even though her little recorder seemed to be functioning just fine.

"And has it always been that way for you? With painting?" she asked.

"Before this past year, I hadn't painted in a very long time—nearly a decade. The last time I painted, I was just out of art school and thought the world was mine to devour. But I guess I'd say that, no, that is not how I painted back then." She paused and tried to remember painting in Italy. "When I was younger, I think there was more of a competitive drive motivating my work. I was passionate and wanted to capture beauty, but there was a sense of urgency, like, if I didn't paint enough or didn't paint in a certain way, I may not become successful." She had never fully realized the psychology of her art school mentality before, but after a year in Bluewater, a lot of things from her life were brought into clarity.

"That's fascinating. What changed? Aside from the ten years passing by?" Harriet smiled and waited anxiously for an answer.

"I think it's *because* I took that time away. And then, when I allowed myself to paint again, it was for me and not for anyone else. It wasn't for fame or success; it was just raw and pure. I live in a place now where I'm surrounded by unimaginable beauty, and I think that overpowers my intentional thought. I surrender to it, and this is what happens." Katherine gestured around the room.

"I have to say, Katherine, I think you are the first artist I've interviewed to answer so frankly." She grinned, acknowledging Katherine's nervousness. "It's a good thing—it's refreshing. No bells or whistles. You relinquish your control, and you speak, and obviously paint, with honesty." Harriet spoke as she wrote. *Was she writing what she was saying? Or was she speaking one thing and writing another? That would be impressive.*

Harriet asked a few more questions regarding Katherine's technique and inspiration for the show, and then she asked Katherine to walk her through the gallery and say a few words about each painting. They laughed a lot, and Katherine eased into the interview quite comfortably. Harriet was friendly and had some remarkably kind things to say regarding her work. She particularly enjoyed the *Fall* series and the fiery romantic colors.

As they finished discussing the *Spring* wall, Harriet called in her photographer, Jasper, to take some shots of Katherine in the gallery, standing alongside certain paintings and sitting pensively on the bench. At the end of the interview, Harriet hugged Katherine and thanked her for the opportunity.

"I will be at the opening tomorrow. My editor is coming too!" she declared enthusiastically. "Congratulations, Katherine. You are a master painter, and the best part is you don't even know it." She winked as she tucked her recorder back into her pocket and wandered casually out of the gallery.

"Oh, my gosh! Am I in heaven?" Katherine gasped as she followed the secretary into Sebastian's enormous office. To Katherine's surprise, Sebastian and Andi had hired out a catered lunch, and small tables were set up with white table cloths and covered with beautiful platters of shrimp cocktail, sushi, assorted salads, French rolls and butter, and ice cold Perrier. Another table in the corner was delightfully covered in an array of colorful and delicate pastries.

"Well, we figured you should fuel up for your next meeting." Andi grinned and poured a glass of sparkling water for Katherine. Sebastian's office was just as Katherine would have imagined it to be. It was classic, with luscious dark woods and gorgeous velvet upholstery. One entire wall was a built-in bookshelf stacked full with hundreds of fine-art books. The far wall was not a wall at all, but floor-to-ceiling windows overlooking the park. Katherine grabbed a roll, smeared it with the creamy butter, and then stood by the window looking out over the magnificent autumn landscape.

"What a terrible view you have here, Sebastian." She smiled and Sebastian laughed.

"Ah, judging by your ability to make a casual joke, do I dare presume that the interview went well?" Andi remarked, raising her eyebrows expectantly.

"Yes, it did. Harriet is wonderful." Katherine breathed a sigh of relief and loaded a plate with some salmon skin rolls.

"She is indeed. And a fantastic writer. I can't wait to see what she does with your show." Sebastian sipped some water and cleared his throat. "Now, after lunch, I will bring you back to the gallery to meet Duncan Bristow, Curator of Contemporary Arts at the Tate." He paused. "Duncan is extremely selective about which art events he attends throughout the year, and he is a notorious snob. So it says something that he is here to see you—to see your work."

"Annnnnd, I'm nervous again," Katherine said with a mouthful of shrimp.

"Don't sweat it, lady. You've already locked in the Met, and you've wooed the *Times* with ease. Some snooty British guy doesn't stand a chance." Andi spoke confidently with a mouthful of puff pastry. Sebastian regarded her lovingly.

After lunch, Sebastian and Andi accompanied Katherine back to the gallery. When they first walked in, the room appeared to be empty, but then Katherine noticed a tall gentleman standing quietly in the corner, closely studying one of her more colorful and heavily textured *Summer* pieces. He wore a beautiful, tailored suit and stood with his hands behind his back, as one is instructed to do at a young age when leaning in to look at important art in museums.

"Ah, Duncan!" Sebastian walked over to the man, and they shook hands amicably.

When the man turned around, Katherine was surprised to see that he was quite young; he couldn't be much older than she, and he was quite handsome. He had a strong, classic brow and Greek nose, with auburn hair and green eyes.

"Sebastian! Good to see you!" Duncan responded with a thick British accent and a huge smile.

"Duncan, this is Katherine Ross," Sebastian said proudly, as Katherine walked over.

Duncan's eyes lit up and he smiled widely. "Katherine. It is my profound pleasure to meet you." He took her hand in both of his. "Your work has captivated me and my staff over the past few months, and I'm delighted to finally see it in person."

"Thank you, Mr. Bristow. Thank you so much. It's an honor." She felt her cheeks warm. It was probably his accent and his impeccable attire, but she felt like she was shaking hands with royalty.

"And this is my girlfriend, Andi." Sebastian brought Andi over to stand next to Katherine.

"Lovely to meet you, Andi. You are more beautiful than Sebastian let on." Duncan kissed her hand.

"So are you." Andi joked and they all laughed. She was always brilliant at breaking the ice.

For the next hour, they all walked around the room, their voices echoing as they discussed certain pieces from Katherine's collection. Duncan would observe some of the paintings intently without saying a word and then ask several pointed questions about others. Sebastian and Andi followed behind, remaining quiet for the most part, but joining in on casual conversation when appropriate. As they walked and talked, Katherine became more comfortable with Duncan. She still found him intimidating, but his disposition was kind and warm. He was honest, too, and would openly tell her why he thought certain pieces were stronger than others.

As they circled around to where they began, Duncan stopped in front of the largest piece in the show, a five-foot square *Spring* canvas. Katherine had painted it in the gazebo one rainy morning. A dense fog had hovered over the lake, and some of the spring flowers had started to pop up along the shoreline. Some would undoubtedly find the overwhelmingly gray palette of the painting sad or depressing, but Katherine found it to be extremely peaceful and refreshing. She could smell the wet grass and the damp spring air in Bluewater as she stood and looked at it. And the flowers signified new beginnings, with subtle but resilient hues of purple and yellow and green peering through the fog.

"I will be purchasing this piece for the permanent collection at the Tate Modern," Duncan said matter-of-factly. He smiled over his shoulder at Katherine, who stared back at him, dumbfounded. She couldn't believe what she had heard. One of *her* paintings would be in the permanent collection at the Tate in London!

Andi cleared her throat and jabbed Katherine in her side with her elbow. Katherine snapped out of her stupor. "Mr. Bristow, I don't know what to say!"

Duncan laughed. "Please, call me Duncan." They continued to stand in front of the large painting. "And I have more I'd like to discuss with you. Can we all do dinner tonight?" He looked at Sebastian hopefully.

"Yes, of course, Duncan. I'll have my assistant make the arrangements." Sebastian shook his hand and strolled out of the gallery.

"Wonderful. I'll see you ladies this evening." Duncan bowed his head and walked out behind Sebastian, reaching for his cell to make some calls.

"Oh, my God!" Andi cried as she and Katherine hugged and jumped up and down when they were sure Duncan had gone.

"Katherine, you're going to be in the *Tate*! It's unbelievable!" Andi smiled and continued. "Well, I mean . . . It's *completely* believable—look at this!

You're amazing! I'm so proud of you!" She gestured toward the painting.

"Thank you, Andi." Katherine choked back tears, trying not to get emotional. "None of it would have happened without you." She hugged her friend tightly as one of Sebastian's assistants walked in and placed a small red "SOLD" sticker on the label for the spring painting. Katherine paused and smiled at the red dot. *It's just a tiny little sticker. It seems so insignificant, but it means so much.*

As they walked out of the gallery, she tried to call Will. She wanted to tell him the exciting news. But his phone went straight to voicemail. They hadn't actually spoken to one another since she arrived in New York. He had tried to call her that morning, but her phone was on silent during her interview with Harriet, and he didn't leave a message. They had sent a couple of texts back and forth, but she hadn't heard his voice since he dropped her off at the airport.

Katherine sighed. She missed Will. She wanted to hear his voice. But she was grateful for the distractions. They would do dinner with Duncan tonight, and the exhibition would open tomorrow. Her stomach tumbled as she thought about the show. Sebastian said it was forecasted to have record attendance. And she still couldn't believe one of her paintings would forever live in the world famous collection at the Tate. The thought made her pause. Duncan had said, "He had more to discuss with her." They had spent the entire afternoon in the gallery, discussing her work. *What else was there left to discuss?*

CHAPTER 32

"Here's to the lovely Miss Ross and her marvelous work!" Duncan announced as he lifted his glass of champagne.

"Here, here!" Sebastian chimed in.

Katherine's cheeks burned. She sat between Andi and Duncan in an intimate booth at some lavish Japanese restaurant in the Upper West Side.

"Thank you, Mr. Bris . . . I mean, Duncan." Katherine didn't know why she felt so nervous. The hard part was over. The show was installed, she had survived the interview with the *New York Times*, and she had already sold her largest painting to the Tate. She should be relieved; she should be ecstatic. But there was something about Duncan and his proximity to her that made her feel uneasy. He was very kind and frequently smiled warmly at her as they sat and sampled Japanese delicacies, courtesy of the restaurant's owner, Mr. Murakami, a friend of Sebastian's.

"Now then, I guess we should get on to some business." Duncan smiled and turned toward Katherine. "I've been conferencing with my colleagues, and we have a proposition for you," he said, sipping his champagne.

Before he could continue, Andi interjected, "Oh Sebastian, I think I see Mr. Sanchez at the bar. Be a dear and come say hello with me." She fixed her eyes intensely on Sebastian's, not so nonchalantly hinting that they leave the table.

"Mr. San? Are you sure? That doesn't look like—" Sebastian began to object, but Andi must have kicked his shin under the table, because he stopped abruptly and corrected himself. "Oh, *Mr. Sanchez.* Yes, I see him now." He looked like he was in pain and also very confused. But Andi pushed him out of the booth and grabbed his hand, dragging him toward the elegant low-lit bar.

Katherine felt warm and slightly panicked. Duncan smiled and seemed perfectly at ease.

"Anyhow, as I was saying, we have something we'd like to propose to you." He shifted in his seat so that his body was facing Katherine's.

"We are very pleased to include the painting in our permanent collection. But we are greedy Brits, and we want more." He grinned, trying to lighten the mood. "Katherine, we haven't encountered work like yours for a long time, if ever. And the fact that it comes from someone so young, someone so real . . . It's just . . . Well, it's fascinating, is what it is." His eyes became serious, and he looked deeply at her. "You're this wonderfully pure, untainted, artistic genius. And, well, it would be irresponsible of me to just let you slip away."

She realized at that moment that she didn't know if Duncan was speaking on a personal level or strictly business. *Was he flirting with her?* At first, she thought he was just being nice, but something about the way he looked at her made her sense something more. Katherine remained speechless. To Duncan, it probably seemed like she was playing it cool, patiently waiting for him to go on. But she simply could not sort her thoughts fast enough to formulate any kind of response.

Duncan took a deep breath and continued, "We'd like to offer you a year-long residency at the Tate. We feel that people should see you in action, that the art-adoring public should witness the magic itself, the brilliance of your process. You painting . . ." He trailed off, trying to read Katherine's reaction. But she just stared at him with wide eyes. "Of course, you will be handsomely paid. And the museum would put you up in a beautiful flat nearby. We'd help you travel all around Europe. You could spend a weekend painting in Paris and another in Tuscany. The possibilities are endless. We'll wine and dine you. You wouldn't spend a dime. To the Tate, you'd be royalty."

Katherine cleared her throat and reached for a glass of water. She had received so many offers when the *Denver Post* article was published all those months ago, but nothing on such a grand scale. It wasn't the money that enticed her, but the idea of living in Europe for a year, painting at one of the biggest museums in the world. *She could paint in Florence again.*

"You are already making a splash in the art world, Katherine. We want to help you make your mark on history. Your work deserves to be seen, to be experienced. It would be a tremendous honor for me to have you there." Duncan continued to hold her gaze, and he gently took her hand in his.

Katherine sat paralyzed for a moment. Perhaps it was the Japanese champagne, but she suddenly felt very dizzy. When she put her head down to breathe, she saw Duncan's hand holding hers, and she quickly pulled her hand away.

What am I doing?

"I'm sorry. I didn't mean to upset you." Duncan looked stunned. "Katherine, are you alright?" He was obviously concerned.

"I-I don't know. I, um . . . I need some air." She excused herself from the booth just as Andi and Sebastian were walking back over, laughing, with fresh cocktails in hand.

"Katherine? Where are you going?" Andi asked as Katherine pushed by them.

She shivered, breathing in the cold night air outside the restaurant, losing herself in the chaotic New York street noise—a modern nighttime symphony of car horns, passing conversations, and some kind of heavy bass rap music thumping from a parked Escalade down by the corner.

Katherine didn't like the effect Duncan had on her. But it wasn't his fault—it was hers. He was perfectly kind, and he didn't know she was involved with someone else. In another time, if there were no Bluewater, if there were no Will, Duncan would be perfect for Katherine, and she was mad at herself for how *she* felt about him.

She loved Will; she loved him so much that it hurt. But he wasn't here, and for the first time since she left Bluewater, Katherine let herself feel angry. She knew why he couldn't come, but she wanted to be more important to him. She wanted to be worth him facing his past and conquering his pain. She had let herself feel tempted by Duncan because she was mad at Will.

"Katherine?" Duncan stepped out onto the sidewalk and stood nervously in front of her. "Katherine, I am so sorry. I didn't mean to cross the line. I came here for the show, for the paintings. I didn't expect you to be so beautiful, and I forgot my place. Please . . . please don't let my behavior affect your decision about the residency. I promise it won't happen again." He spoke so sincerely and remorsefully. His eyes begged her for forgiveness.

"Duncan, I—" Katherine began to speak, but he interrupted.

"Look. It's a big decision. Why don't you think on it and we'll touch base tomorrow, okay?"

"Okay, tomorrow." Katherine gave him a courtesy smile. Too much had happened that day, and she welcomed the mental reprieve. They walked back inside to join Sebastian and Andi, and the foursome kept the conversation light as the evening hours grew late. Duncan generously picked up the tab and thanked Sebastian as they walked outside.

"I will see you all tomorrow at the big event." He smiled shyly, apologetically, at Katherine and climbed into the back of a private car. And then he was gone.

"Okay. Spill it." Andi demanded eagerly as Sebastian called their driver.

"Spill what?" Katherine asked, exhausted and desperate to lie down.

"Oh, don't be coy. What did Duncan want to talk about?" Andi wrapped her arm through Katherine's and looked at her expectantly, like a fifteen-year-old girl in the locker room wanting the gory details from a first kiss.

Suddenly, Katherine had a strange feeling.

"Did you know?" she asked Andi flatly.

"Know what?" Andi suddenly appeared anxious and avoided eye contact.

"Did you *know* what Duncan was going to propose?" Katherine asked, refusing to leave the sidewalk even though the car had arrived and Sebastian waited patiently with the door open.

"No! Well, not exactly . . ." Andi looked around at the passersby. Katherine remained still with her arms crossed, waiting for an explanation.

"Look. Sebastian and Duncan talked this afternoon, after we left the gallery. I guess Duncan mentioned something about you coming to work at the Tate, but Sebastian didn't elaborate." Andi sighed. "I'm sorry. I didn't know it would upset you. We wanted it to be a surprise. Wait. Isn't this *good* news?" She looked perplexed.

"You know how I feel about leaving Bluewater, Andi! You know where I stand. This week—this show—was special. It's the Met! *This show* was the exception, only this one." She nearly yelled. "How dare you dangle this in front of me?" Katherine looked over at Sebastian, who was completely stupefied and remained motionless by the car. Katherine looked back at Andi. "What about Will, Andi?" She stared intensely at her friend, daring her to answer.

"What *about* Will, Katherine?! He isn't even here. He didn't come to support you for potentially the biggest moment of your life! Is that how it's going to be forever? You deserve more than that. He's holding you back!" Tears sprang into Andi's eyes. "Are you seriously going to walk away from your dreams, from *the Tate,* for some *guy* who can't even get over his own baggage?" Andi's eyes widened, and she put her hand over her open mouth. She couldn't believe what she just said.

Katherine didn't speak. But her icy glare said everything. Andi floundered, desperately trying to recover from her huge misstep, "Katherine, I . . . I'm so sorry. I didn't mean . . ."

"It's fine," Katherine said coldly. "I think I'm going to walk. See you at home."

Only with her back turned and at a safe distance away, did she allow the tears to pour down her face.

It was nearly midnight when she returned to the apartment. When the elevator door opened to the living room, she found Andi sitting in her robe on the couch, her cheeks stained with mascara-tinted tears. Katherine sat down on the other end of the couch and wrapped herself in a blanket as she looked silently at her friend.

"Oh, Katherine, I'm so sorry," Andi whispered, her voice raspy from crying. "I had no right to say what I said. I feel terrible." She sniffled.

Katherine sighed as she shivered under the warmth and softness of the blanket. "It's okay." She grinned wearily at Andi.

"No, it's not okay. I'm a monster. I know Will means the world to you!" She began to cry again. "I just . . . I miss you so much, and I'm so proud of you. I want you to have everything you've ever dreamed of."

"I know. And, yes, Will does mean the world to me. But . . ." She paused, carefully contemplating what she was about to say. "But maybe you're right." She looked down at her hands. The words didn't taste good in her mouth.

Andi looked confused. "What do you mean?"

Katherine took a deep shaky breath. "Well, I mean maybe I should consider the residency." Her heart hurt as she spoke. Part of her knew she was happy in Bluewater, that she loved her life there, and that she was happy with Will. But now, another part of her worried that Will's past would haunt them forever, that his pain would become her pain. She had felt free, freer than ever when she was with him. But that was when they were in Bluewater. *If Will refused to leave, ever, even for her, would that freedom begin to feel like a prison?*

Deep in her heart, Katherine knew that she didn't want to go to London. Tate or no Tate, she didn't want to leave Bluewater. But if Will refused to commit his whole self to her, if he really could not let go of his past, would their future ever truly belong to them? If she decided to accept Duncan's offer, at least she would be taking charge of her own future.

She yawned. Her thoughts twisted into a thick fog in her mind, and her body ached. "I don't know. I need to sleep on it. Big day tomorrow." She stood and folded the blanket. Andi stood nervously, still looking devastated and ashamed. Katherine wrapped her arms tightly around her. "Thank you."

"For what?" Andi asked.

"For always looking out for me." Katherine smiled. "It may drive me crazy sometimes, but I love you for it."

CHAPTER 33

As she climbed into bed, her heart pounded. *Could she really consider leaving Bluewater?* She reached for her phone. No messages. She dialed Will's number. Maybe he would answer and they would talk, and maybe after hearing his voice, she would remember her place—she would remember her heart.

She had found herself in Bluewater; she felt grounded and safe and fulfilled for the first time in her life. Did the hype of the show and the *New York Times* and Duncan and the Tate really have the power to shake her from her newfound strength?

Ring.

Ring.

No answer.

Katherine held the phone tightly to her chest, hoping Will would call right back. She couldn't keep her heavy eyes open another moment, and her exhausted body succumbed to sleep.

~*~

Knock. Knock.

"Katherine?" Andi's voice beckoned from the door. "Are you awake?"

Katherine was in the same exact position; she hadn't moved a muscle the entire night. Her phone was still tightly wrapped in her hands against her chest. She blinked the sleep from her eyes and looked at the screen. There was a text from Will:

Good morning, beautiful. Break a leg tonight.

I love you.

"Katherine?" Andi knocked again.

"Yes. Hi. I'm awake." Her voice was groggy and she cleared her throat. "Come on in."

Andi slowly opened the door. She was already dressed for the day, and she carried a beautiful Tiffany's breakfast tray. She smiled humbly, the way that best friends smile at one another after a big fight.

"Breakfast in bed for the artiste!" She carefully placed the tray next to Katherine on the bed. It was decadent: steaming croissants, fresh fruit, and hot coffee, with a tiny blue vase and one pink peony.

"Oh, Andi, you didn't have to . . ." Katherine sat up and tried not to let drool escape from her mouth. She realized that in the midst of the excitement and the unexpected escapade with Duncan the night before, she had barely eaten any dinner.

"Of course I did! Anything for you!" She smiled and stole a blueberry, popping it in her mouth. They laughed, and Sebastian knocked outside the door.

"Everyone decent?" he asked politely.

"Depends on what you consider *decent*," Andi joked, and he entered carrying another tray filled with exquisite pastries, setting it down by Andi.

"Katherine, I, . . ." he spoke hesitantly.

"No," she interjected. "Sebastian, I am so, so sorry. I didn't mean to lose my temper with you. I'm completely mortified. You have been so generous and gracious, and I owe you everything."

"Yeah, honey, don't worry. It's me she hates," Andi teased and winked at Katherine. Katherine blushed and continued to devour a croissant.

"Water under the bridge." Sebastian smiled and kissed Andi sweetly before walking back toward the door. "Big day, ladies. Enjoy your breakfast." He smiled and left the room.

"So, how are you feeling?" Andi asked tentatively as they enjoyed their feast. "Any thoughts about . . .?"

Katherine sighed and looked again at Will's text. She was glad to hear from him, but his text felt like a hollow gesture. They were just words.

"I don't know. It breaks my heart to even think about leaving Bluewater. But it would only be for a year, right? A year isn't so bad, and then I could go back." Katherine spoke aloud as she reasoned in her mind. "It *is* the opportunity of a lifetime. Maybe Will and I could use the time apart to reevaluate, recharge . . . you know, figure out our priorities." She rambled on and Andi nodded silently. Katherine paused and sipped her coffee as she stared blankly out the window.

"I have something for you," Andi said, changing the subject. She was suddenly beaming with excitement and pride. She hopped off the bed and stepped out into the hall. Katherine sighed, trying to push thoughts of Will and Duncan and London out of her head. The opening reception was tonight. This was *her* day, and she resolved to savor every moment.

"Ready?" Andi peeked her head around the door, wearing a silly grin on her face.

"I think so?" Katherine replied nervously. She hated surprises.

"Ta-da!" Andi walked in, carrying Katherine's old beat-up travel easel from art school.

"Oh, my God! Andi!" Katherine gasped at the sight of the easel, and memories from Italy and her old painting studio instantly flooded her mind. Her eyes filled with tears. She felt like she was reuniting with a dear old friend after spending years apart.

"I found it when I was moving your things to our new storage. I remember you carrying this thing around when we first met." Andi smiled nostalgically down at the broken, weathered box, splattered with dry colorful paint. "I don't know. There was something beautifully symbolic about it, about finding it right now—at this time, you know?" She smiled shyly.

Katherine jumped out of bed, and Andi handed her the easel. The hinge was still broken, and the leather carrying-strap was worn down so that the threads dangled from its edges. Katherine sat with the easel on the floor and ran her fingers gently over the paint stains, recalling the specific colors she had mixed while sipping Chianti and painting in the studio, or while working on-sight painting *en plein* air at the Boboli gardens.

She smiled, remembering her younger self, so passionate, ambitious, and focused. She was going to conquer the world with her paintings, she was going to be a true artist, crazy and obsessed, and she would one day be discovered and her work would be celebrated.

Katherine could feel what she felt all those years ago, silently marveling at the incredible power of time and fate. In those innocent days, she'd never imagined her life turning out the way it did. Young art student Katherine could never fathom being a divorcee or moving to some strange little town in Colorado or finding love with someone like Will. But on the other hand, her dreams for her art *were* coming true; it all just happened in an unexpected way, after following a different road from the one she had planned.

Katherine smiled. Suddenly, she knew what she was going to do.

"It's perfect." Katherine hugged her friend. "Thank you, Andi."

~*~

After breakfast, they met with Andi's close friend, Raul, a highly sought-after and thoroughly entertaining dress designer for Manhattan's finest.

"Raul is the best. People wait up to a year to get in with him, but I just sold him his fabulous place on 5th after elbowing out seven other offers, so he owes me," Andi said proudly as they walked through the gold-plated doors to Raul's studio.

"Ah! Andi *daaaaarling*! Get over here, you exquisite creature!" Raul was all of ninety pounds and wore a fuchsia cashmere sweater with black skinny jeans and silver leather shoes. He was bald with a pointy black goatee and a huge smile revealing flawless white teeth.

After kissing each other's cheeks about five times, Andi turned and gestured grandly toward Katherine.

"Raul, this is Katherine Ross. The artiste!"

"It is my pleasure, Miss Ross," Raul said with a low bow.

"We will need something—by tonight, of course—for the opening reception. You're coming, right?" Andi confirmed with Raul.

"Are you kidding? The most highly anticipated art show of the year?! I wouldn't miss it, *cherie*! I'm bringing Francois. We are going to wear delicious coordinating suits. The red carpet is just going to die!" Raul talked about fashion with the same enthusiasm as a child talking about cotton candy. Katherine smiled, appreciating his energy.

Raul escorted Katherine to the pedestal in the middle of the room and asked her to turn slowly.

"Okay, my lady, what do you envision on your gorgeous body for this fantastic event?" Raul was studying her hips and calves unabashedly as he spoke.

Katherine hadn't thought about what she would wear. She knew Andi was gifting her a dress from Raul's studio, but she hadn't considered what she'd want it to look like.

"Um, I'm not sure. Maybe something black?" Katherine suggested uncertainly.

"*Black?* Oh, mon Dieu, *no*! These curves deserve more than black!" Raul ranted passionately.

Katherine looked uncomfortably at Andi, who giggled and shrugged.

"Well, many of my paintings have vivid blue colors in them. An incredible blue lake was my subject focus for the show." Katherine searched her mind for ideas.

"Cobalt! *YES*!!!" Raul shouted abruptly, making Katherine jump nearly a foot into the air. "With your eyes and your hair, cobalt will make you look as though you are swimming among the paintings!"

For the next hour, Raul and his assistants wrapped various blue fabrics around Katherine's body, playing with length and fit, sticking pins around folded sections under her arms and along her back. Andi relaxed on Raul's gold silk couch, sipping mimosas and answering emails.

They ordered-in lunch while Raul worked in the back, feverishly assembling his creation. And finally, he reappeared with the precious garment delicately draped over his arms. He looked exhausted but exceedingly pleased with himself.

"My dear Katherine, let's have a look shall we?" he asked, his eyes hungry with anticipation.

When she walked out from behind the dressing partition, everyone gasped. She ambled carefully up to the pedestal where she could see herself in the mirrors.

Raul was an artistic genius. In just a few hours, he had created the most stunning piece of clothing Katherine had ever worn. The strapless cobalt dress hugged her body so naturally. She felt sexy and comfortable at the same time, with the rich blue fabric reaching to the middle of her thighs. Around her waist, Raul had attached a floor-length train of divine cerulean silk, which remained open in the front to show her legs. The dress was simple, but it was perfectly elegant. It was as if Raul had studied her for years, developing a deep awareness of her character. But they had only just met.

"Well?!" Raul was nearly bouncing up and down, awaiting her approval. "You're killing me here!"

Katherine couldn't tear her eyes away from the mirror. "Raul, you are an artist. It is beyond anything I could have imagined!" She smiled at him warmly, and Andi squealed with delight, hugging Raul as they jumped with happiness.

"I couldn't get the vision of 'Katherine the Mermaid' out of my head once you mentioned the lake. And so here you are, Raul's very own interpretation of a mystical mermaid goddess!" Tears filled his eyes as he stood savoring his creation.

"Oh my! I nearly forgot!" Raul said, suddenly running to the back room. He reemerged holding a pair of strappy gold stilettos. As he handed them to Katherine, she noticed a delicate line of blue sapphires along each strap.

"These will be perfect, I think." Raul remarked, beaming with pride.

"Thank you, Raul. Thank you so much!" Katherine slipped on the shoes, and they fit perfectly. She felt like Cinderella heading to the ball.

Only she realized sadly that there would be no prince awaiting her.

~*~

Back at the apartment, they began to get ready for the big night. Katherine became more nervous every

314

minute, with butterflies dancing in her stomach and her heart beating wildly. She decided to wear her hair down and loosely curled. She couldn't get Raul's "mermaid" theme out of her mind—she quite liked it. Keeping her makeup to a minimum, with mascara, slight blush, and gloss on her lips, she carefully pulled Raul's dress over her head, treating it like the fragile treasure it was. And she finished off the presentation with the exquisite shoes. She stepped back and looked at herself in the full-length mirror behind the door. She felt beautiful, more beautiful than she had ever felt in her life.

If only Will were here to see her . . .

Andi had been speaking to Sebastian throughout the day, and it sounded like everything was ready at the museum. Some of the VIPs had arrived early to enjoy a sneak peek of the show before it became too crowded. According to Sebastian, the Mayor of New York was already there, strongly considering one of the spring paintings for his office, and rumors swirled that George Lucas was sending his private art dealer to the event to scout out some potential additions for his private collection.

"Oh, Katherine! You look absolutely stunning!" Andi said from the door and stepped into the room. She walked over behind Katherine, securing the zipper on the back of her dress. "Are you ready?" Andi asked, as their eyes met in the mirror.

Katherine took a big shaky breath.

"Yes. Let's go."

CHAPTER 34

As the car turned onto Fifth Avenue, Katherine couldn't believe her eyes. At least 200 people stood on the stairs of the Met, dressed to the nines, smiling for the army of flashing cameras. A red carpet had been laid down the entire stairway, and limos lined up along Fifth, waiting to deliver their passengers.

"Is there something else going on at the Met tonight?" she asked Andi hopefully. "Some kind of gala or something?"

Andi laughed. "You're cute."

"You mean all of this . . . This is all for my show?" Katherine's mouth became suddenly dry, and she found it difficult to swallow.

"Yes, silly. That's what we've been trying to tell you all week! You're kind of a big deal." Andi winked and squeezed her hand as their car pulled up in front of the carpet.

"I think I might be sick." Katherine felt paralyzed in the safety of the back seat, protected behind the tinted windows.

"You are going to be great. This is your *dream,* Katherine! Own it." Andi smiled and nodded toward the window. "Here comes Sebastian. He will escort you to the gallery, and I'll be right behind you. The press will bombard you with a million questions, but just smile and keep on walking. Sebastian will help you, you know, so you don't trip and fall on your face." Andi smirked playfully.

Sebastian tapped on the window. He was dressed magnificently in a timeless tux, and he smiled calmly, waiting for Katherine to work up the nerve to exit the vehicle.

She took one more deep breath and opened the door. *It's now or never, I guess.* Sebastian took her hand and wrapped it tightly through his arm.

"Katherine, you are a vision." He tapped her hand with his. "This is going to be a night to remember." He winked, and they began to walk slowly toward the stairs. Andi was right—the very second Katherine stepped onto the carpet, the press exploded with flashing cameras and a chaotic tangle of bellowing questions, one overlapping the next:

"Miss Ross! Which is your favorite painting?"

"Miss Ross! Do you have a muse?"

"Miss Ross! There are rumors that you will take this show to the Tate next! Are the rumors true?"

"Miss Ross! Are you dating anyone?"

"Miss Ross! Who are you wearing?"

As Andi instructed, Katherine simply smiled into the onslaught of flashing lights, as she held on tightly to Sebastian's arm. After what felt like an eternity, they made it to the lobby, and Sebastian quickly guided her through the secret door to the secret white hallways. With the door shut safely behind them, they paused and Sebastian and Andi laughed out loud.

"Well done, Katherine! You survived the gauntlet." Sebastian applauded, the sound echoing in the silent narrow walkway.

Katherine leaned against the wall, trying to catch her breath and blink away the residual blue patches dancing inside her eyelids from all of the blinding camera flashes. *This is what a seizure must feel like*, she thought.

Sebastian offered his arm again. "Shall we, ladies?"

"Wait." Katherine halted after only a few steps. "Sebastian, can we make a quick stop along the way?"

Andi and Sebastian looked curiously at one another and then at Katherine.

"Stop? Where?" Andi asked, perplexed. "We're in the underground hallways of the Met, where could you possibly want to stop?"

"There's a small painting I'd like to see. It's in the European Painting wing. I won't be long, I promise."

Sebastian checked his watch and glanced at Andi.

"Of course. We can spare a few moments." Sebastian smiled patiently. "Right this way."

Katherine and Andi followed Sebastian down a few of the unmarked hallways, all three of them quickening their pace. Sebastian stopped in front of a modest door labeled *European Paintings—Gallery 7* and retrieved his key card.

"Here we are," he said as he held the door. Katherine stepped out into the gallery and looked around, trying to get her bearings. The European Paintings Collection was vast and displayed among several galleries. She closed her eyes and tried to visualize where the painting was. Then, without a word, she walked through the gallery and turned right through the next gallery, her heels echoing loudly through the empty halls. Andi and Sebastian followed silently behind. Katherine looked left and then right and walked quickly left through a third gallery and then down an open corridor, before stopping in front of a small painting hanging on the wall to the left.

"Ah, Monet's *The Valley of the Nervia,* a delightful little piece.*"* Sebastian stood behind her, his voice echoing in the empty hall though he was speaking quietly. "It is often overlooked." He frowned, wondering why she *had* to see this particular painting.

Katherine stood in front of the small unimposing painting that changed her entire life over a year ago, and tears began to stream down her cheeks.

"Katherine?" Andi walked over to stand next to her, handing her a tissue.

Katherine smiled at Andi and gently blotted the tears from her face. "It's all because of this painting." She nodded. Andi searched her eyes, trying to understand.

"Everything . . . Everything that's happened—Bluewater, Will, this show—it all started right here." She turned back to the painting, silently thanking Monet for giving her the push she needed.

The painting sat quietly nestled between two larger, more powerful works, just as it had when she first discovered it, when nothing else in her life made sense. The gentle stream still crept peacefully along the canvas, while the majestic snow-covered mountains governed over the quiet land. Katherine closed her eyes and pictured Bluewater; the glowing lake and the giant mountain watching over the town. She had found her very own *Valley of the Nervia*, and no matter what happened tonight, she would always be grateful for the time she had there.

Sebastian cleared his throat nervously. "I'm sorry, Katherine. We really must be going."

She took in one last glance at the painting and sighed contentedly. "Yes, of course. Thank you for bringing me here. We can go now."

Before they opened the door to *Contemporary Gallery #4*, Sebastian explained the scene. "I will escort you inside, and I will introduce you to the room. Andi will get you something to drink, and from there, you are free to wander or sit and talk to whomever you like." He smiled. "This is the moment we've been waiting for, Katherine. This is *your* moment."

Andi gave Katherine's hand one more squeeze as Sebastian slowly opened the door. The quiet hallway immediately flooded with a sea of voices, laughter, and the clinking of glasses. Katherine closed her eyes and took one final deep breath.

Here we go.

As soon as they walked through the door, the crowd parted, and the museum staff began to applaud their arrival. The press members and guests followed suit and everyone stood on their toes, clapping and trying to catch a glimpse of the artist. The gallery was packed. Katherine looked around, smiling and nodding, marveling at the sheer magnitude of attendees. She didn't think it was physically possible to fit another body in the room.

Was that Meryl Streep standing in the corner?! It couldn't be.

Sebastian tapped his champagne glass with a spoon, and the massive room filled with bodies became silent, aside from a muted whisper here and a muffled cough there.

"Ladies and gentlemen, on behalf of the Metropolitan Museum of Art, I welcome you to tonight's event celebrating one of today's most coveted artists, Katherine Ross." As he said her name, he reached out for Katherine's hand. Her heart beat so violently she thought someone might be able to see it threatening to pound right out of her chest. Her hand shook visibly, as she took hold of Sebastian's. She stood alongside him and gave a little nod and wave, and the room erupted into applause once again. Sebastian continued, "Now, let's eat, drink, and be the art lovers we are. Cheers!"

"Cheers!" The audience saluted back and applauded once more before the crowd dispersed, and the superbly attired guests began studying and discussing the paintings along each of the four walls.

"See? That wasn't so bad." Andi nudged Katherine and handed her a cold glass of champagne. Katherine was terrified to spill any on her beautiful dress, but gladly welcomed the drink.

She looked around the room, trying to permanently imprint each image in her mind so that she could remember this night for the rest of her life. The guests ranged in age from early twenties to eighties or nineties, and everyone looked either extremely important or incredibly artistic in their own right. She thought she recognized a few celebrities wandering around, but it was so incredibly crowded and her head was spinning with so much adrenaline that it was difficult for her to focus on just one single person. Strategically placed Mct staff members sentineled the room, still as statues, with pleasant smiles on their faces, holding binders meant to discreetly record buyers' names and payment accounts for purchased pieces.

Katherine stood near the wall with her biography, as suggested by Sebastian, and for nearly an hour, she exchanged colorful conversations with press members, politicians, theater directors, and international art collectors. Harriet Hughes from the *New York Times* came over and gave Katherine a warm hug and congratulations and introduced her to her editor. "The story runs tomorrow!" Harriet exclaimed with excitement before wandering off to show her editor some of her favorite pieces.

The strappy gold heels from Raul were surprisingly comfortable, for which Katherine was very grateful, and she received countless compliments on her dress and the way it "fit" perfectly with the exhibition.

"Oh, Miss Ross! *Who* designed that heavenly ensemble for you?" Raul teased as he walked up to Katherine, kissing her cheeks and introducing her to his partner, Francois. As promised, they wore coordinating suits of gray and teal. Raul's jacket gray with teal pants, and Francois's the reverse. "By the way, darling, I wanted to buy one of your masterpieces for our home in the Hamptons, but I was informed they've all been spoken for, so I suppose I will have to commission something special from you!" He winked and sipped a cosmo.

"What do you mean? They're all spoken for?" Katherine glanced at Andi, who shrugged and looked just as confused.

"What he means is it is a *sold-out* show. Every piece sold," Sebastian declared proudly as he walked up behind them.

"But, how? I mean the show just opened an hour ago!" Katherine couldn't believe what she was hearing.

"Yes. This has never happened before. We've had sell-out exhibitions, of course, but only after a month of display time and heavy marketing. We have never hosted an artist who sold *every* piece the first night. Never." Sebastian was giddy. It was the first time Katherine saw him giggle. "Congratulations, Katherine. Brava, brava!" He bowed toward her and walked off to talk with a gentleman who bore a striking resemblance to Ralph Lauren—*but it couldn't be . . . could it?*

"My goodness—a sold-out show. I'll drink to that!" Andi touched her glass to Katherine's, and they tried to maintain some composure in spite of the exciting news. Katherine savored the bubbles dancing around her mouth and down her throat.

It all felt like a fairy tale. How could she be certain it was real?

CHAPTER 35

"Katherine!"

She heard a familiar voice shouting through the crowd.

"Katherine! There she is!"

It was Ginger! Katherine saw her head popping up over the throng on the far side of the gallery. Then she saw Matt following closely behind her. Ginger politely pushed her way through the other guests, dragging Matt by the hand as she ran over to Katherine, hugging her so exuberantly they nearly tumbled to the floor.

"Ginger! Oh my gosh!" Katherine's eyes filled with tears. She had been so engulfed in preparations for the show that she completely forgot that Ginger had promised to be there. Her heart leapt with joy at the sight of her Bluewater friends, but it also ached, longing for Will to be with them.

"Katherine, this is . . . Wow. Just, wow!" Ginger was ecstatic as she gestured around the room. She looked just like the elegant socialite 'Ginger Mayrose' they used to read about in the papers—dressed like royalty in a sheer red gown, her hair perfectly tied up in artistically crafted knots on top of her head. And Matt was nearly unrecognizable in his tux. He was perhaps the largest man in the room, but he wore the suit quite handsomely. He kept fidgeting with the bow tie, and Ginger kept swatting his hand away.

"I can't believe you guys came! Thank you. Thank you so much for being here. It means the world to me!" Katherine hugged Matt, and Andi brought them all fresh glasses of champagne.

"Of course! We couldn't miss this!" Ginger toasted the show, and they all talked about celebrities they had spotted so far at the event. Once in a while, Katherine would look around hopefully; though deep down she knew the person she was looking for was simply not going to be there.

"He feels terrible," Ginger said, as though she could hear the thoughts in Katherine's head. "I've never seen him so torn up."

"Yeah. I feel pretty torn up myself," Katherine said, trying not to sound bitter. She sighed. "I just wish he could be here with me."

"I know," Ginger said and hugged her friend. Then she laughed and changed the subject. "I basically had to tie Gramps to his bed so that he couldn't sneak onto the plane with us! He's such a child—threw a total fit when we refused to let him come along."

Katherine laughed, imagining stubborn Mr. Trust objecting to his doctor's orders not to fly. "Poor Mr. Trust, he would just love all this excitement."

"He sure would." Ginger smiled. "Well, I'm going to walk around with Matty and try to get him some food. He's grumpy from the flight," Ginger teased, as Matt rolled his eyes.

"Congratulations, little lady. We're damn proud of you." Matt hugged Katherine so hard he lifted her off the floor.

"Thanks, Matt." She smiled as she watched the couple stroll off hand-in-hand toward a waiter carrying a tray of hors d'oeuvres. Seeing Ginger and Matt made her realize how much she missed Bluewater. She had only been gone a week, but she missed the little town and the inn and the lake. She missed the simplicity; she missed the quiet.

The naïve girl inside her still had hoped maybe, just maybe, Will would show up and sweep her off her feet. But the reception was winding down, and it was becoming obvious to Katherine that no such sweeping would happen tonight. She hadn't seen Duncan at the show either. It was still packed inside, and he could be anywhere, but she hadn't yet encountered him. During a quiet moment, she finished her champagne and rehearsed what she would say to Duncan regarding the Tate residency. Her heart was torn, but she had made a decision, and it was time to move forward.

Katherine decided to wander through the exhibition one last time and bid farewell to her paintings. She had a special connection with each and every work, and the fact was just hitting her that, after tonight, she would never see many of these paintings again. She decided she would start with *Spring*, and walk in a circle to *Summer* followed by *Fall*, and then finish with *Winter*.

As she strolled past her work, people would stop her to talk or to shake her hand and congratulate her.

Some would ask her questions about the motivations behind a particular piece.

Eventually she made her way to the *Winter* wall, and she stopped in front of the small painting she did on the beach alongside the icy lake, the day she fell and literally found herself in Will's arms. Just as she began to study the work, she noticed Duncan making his way across the gallery. He had obviously seen her standing there, and it was time for them to talk about the residency. Luckily, Sebastian stopped him in the middle of the room, introducing him to some of the VIP guests. Katherine turned back to her painting, glad for the delay.

For a moment, she let herself get lost in the brush strokes, remembering the slippery rocks she had to climb down, racing against the rising sun, and the elation she felt when the morning light kissed the far side of the frozen lake, when she was able to capture the divine moment on her canvas. Looking at the painting now, she was deeply saddened to notice a tiny red 'SOLD' dot on its label. Suddenly, she regretted putting it in the show.

She should have kept this painting for herself.

This one painting, above all the others, meant the most to her.

"Well, clearly, I couldn't let anyone else have this one." His voice was close behind her.

Katherine's heart leapt to her throat as she spun around to see Will.

"It's still my favorite." He smiled, obviously quite pleased with himself.

"Will!" She couldn't believe it. *Was it a dream?*

Will took her into his arms and held her tightly as he kissed her lips with an intense passion that said, "I'm so sorry" and "I love you" and "I'm here" all at once.

She didn't let him go. Even as they pulled their lips apart, she kept her arms wrapped tightly around his back, fearing that, if she loosened her grasp, he would disappear. He wore a tux and his hair was combed, and he had shaved. He was breathtaking; he was perfect.

"What are you doing here?!" Tears poured down Katherine's face as she looked up into the wild blue eyes she had missed so much.

"I really didn't think I would come." Will looked down at her, his voice filled with shame. "I didn't think I *could* come." He kissed her again; this time it was tender and soft.

"But I was trying to write at home, and everything hurt. I felt sick. My head was going crazy." He kissed her cheeks and pulled away, keeping his hands on her waist. "God, you are so beautiful," he said as he looked at her from head to toe.

Katherine was speechless. She just stood there, crying and laughing and drinking in the sight of him. *It was Will! He was here! He came!*

"Anyway, before I knew it, I was on a plane. And here I am. I called Sebastian yesterday and asked him to hold this painting for me, but he didn't know I was coming. *I* didn't know I was coming." He gestured toward the painting, toward *their* painting.

He put his hands on her cheeks and looked into her eyes. Her knees felt weak as she stared back at him.

"Katherine, I was just fine before you came to Bluewater. But now that I've met you, I can't live without you. Life is nothing when you are gone, and I can't stand it. I'm so sorry, Katherine. I'm so sorry—I've been a damn fool." He shook his head, letting his thoughts spill out into the small space between them. He spoke seriously, urgently, as though he were racing against time.

"You are the only thing that makes sense to me; you are the only thing that matters. I have to marry you, Katherine. Will you marry me?" He pulled her face to his and kissed her like he never wanted to let go.

"Ahem."

They turned to see Duncan standing next to them.

"I'm so sorry to interrupt, but I'm afraid I have a plane to catch." He smiled awkwardly at Katherine.

"Yes, of course." Katherine cleared her throat and stepped back. "Will, I'd like you to meet Duncan Bristow. Duncan is the Curator for Contemporary Works at the Tate Modern in London."

"Pleased to make your acquaintance." Duncan smiled politely at Will as they shook hands. Katherine could feel the heat rising in her chest and face as she wiped the lingering tears from her cheeks.

"Katherine, I wondered if you might have a decision for me?" Duncan asked cautiously, not knowing if it was okay to discuss business in front of Will.

Will looked at Katherine with curiosity as he placed his hand on her lower back. Katherine took a deep breath and smiled at Duncan.

"Yes, I do," she started.

Just five minutes ago, she was going to accept Duncan's offer. She was going to take the residency. But then Will showed up.

"Duncan, working in the Tate, having my paintings there, would be a dream," she began, as Will's expression became anxious. "But it was a dream of my past. My dreams have changed." She smiled at Will. "I'm sorry, but I must decline."

Duncan smiled respectfully. "I understand."

"I'm so thankful to have met you, and I thank you from the bottom of my heart for purchasing a painting for your museum. I hope to visit someday." Katherine put her hand out to Duncan.

As he took her hand in his, he spoke with warm sincerity, "We are honored to have your work in our collection, Miss Ross. And, well, you are an absolute joy. I wish you the best of luck." And with that, Duncan nodded at Will and kissed Katherine's hand. Then he turned and walked out of the gallery.

"Wow. The Tate?" Will asked as he turned back to face her.

Katherine blushed, looking down at her feet. Then she smiled up at Will. "Yeah, the Tate."

For a moment, they just smiled at one another as Will took Katherine's hands in his. The gallery was still full of lingering guests. Hors d'oeuvres still circled on trays, and the party continued onward. But for Will and Katherine, everything fell silent around them, and they were all that existed in the world.

"So, where were we?" Will grinned.

"Well, I think you just asked me to marry you." Katherine looked up at him, hoping she was right and that the champagne hadn't played some evil trick on her short-term memory.

"Oh, that's right." Will wrapped his arms around her waist, pulling her face close to his. "Let's try that again, shall we?"

He kissed her softly and whispered, "Katherine Ross, will you marry me?"

"Yes."

EPILOGUE

One Year Later

Katherine pulled her scarf tighter around her shoulders as the cool fall breeze danced across the water, stirring the fallen leaves from the path leading down to the gazebo. It was a cloudless day, and the sun was so vibrant it appeared to ignite the autumn colors surrounding the lake into a fiery blaze of red and gold. A simple gold ring shone brightly upon her left hand as she gently draped the bouquet of fresh red roses across the newly installed plaque. Tracing the engraved letters with her fingers, Katherine sighed and closed her eyes, just before the tears could begin to escape again.

"He would have loved this day," Will said as he walked up behind her and took her hand in his. Katherine sunk into his shoulder and smiled. "He really would have. A perfect Bluewater day . . ." The air smelled faintly of snow and cinnamon. The bakery had begun making its signature fall spice muffins.

Will stepped forward and placed another bouquet of roses upon the plaque for Jacqueline. "They're finally together again."

Eli Trust had passed away peacefully in his sleep, holding a picture of Jacqueline on his chest. As per his requests, Ginger and Murray sprinkled his ashes into the lake where he had done the same for Jacqueline years before, and Will installed an identical plaque for Eli alongside Jacqueline's at the gazebo.

For Eli,

This man knew love.

This man was love.

And this town loved him.

Everyone gathered at the shoreline to place wreathes of wild flowers on the calm water. As Tony bent down to release his haphazard bundle of dandelions, Matt shoved him from behind, sending him flying into the water with a massive splash. Ginger laughed out loud, covering her mouth when Tony surfaced and glared furiously back at Matt. Andi and Sebastian suppressed their giggles too. They had flown out to celebrate the man they had hardly known, but who had made a lasting impression on them the way he had on so many others. Lolo tearfully knelt on the sand and gracefully sent off the most beautiful wreath of columbines and fairy trumpet flowers, before offering her hand to a drenched Tony, who waded inland and covered her with a sopping wet hug.

Murray chuckled, as he walked around with a tray of Mr. Trust's favorite lemon butter cookies. He would be taking over the inn, with the help of Ginger and Matt, just as Mr. Trust had insisted only weeks before when they all celebrated Ginger and Matt's engagement. Mr. Trust had happily given Matt his blessing, "On one condition, young man. You love my granddaughter more than anything else. With each passing moment, you love her more. You take care of her, son. And you help Murray when I'm gone . . ."

Katherine looked around at the people she loved and at the beautiful flowers drifting atop Bluewater Lake, and she smiled. She remembered the morning she had encountered Mr. Trust sitting there in the gazebo, the day he told her about true love. She had finally found her love, the one she deserved, and the one that made her want to hold on and never let go. "Breathe it in every single day," Mr. Trust had advised all those months ago.

She still couldn't believe all that happened over the past two years. And despite the magnitude of her show at the Met, the highlight for Katherine had been her wedding day that following spring. She and Will had married in the gazebo, with all their friends in attendance. It was a small ceremony, simple, perfect. Mr. Trust officiated and had everyone laughing and in tears.

"I'm going to miss him," Katherine said, just as a fish jumped out of the flower-covered water beyond the gazebo.

"Me too. But he'll always be here with us. I'm sure of it," Will whispered as he wrapped his arms around Katherine's growing belly. They laughed when the baby kicked playfully inside.

"Our son." Katherine smiled.

Will grinned proudly and kissed her cheek. "Let's name him Eli."

ACKNOWLEDGMENTS

I'd like to thank my mother, aka my first reader, aka my first editor. Thank you for bearing with me chapter by chapter, and for introducing me to our very own "Bluewater Lake" all those years ago.

I also have to thank my dear friend, and the best cheerleader ever, Julee. I seriously don't think I would have finished this story without your relentless encouragement and support. I love you, girl!

And to the incredible JB Salsbury—what would I do without you? Thank you for your guidance, and thank you for inspiring me to pursue this dream.

Many thanks to Allison, Jen, and Elisa—you all helped me to believe in this book!

Thank you to Cassy at Pink Ink Designs for bringing my vision to life for this book cover. It's beautiful!

Thank you to my wonderful editor, Theresa Wegand, for holding my hand through this very intimidating process, and for teaching me the difference between stomach and abdomen.

And finally, to my ridiculously supportive husband: Thank you for letting me disappear to the coffee shop for hours at a time, where I spent a good portion of our life savings on cappuccinos. You are my rock. You are my heart. I love you.

ABOUT THE AUTHOR

Painting Blue Water is the debut novel for Leigh Fossan. A creative soul at heart, Leigh grew up with a paintbrush in her hand and went on to study the arts in Florence, Italy. While abroad, Leigh was one of the few recipients of the *Coluccio Salutati* Award for Creative Writing. Today, Leigh is a professional artist, and her paintings are collected around the world. She lives in Colorado with her artist husband and their young daughter, who wants to be a scientist.

Follow Leigh Fossan

Facebook:

https://www.facebook.com/leighfossanauthor

Instagram:

@leighfossanauthor

www.leighfossanauthor.com